A WOMAN'S LIFE

Guy de Maupassant was born in Normandy in 1850.
At his parents' separation he stayed with his mother,
who was a friend of Flaubert. As a young man he
was lively and athletic, but the first symptoms of
syphilis appeared in the late 1870s. By this time
Maupassant had become Flaubert's pupil in the art
of prose. On the publication of the first short story to
which he put his name, 'Boule de suif', he left his
job in the civil service and his temporary alliance with
the disciples of Zola at Médan, and devoted his
energy to professional writing. In the next eleven
years he published dozens of articles, nearly three
hundred stories and six novels, the best known of
which are *A Woman's Life, Bel-Ami* and *Pierre and
Jean*. He led a hectic social life, lived up to his reputation for womanizing and fought his disease. By
1889 his friends saw that his mind was in danger,
and in 1891 he attempted suicide and was committed
to an asylum in Paris, where he died two years later.

GUY de MAUPASSANT

A WOMAN'S LIFE

TRANSLATED
WITH AN INTRODUCTION BY
H. N. P. SLOMAN

PENGUIN BOOKS

Penguin Books Ltd, Harmondsworth, Middlesex, England
Viking Penguin Inc., 40 West 23rd Street, New York, New York 10010, U.S.A.
Penguin Books Australia Ltd, Ringwood, Victoria, Australia
Penguin Books Canada Limited, 2801 John Street, Markham, Ontario, Canada L3R 1B4
Penguin Books (N.Z.) Ltd, 182–190 Wairau Road, Auckland 10, New Zealand

—

This translation first published 1965
Reprinted 1967, 1970, 1977, 1979, 1980, 1982, 1985, 1986

—

Copyright © H. N. P. Sloman, 1965
All rights reserved

—

Made and printed in Great Britain by
Hazell Watson & Viney Limited,
Member of the BPCC Group,
Aylesbury, Bucks
Set in Linotype Granjon

INTRODUCTION

GUY de MAUPASSANT was born in 1850 at the Château de Miromesnil, a seventeenth-century mansion situated in a magnificent park in Normandy some six miles south of Dieppe; his father had rented the property for a few years and it was here first, and later at his mother's house at Étretat, that Maupassant passed his childhood. He was educated at the Seminary at Yvetot and at the private Institution Leroy-Petit and later at the Lycée Corneille at Rouen. He entered the Civil Service after a period in the army as a conscript, which coincided with the Franco-Prussian War of 1870, though he saw no actual fighting. He worked in the Ministries of Marine and Public Instruction in Paris for ten years. Thus the background of most of his stories, though not of this volume, is the France of the Third Republic from 1870 to 1890.

He was encouraged to write by his old friend and mentor, the great stylist Flaubert, and in 1880 he published both a volume of poems and, in a book of war stories brought out under Zola's aegis, *Boule de Suif,* probably his greatest *nouvelle* or long short story. From this date till his early death in 1893 – he died of syphilis in an asylum to which he had been committed suffering from general paralysis of the insane – he lived by his pen.

His output was phenomenal; in thirteen years he wrote in addition to his verse six full-length novels, including the present volume, three volumes of travel sketches, four plays, and more than 300 short stories. His verse and his plays have been forgotten; it is as a writer of novels and short stories that his immortality is secure, and his influence on other writers in these *genres,* abroad as well as in France, has been immeasurable.

Guy de Maupassant received his training as a writer from Flaubert, who himself carried further the principles of the realist novel of Balzac. His observation of life is keen and detailed, if sometimes cynical and even coarse; he studied all classes of contemporary France with equal interest and detachment, from the Normandy peasants to all ranks of Parisian society: prostitutes, civil servants, journalists, artists, soldiers, and members of the old noble families of the *ancien régime*, as well as of the *bourgeoisie*, to which he himself belonged and in which he was always most at home.

His six full-length novels, especially *Pierre and Jean* and the present volume, *A Woman's Life*, published in 1883, are still widely popular. Here we have in minute detail the life of a woman, Jeanne, a member of the old Normandy gentry, from her departure in 1819 from the Rouen convent where she had been educated to her late middle age about 1855. The first three-quarters of the book deals with only the first six years, up to the violent death of her husband, Julien, when their son Paul is only five years old and Jeanne herself twenty-five; the last quarter shows us Jeanne's subsequent life of increasing loneliness as her parents die and her son's extravagances force her to sell the Poplars, the family mansion.

The whole of Jeanne's adult life is in fact a succession of misfortunes, which hurt her all the more in that she finishes her schooling innocent, trusting and vulnerable. Her husband is a vulgar little lecher; her parish priest is a cynical *bon vivant* and his successor a fanatical ascetic; her mother, as she discovers after her death, had been unfaithful to her father; her son turns out to be a swindler and spendthrift who never writes to her except to ask for money, and who eventually brings her to the verge of ruin.

Yet if *A Woman's Life* is steeped in the pessimism and melancholy characteristic of Maupassant's later years, its heroine is portrayed with unusual sympathy and tenderness. Just as the author's description of the Poplars was inspired by his memories of the Château de Miromesnil, Jeanne herself may indeed be a portrait of his mother. Certainly *A Woman's Life* was one of Maupassant's favourites among his own works, and it has lost nothing of its melancholy charm with the passage of time.

H.N.P.S.

CHAPTER ONE

JEANNE finished her packing and went over to the window, but the rain showed no sign of stopping. The downpour had rattled all night against the panes and the roof. The lowering sky, full of water, seemed to have burst, drenching the earth and reducing it to a muddy paste like melted sugar. Furious gusts of wind were blowing, laden with stuffy heat, and the roar of flooded gutters filled the empty streets, where the houses like sponges sucked up the damp, which found its way inside and made the walls sweat from cellar to attic.

Jeanne had left the convent the day before, free for ever at last and ready to grasp all the joys of life of which she had long dreamt, but she was afraid that her father might hesitate to start, unless the weather cleared, and for the hundredth time that morning she scanned the horizon anxiously. Suddenly she noticed that she had forgotten to put her calendar into her suitcase, and she took down from the wall the little piece of cardboard divided into months with the date of the current year, 1819, emblazoned in gold figures at the top. Then she scratched out with a pencil in the first four columns the names of all the saints up to 2 May, the day she had left the convent.

A voice outside the door called : 'Jeanne dear !'

'Come in, Papa !' she replied, and her father appeared.

Baron Simon-Jacques Le Perthuis des Vauds was a nobleman of the previous age, a kindly crank. A fanatical disciple of Jean-Jacques Rousseau, he had a lover's affection for nature, the fields, the woods, and the animals. An aristocrat by birth, he had an instinctive hatred of '93; but being philosophically inclined and liberal by education, though he hated tyranny, his hatred was innocuous and confined to words.

His generosity was his great strength and his great weakness; he had not enough hands to caress, to embrace, to give; it was the generosity of a creative power, without method and without toughness, which as it were sapped the muscles of his

7

will and almost amounted to a vice. In accordance with his theories he had mapped out his daughter's education with the object of rendering her happy, virtuous, honest, and affectionate. Up to the age of twelve he had kept her at home; then, in spite of her mother's tears, she had been sent to the Convent of the Sacred Heart, where she stayed strictly shut up, cloistered, hidden away, knowing nothing of the facts of life. He wanted her to come back to him at the age of seventeen a virgin, intending to give her himself a baptism of romantic reason; in the fields of the fruitful earth he would open her soul and enlighten her ignorance by the sight of the innocent loves and natural mating of animals in accordance with the gentle laws of life.

Now she was leaving the convent, radiant, bursting with life, thirsting for happiness, ready for all the joys and all the risks, which she had already anticipated in imagination in days of idleness and in the long hours of the night with no one to share her hopes. She looked like a portrait by Veronese, with her glossy fair hair which seemed to have caught the sheen of her skin, the skin of an aristocrat with the faintest tinge of pink and a shadow of light down like pale velvet just visible under the caress of the sunlight. Her eyes were blue, the dark blue of Dutch delft figures. On the left nostril there was a tiny beauty spot and another on the right side of the chin, on which grew a few curly hairs hardly noticeable against her skin. She was tall with a developed bust and a supple figure, and she often raised both hands to her temples in a natural gesture as if to smooth her hair.

She ran to her father, flung her arms round him and kissed him, crying: 'Well, are we starting?'

He smiled, shaking his head with its long white hair, saying as he pointed to the window: 'How can we go in this sort of weather?'

But she pressed him with tender coaxing: 'Oh! Papa, do let's go, *please*! It'll be fine in the afternoon.'

'But your mother will never agree.'

'Oh yes, she will, I promise you; I'll see to that!'

'If you succeed in persuading your mother, I have no objection.'

She hurried to the Baroness's room, for she had been waiting for the day of her release with ever increasing impatience.

Since she had entered the Sacred Heart, she had not been out of Rouen, her father having forbidden any distraction before she reached the age he had fixed. She had only twice been taken to Paris for a fortnight; but Paris was a city and all her dreams were of the country. Now she was going to spend the summer at their country place, the Poplars, an old family mansion on the cliff near Yport, and she was looking forward with joyful anticipation to the freedom of this life close to the sea. Moreover it had been decided that this manor house should be made over to her and that she should live there when she married.

This rain, which had been falling without a break since the previous evening, was the first serious disappointment of her life. But three minutes later she ran out of her mother's room shouting all over the house: 'Papa, Papa! Mama agrees! Get the barouche harnessed!'

The downpour continued, indeed it seemed to be getting worse when the barouche appeared at the door. Jeanne was ready to get in, when the Baroness came downstairs, supported on one side by her husband and on the other by a tall chambermaid, a strong strapping lass like a boy. She was a Normandy girl from the Caux neighbourhood and looked at least twenty, though she was only eighteen. She lived like one of the family, a second daughter, for she had been Jeanne's foster-sister; her name was Rosalie. Moreover her main job was to support her mistress when she walked, for she had become very heavy in recent years as the result of cardiac hypertrophy, of which she was always complaining.

The Baroness reached the terrace steps in front of the old mansion and saw the courtyard streaming with water. 'It's quite ridiculous going out in this,' she murmured. Her husband replied with his usual smile: 'The decision is yours, Madame Adélaïde.'

As she bore the high-sounding name of Adélaïde, he always prefixed the 'Madame' with a slightly ironical hint of respect.

She made her way down the steps with some difficulty and struggled into the carriage, the springs bending under her weight. The Baron sat down by her side with Jeanne and Rosalie opposite with their backs to the horses. The cook Ludivine brought an armful of cloaks, which they spread over their knees, and two baskets, which were stowed away under their feet; then she climbed on to the box by the side of old Simon and wrapped herself up in a large rug which covered her head. The porter with his wife came to say good-bye as he closed the door. They were given the last instructions about the baggage, which was to follow on a cart, and the party moved off. Old Simon the coachman, lowering his head and humping his back, snuggled into his box-coat with its triple cape. The howling wind drove the rattling rain against the windows and flooded the roadway. The barouche travelled at a brisk pace, as the two horses trotted down to the sea-front, passing the line of big ships, whose masts, yards, and tackle were outlined grimly against the dripping sky like dead trees. Then it turned off into the long boulevard of Mont Riboudet.

Presently they were crossing open fields and here and there a drenched willow with branches sprawling like the limbs of a corpse was depressingly visible through the curtain of rain. The horses' shoes splashed through the puddles and the four wheels threw up showers of mud.

There was silence in the carriage; their minds seemed drowned like the earth. Mama was leaning back with closed eyes supporting her head; the Baron kept a gloomy eye on the featureless soaked country-side, and Rosalie with a parcel on her knee was dreaming the sub-human dreams of peasant folk. But under the warm downpour Jeanne was conscious of new life like a plant long shut up and now restored to the fresh air; the intensity of her happiness was like foliage shielding her heart from depression. Though she did not speak, she would have liked to sing and put her head out of the window to catch and drink the rain, and she enjoyed the speed of the horses, watching the desolate country-side and feeling quite safe in the deluge. Under the lashing of the storm the shiny haunches of the two horses were steaming like water boiling.

The Baroness gradually went off to sleep; her face, framed by six plaits of hair hanging down, slowly dropped, insufficiently supported by the three great waves of her neck, whose last curves were lost in the ocean of her breast. Her head rose and fell with each breath and her cheeks puffed out, as a loud snore issued from her half-open lips. Her husband leant over towards her and gently placed in her hands, which were crossed on the ample curves of her stomach, a small leather wallet. The touch woke her up and she looked down at it, puzzled, with the dazed glance of one just waking up. The wallet fell down and opened; gold and bank notes were scattered all over the floor. This woke her up completely and her daughter's amusement expressed itself in a burst of laughter. The Baron picked up the money and put it on her lap: 'There, dearest, that's all that is left of my farm at Eletot. I sold it to have money for the renovation of the Poplars, where we shall be spending a lot of time in the future.'

She counted 6,400* francs and put the money quietly in her pocket.

This was the ninth farm to be sold of the thirty-one inherited from their parents. But they still had an income of about 20,000 francs from landed property, which could easily have brought in 30,000 francs if properly developed. But as they lived simply, what they had would have been enough, if there had not been in the house a bottomless and ever-open outlet, the Baron's generosity; this was always drying up the money in their hands as the sun dries up the water in the marshes. As it was, their cash drained away imperceptibly and disappeared. How? No one knew. One of them was always saying: 'I don't know how it happened; I've spent 100 francs today and I didn't buy anything to speak of.' However, this carelessness about money matters was one of the joys of their life; they were agreed on this point to a magnificent extent – it was quite touching.

'Won't my mansion be wonderful now?' asked Jeanne.

'You'll see presently, my girl!' replied the Baron with a smile.

The violence of the storm was abating gradually; soon it was only a kind of drizzle, a fine mist of flying rain-drops. The cloud-ceiling began to rise and clear, and suddenly through an invisible opening a long slanting gleam of sunlight shone down

* It is hard to assess the value of the franc in 1819, but 1,000 francs then may be estimated at between £150 and £200 in purchasing power today.

on the fields. As the clouds parted, the blue depths of the sky appeared; then the rent broadened like a torn veil and a lovely clear expanse of sky spread over the whole earth. A gentle fresh breeze rose like a sigh of relief from the ground, and as they drove past gardens and woods, the cheerful song of a bird as it dried its wings was audible. It was getting dark and now everyone in the carriage was asleep except Jeanne. Twice they stopped at inns to allow the horses a breather and give them some oats and a drink of water.

The sun had set and bells were ringing in the distance. In one tiny village the street-lamps had been lit and the sky was studded with a host of stars. Here and there houses were lit up and threw a beam of light through the darkness, and suddenly behind a hill, through the branches of the pines, a great red moon rose sleepily.

It was so mild that the windows had been left open. After running through all her dreams Jeanne had now gone to sleep, having exhausted all her visions of happiness. Now and then the numbness caused by a prolonged stay in one position made her open her eyes and, looking out in the half-light, she saw the trees of a farm pass by or a few cows scattered over a field raise their heads. After changing her position she tried to recapture the thread of a dream, but the continuous rumble of the wheels filled her ears and paralysed her thinking, till she closed her eyes again, tired out mentally as well as physically.

Suddenly the carriage stopped. There were men and women standing in front of the door with lanterns in their hands. They had arrived. Jeanne woke with a start and jumped out quickly, while Papa and Rosalie, lighted by a farmer, almost lifted the Baroness out, now completely exhausted, groaning with pain and repeating over and over again in a low, scarcely audible voice: 'Oh my God! My poor children!' She would have nothing to eat or drink, but went straight to bed and fell asleep. Jeanne and the Baron had supper alone. Looking at each other, they smiled and grasped hands across the table; after the meal they started to go all over the renovated mansion with childish pleasure.

It was one of those vast tall Normandy houses, combining the farm-house and the mansion, built of white stone weathered grey, large enough to accommodate a whole clan. A great hall divided the house in two, running through it from one side to the other with great doors opening on the front and back. A double staircase spanned the front door, leaving the centre open, and the two flights joined on the first floor like a bridge. On the ground floor to the right was the door into the huge drawing-room, the walls of which were lined with tapestry with birds flitting about in leafy trees. All the furniture was upholstered in *petit-point*, illustrating La Fontaine's Fables, and Jeanne gave a start of pleasure when she found a chair that she had loved as a small child, representing the story of the Fox and the Stork. Out of the drawing-room opened the library, full of old books, and two other rooms which were unfurnished. To the left was the dining-room, newly panelled in wood, the linen-room, the pantry, the kitchen, and a small room with a bath. On the first floor a passage ran down the centre with ten bedroom doors opening off it. At the far end on the right was Jeanne's room, which they entered together.

The Baron had just had it done up, simply using the hangings and furniture that had been lying unused in the attics. Tapestries of Flemish origin peopled the walls with strange figures. But when she caught sight of her bed, the girl uttered cries of joy; the bed itself was supported at the four corners by four large birds in oak, black and highly polished, which seemed to be on guard. The sides were carved in two broad wreaths of flowers and fruits; and four delicately fluted pillars with Corinthian capitals held a cornice of roses and cupids intertwined. The whole effect was grandiose but at the same time attractive in spite of the severity of the wood darkened by age. The coverlet and the canopy of the bed shone like two skies; they were of dark blue antique silk, studded with large fleurs-de-lis embroidered in gold thread.

After admiring the bed Jeanne raised her candle to examine the tapestries and make out their subjects. A young nobleman and a young lady, very oddly dressed in green, red, and yellow, were talking under a blue tree, on which white fruits were ripening; a fat rabbit of the same colour was grubbing in a patch of grey grass. Just above the two figures in a conventional distance were visible five small round houses with pointed roofs, and above them almost in the sky a bright red windmill. The whole was framed in a magnificent floral design. The other two panels were like the first except that one noticed coming out of the houses four strange little men dressed in the Flemish fashion, raising their arms to heaven as if registering extreme astonishment and anger. But the third tapestry was a dramatic scene. Near the rabbit, which was grubbing as before, the young man lay outstretched and apparently dead, while the young lady with her eyes fixed on him was thrusting a sword into her breast, and the fruit on the tree had turned black.

Jeanne was giving up her attempt to unravel the story when in one corner she caught sight of a tiny creature, which the rabbit could have gobbled up like a blade of grass, if he had been alive. But it was a lion. From this she realized that it was the tragedy of Pyramus and Thisbe; and although the naïveté of the drawing made her smile, she was glad that she was to be shut up with this love-story, which would always recall her cherished hopes, while this ancient legend of love kept watch over her sleep every night.

The rest of the furniture was a mixture of styles. It consisted of the pieces which each generation leaves behind in the family and which turn old houses into a kind of museum of every out-of-date fashion. A magnificent Louis XIV chest-of-drawers, plated with gleaming copper, was flanked by two Louis XV arm-chairs, still upholstered in flowered silk. A rose-wood writing-table faced the chimney-piece, on which stood an Empire clock under a glass globe. It was a bronze bee-hive raised on four marble pillars above a garden of gilded flowers. From a slender pendulum, which projected from the hive through a wide slit, a tiny bee with enamel wings swung backwards and forwards, and the painted china clock-face was let into the side of the hive.

The clock began to strike eleven. The Baron kissed his daughter and went to his room, while Jeanne regretfully got into bed. After a last look round the room she blew out her candle. But the bed, of which only the head was against the wall, had a window on its left, through which a flood of moonlight cast a bright patch on the floor; this was reflected on the walls, dimly lighting up the love-story of Pyramus and Thisbe.

Through the other window facing the foot of the bed Jeanne noticed a tall tree bathed in the soft light. Turning on her side, she closed her eyes, but after a minute or two opened them again. She felt as if she was still being shaken by the jolting of the carriage, whose motion seemed to go on in her brain. At first she remained without moving, hoping that the rest would at last send her to sleep, but the restlessness of her mind soon affected her body. Her limbs twitched more and more feverishly; and finally she got out of bed with bare arms and feet, in her long nightdress, which made her look like a ghost, and crossed the patch of moonlight on the floor, opened the window and looked out. The night was so bright that one could see as clearly as if it was midday and the girl recognized every detail of the country that she had loved since her earliest childhood.

First of all facing her was a broad lawn as yellow as butter under the night sky. Two tall trees rose up like steeples in front of the house, a plane to the north and a linden to the south. Right on the far side of the stretch of grass a small clump of trees formed the boundary of the park, which was sheltered from the sea-wind by five rows of ancient elms, twisted, bare, like sloping roofs, eroded by the violent gales blowing in from the ocean. This sort of park was bounded on both sides by two long lines of towering abeles, called poplars in Normandy, which separated the owners residence from the two farms next to it, one occupied by the Couillard family, the other by the Martins. It was these poplars which had given the mansion its name. Beyond this enclosed park stretched a vast expanse of uncultivated land covered with scattered gorse-bushes, over which the sea-breezes whistled and scurried by day and night. Then suddenly the coastline dropped in a three hundred foot cliff, white and precipitous, its base washed by the surf.

Jeanne gazed at the broad surface of the sea, which looked like watered silk, sleeping peacefully under the stars. In the quiet of the sunless sky all the scents of the earth rose up into the air. A jessamine climbing round the downstair windows gave off a penetrating scent, which mingled with the fainter smell of the young leaves. Gentle gusts of wind were blowing, laden with the sharp tang of the salt and the heavy sticky reek of seaweed. At first the girl was happy just breathing the night air; the peace of the countryside had the calming effect of a cool bath. All the creatures which wake up every evening and conceal their secret lives in the peacefulness of the night were filling the semi-darkness with their faintly heard movement. Large birds were flitting about noiselessly like black blotches or ghosts and the hum of unseen insects caressed the ear; there were silent scurryings through the dewy grass and the dust of the deserted roads. The only sound was the melancholy monotonous note of the frogs croaking at the moon.

Jeanne felt her heart expanding, full of murmurs like the clear evening, suddenly filled with a thousand desires like the prowling nocturnal animals, whose rustlings were all round her. She felt part of the living poetry of nature, and in the soft brilliance of the night she was conscious of mysterious shivers, a palpitating sense of undefined hopes like a breath of happiness.

She began to dream of love. Love! For the last two years it had been filling her thoughts with anxious anticipations of its advent. Now she was free to love; she had only to meet *him*! What would *he* be like? She did not really know or even ask herself. He would be *him*, that was all. She only knew that she would worship him with all her heart and soul, and he would cherish her with all his strength. They would go for walks together on nights like this in the bright starlight; they would hold hands, pressing close to each other, hearing their heart-beats, feeling the warmth of their bodies, their love melting into the soft clear summer night; they would be so close that the power of their love would enable them to penetrate each other's secret thoughts. This would go on for ever in the serenity of a love too deep for words. Suddenly she seemed to feel *him* there close by her side, and a quick shiver of sensual longing ran over her whole body; she crossed her arms over her breast in an unconscious movement as if to embrace her dream, and, as she stretched out her lips towards the unknown, something seemed to touch them, as if the breath of the spring had printed on them a lover's kiss.

Suddenly, down below behind the house, she heard the sound of footsteps on the road in the darkness; and in the wild throbbing of her heart, in a transport of belief in the impossible, in providential accidents, in inspired presentiments, in romantic contrivances of fate, she thought : 'Supposing it were *he* !' She listened anxiously to the rhythmic steps of the passer-by, sure that he would stop at the gate and ask to be taken in. When he had passed on, she felt the sadness of disappointment, but she realized that it was only the over-excitement of her hopes and smiled at her own folly. Then, pulling herself together, she let her thoughts wander on in a more rational dream, trying to pierce the future and plan her life.

With *him* she would live here in this peaceful mansion overlooking the sea. She would no doubt have two children, a son for him and a daughter for herself. She could see them playing on the lawn between the plane and the linden, while father and mother watched them entranced, exchanging loving glances over their heads. She remained a long, long time dreaming, while the moon having finished its course across the sky was about to set in the sea. The air was growing chilly and the sky was lightening in the east. A cock crowed on the farm on the right, answered by others on the left. Their hoarse voices seemed to come from very far away across the chicken-runs, and the stars were growing dim in the vast vault of heaven, which was imperceptibly brightening. A faint bird-call rang out somewhere. Then twittering, timid at first, was audible in the leaves, and soon all the birds gaining courage were uttering their happy resonant note, which spread from branch to branch and from tree to tree.

Jeanne realized that it was broad daylight, and raising her head which she had hidden in her hands she closed her eyes, dazzled by the brightness of the dawn. A bank of crimson cloud, partly hidden by the long poplar avenue, was casting a blood-red light on the awakened earth. Soon the great blazing orb of the sun appeared, slowly bursting through the breaking clouds and flooding the trees, the plains, the ocean, and the whole sky with fire.

Jeanne felt that she was going mad with happiness, and a delirious joy, an uncontrollable emotion stirred by the beauty of nature swept over her fainting heart. It was *her* sun, *her* dawn, the start of *her* life, the dawn of *her* hopes; she stretched out her arms as if to embrace the sun. She wanted to speak, to cry aloud something as inspired as the dawn, but she remained paralysed by impotent excitement; she felt her eyes filling with tears and she wept from sheer happiness. When she raised her head, the first splendour of the dawn had already faded. She felt soothed, a little tired, as if chilled. Leaving the window open she went and lay down on the bed, dreamed for a few minutes longer and then went to sleep so soundly that at eight o'clock she did not hear her father's call and only woke up when he entered the room.

He wanted to show her the renovation of the mansion, *her* mansion. The front looked out on the central part of the estate and was separated from the road by a vast courtyard planted with apple-trees. The road, a secondary one running between peasants' holdings, joined the main road from Le Havre to Fécamp a little more than a mile further on. A straight drive led from the wooden garden-gate to the front-door steps. Low farm-buildings of sea-shingle with thatched roofs ran on both sides of the yard along ditches which separated it from the farms. All the upholstery had been renovated, the woodwork restored, the walls repaired, the rooms re-papered and the whole house re-painted. The dingy old manor house now had new shutters which shone like white patches and the new plaster showed up against the broad grey façade. The back, on which one of the windows of Jeanne's room opened, had a distant view of the sea over the top of the copse and the wall of elms fretted by the gales.

Arm-in-arm Jeanne and the Baron went over the whole house, not missing a corner; next they strolled along the long poplar avenues enclosing the so-called park. The grass had grown up and formed a green carpet under the trees. The copse at the far end was quite charming with little crooked paths between walls of foliage. A hare darted out, frightening the girl; then, jumping over the bank, it disappeared into the furze towards the cliff. After lunch, as Madame Adélaïde, who was still worn out, declared that she intended to rest, the Baron suggested that he and Jeanne should run down to Yport; so they started by going through the hamlet of Étouvent, in which the Poplars stood. Three peasants greeted them as old friends. Next they descended the wooded slope, which ran down to the sea in a winding valley. Presently the village of Yport came into sight. Women, mending clothes as they sat at their cottage doors, watched them pass. The road, which ran down the hill with a runnel in the centre and piles of rubbish scattered in front of the doors, gave off a strong smell of pickling-brine. Brown nets with gleaming fish-scales sticking to them here and there like tiny silver coins were drying in front of the cottage doors, from which issued the odour of large families crowded together in a single room. A few pigeons were strutting about the edge of the runnel looking for food.

Jeanne watched the scene, which was strange and novel to her like the backcloth of a theatre. But suddenly, as they turned a corner, she saw the sea, a dark unruffled blue stretching to the horizon. They stopped, facing the beach to admire the view. Sails, white as birds' wings, were passing on the open sea. To right and left towered the high cliff; in one direction a sort of cape cut off the view, while in the other the coastline stretched on and on till it dwindled into a scarcely visible line. A cove and a few cottages appeared in an inlet near by, where tiny wavelets fringing the sea with foam were breaking on the shingle with a faint sound. The fishing-boats, hauled up on the rounded pebbles of the sloping beach, were lying on their sides, showing their curved flanks gleaming with tar to the sun. A few fishermen were getting them ready for the evening tide.

A sailor came up to them offering fish, and Jeanne bought a brill, which she insisted on carrying back to the Poplars herself. Then the man suggested taking them for a sail, repeating his name over and over again to impress it on their minds, Lastique, Joséphin Lastique. The Baron promised not to forget him.

After that they started back home. As the weight of the fish tired Jeanne, she stuck her father's stick through its gills and each took one end. They were in cheerful mood, chattering like children, with the breeze in their faces and their eyes shining, while the brill, gradually tiring their arms, swept the grass with its broad tail.

CHAPTER TWO

A DELIGHTFULLY free life now began for Jeanne; she read and dreamed, wandering about by herself in the neighbourhood. She strolled slowly along the roads, deep in her dreams, or else tripped down the winding valleys, the sides of which were draped in a golden cope of gorse in bloom. The strong gentle scent, drawn out by the heat, intoxicated her like the scent of wine, and with the distant breaking of the waves on the shore the surf lulled her mind to sleep. Sometimes a feeling of indolence made her lie down on the close grass of a sloping bank, and sometimes at a bend in the valley, where a triangle of blue sea gleamed in the sun through a funnel of turf with a sail on the horizon, she was seized with an undefined joy as if at the mysterious approach of happiness. Love of solitude flooded her mind in the softness of the cool country-side and the peace of the curving horizon, and she sat so long on the hill-tops that the little wild rabbits scuttled to and fro over her feet. She often ran along the edge of the cliff, urged on by the cool air of the hills, inspired by the exquisite pleasure of effortless movement, like the fishes in the sea or the swallows in the air. She left memories behind her as one sows seeds in the earth, memories whose roots last till death; she seemed to scatter little bits of her heart in all the folds of these valleys.

She took to bathing enthusiastically, swimming far out to sea, for she was strong and fearless; she was happy in the cold, clear, blue water, which supported her on its waves. Far out from the shore she would turn over on her back and fold her arms on her breast, her eyes lost in the deep blue of the sky, across which a swallow darted or the white silhouette of a sea-gull. No sound was audible except the distant murmur of waves breaking on the shingle and the faint whisper of the land gliding over the surface of the rollers with a confused almost imperceptible hum. Then Jeanne sat up and in a wild outburst of joy uttered shrill cries, beating the water with both hands.

Occasionally, when she had ventured out too far, a boat came out to fetch her. She sometimes returned home pale with hunger, but brisk and light-hearted, with a smile on her lips and eyes radiant with happiness.

The Baron for his part was planning important agricultural schemes; he was anxious to start new projects and move with the times, experimenting with modern farm implements and acclimatizing new strains. He spent much of his time discussing his plans with the peasants, who shook their heads, distrusting his new ideas. He often went to sea with the Yport fishermen; after visiting the grottoes, the springs, and the rocky needles in the neighbourhood, he insisted on fishing like an ordinary sailor. On breezy days, when the bellying sail swept the broad hull of the boat on the crest of the waves and dragged to port and starboard the swiftly moving line baited to attract the schools of mackerel, he used to hold in a hand trembling with anxiety the thin line, whose vibrations can be felt as soon as a fish which has taken the bait begins to struggle. He used to go out by moonlight too to take in the nets laid the evening before. He loved to hear the creaking of the mast and breathe the whistling gusts of the night wind, and after tacking about in search of the buoys, steering by a rock crest, the roof of a clock-tower and the Fécamp lighthouse, he enjoyed sitting quietly under the first beams of the rising sun, which made the sticky fan-shaped backs of the large skates and the fat bellies of the turbots gleam on the boat's deck.

At every meal he told the story of his trips with obvious pleasure, and Mama retorted by telling how many times she had walked up and down the long poplar avenue, the one on the right by the Couillards' farm, as the other did not catch enough sun. Having been recommended to take exercise, she could never have enough of walking. As soon as the air warmed up after the night, she came down, leaning on Rosalie's arm, wrapped up in a mantle and two shawls, her head enveloped in a black bonnet covered by a red knitted scarf; then, dragging her left leg, which was rather lame and had already traced two dusty furrows all the way down the path where the grass was worn, one on the outward journey and one on the way back, she started on her interminable walk straight from the corner of the house to the first bushes of the shrubbery. She had had a bench placed at each end of her path, and every five minutes she stopped, saying to the poor patient maid supporting her: 'Let's sit down, my dear, I'm a bit tired.'

At each pause she left on one of the benches first the knitted scarf covering her head, next one shawl, then the other, then her bonnet and finally her mantle. This left at both ends of the avenue a large heap of garments, which Rosalie took back to the house on her free arm when they went in to lunch. In the afternoon the Baroness repeated the same programme, only more slowly with longer rests, even dozing from time to time on a couch, which had been wheeled out for her. She always referred to this practice as *her* exercise just as she spoke of *her* hypertrophy.

A doctor, consulted ten years before because she was suffering from shortness of breath, had spoken of hypertrophy, and ever since, the word, whose meaning she hardly understood, had fixed itself in her head. She was continually insisting on the Baron, Jeanne, and Rosalie feeling her heart, which no one could in fact feel owing to the puffiness of her breast; but she absolutely refused to let another doctor examine her, fearing that he might discover some other complaint, and she talked of *her* hypertrophy on every possible occasion, so often that it seemed that this condition was something peculiar to her and belonged to her as a private possession, to which no one else had any right. The Baron spoke of 'my wife's hypertrophy' and Jeanne of 'Mama's hypertrophy', as they might have mentioned her dress or her hat or her umbrella.

In her young days she had been very pretty, as slim as a reed. After waltzing in the arms of all the officers of the Empire, she had read *Corinne*, which had made her weep; the novel had left a lasting impression on her mind. As her figure coarsened, her soul became ever more romantic, and when her corpulence riveted her to her chair, her imagination continued to wander through tender adventures, of which she was the heroine. She had her favourite dreams, which were always coming back, as a musical-box always repeats the same tune when it is wound up. Sentimental romances about prisoners and swallows invariably reduced her to tears; she even liked some

22

of Béranger's bawdy songs because of the regrets which they voice. She often remained for hours without moving, far away in dreamland, and she enjoyed life at the Poplars immensely, because it provided a background for her soul's romances, and with the woods all round, the uncultivated moors and the proximity of the sea, it reminded her of Walter Scott's novels which she had recently been reading.

On wet days she stayed shut up in her room, going through what she called 'her relics'. They were all her old letters, letters from her father and mother, the Baron's letters during their engagement, and many others. She kept them shut up in a mahogany writing-table with bronze sphinxes at the corners, and she used to say in a special tone of voice: 'Rosalie, my dear, bring me my relic drawer.' The girl opened the bureau, took out the drawer and put it on a chair by the side of her mistress, who began to read the letters slowly, shedding a tear from time to time.

Jeanne sometimes replaced Rosalie and took Mama out for her walk, when she recalled memories of her childhood. The girl often recognized herself in these old reminiscences, surprised by the similarity of their thoughts and the likeness of their desires; for every heart imagines that it has been stirred in the same way by those feelings which have made the hearts of primitive man beat and will continue to affect men and women till the end of time. The slowness of their walks matched the slowness of their stories, which were interrupted by brief fits of breathlessness. Then Jeanne's heart leapt forward beyond the incidents of the old lady's past and plunged into the joys of anticipation and the luxury of hopes.

As they were resting one afternoon at the end of the avenue, they suddenly saw at the other end a portly priest coming towards them. He greeted them while still some distance away, smiled and then, when three paces from them, bowed again, crying: 'Well, Baroness, and how are we today?' It was the parish priest. Mama, born in an age of reason and brought up by a father without religious convictions in the Revolutionary period, rarely went to church, though a woman's instinctive religion made her well-disposed towards priests. She had entirely forgotten the Abbé Picot, their parish priest, and she blushed when

23

she saw him. She made excuses for not having told him of her coming to the Poplars, but the kindly soul did not seem offended. He looked at Jeanne, complimented her on looking so well, and sat down with his clerical hat on his knee mopping his brow. He was very fat and red in the face and was perspiring profusely; he was continually taking from his pocket a very large check handkerchief soaked in sweat and wiping his face and neck. But hardly had the damp cloth been put back in his pocket, when new beads of perspiration appeared on his brow and falling on the cassock stretched tightly over his stomach, fixed the dust from the roads in little round stains.

He was a typical country priest, cheerful, tolerant, and talkative, in fact a good soul. He was full of the village gossip and seemed unaware that his two lady parishioners had not yet come to church. Her natural indolence as well as the vagueness of her religious convictions accounted for the Baroness's absence, while Jeanne was only too happy to have escaped from the convent, where she had had her fill of church ceremonial.

Presently the Baron, whose pantheistic philosophy rendered him quite indifferent to dogma, appeared. He was always polite to the Abbé, though he saw little of him, and he kept him to dinner. The priest knew how to make himself welcome, with that instinctive cunning which dealing with human souls gives to the most ordinary men who are called by the hazard of circumstances to exercise authority over their fellows. The Baroness made much of him, attracted perhaps by the similarity of their physical natures, for the portly priest's red face and shortness of breath flattered her panting corpulence. As they reached dessert, he showed something of the gaiety of a priest on the spree, the uninhibited familiarity common at the end of a good dinner, and suddenly, as if a happy thought had just struck him, he cried: 'But I've got a new parishioner to introduce to you – Monsieur le Vicomte de Lamare.'

The Baroness, with all the noble families of the neighbourhood at her finger-tips, asked: 'Is he one of the Lamare family of the Eure?'

The priest bowed: 'Yes, Madame; he is the son of the Vicomte Jean de Lamare, who died last year.'

Then Madame Adélaïde, who liked the nobility above every-

24

thing else, asked a string of questions, and learnt that after paying his father's debts the young man had sold the family mansion and fixed up a hunting-box on one of three farms near Étouvent. He had an income of between five and six thousand francs a year from landed property, and he meant to live the simple life for two or three years in this modest cottage in order to accumulate enough to cut a figure in society and make a good marriage, without getting into debt or mortgaging his farms.

'He is a very charming young man,' added the priest, 'of settled habits and fond of the quiet life, but the country does not really amuse him.'

'Well, bring him along to our house,' replied the Baron. 'That may afford him a distraction from time to time.'

After that they talked of other things. When they went into the drawing-room after coffee, the Abbé asked if he might take a turn in the garden, being used to a little exercise after meals. The Baron accompanied him and they strolled slowly along the whole length of the white frontage of the mansion and back again. Their shadows, one thin, the other broad with a mushroom-like growth on the head, moved this way and that, now in front of them, now behind, according to whether they were walking with the moon before or behind. The priest was chewing a kind of cigarette which he took out of his pocket. He explained the purpose of this with a peasant's frankness : 'It's to induce belching, as my digestion is inclined to be sluggish.'

Then looking up to where a bright moon was travelling across the sky he said solemnly : 'This is a sight one never tires of.'

With that he went into the house to take leave of the ladies.

CHAPTER THREE

THE following Sunday the Baroness and Jeanne went to Mass out of a delicate feeling of respect for the priest. After the service they waited for him to ask him to lunch on Thursday. He came out of the vestry arm-in-arm with a tall, well-dressed young man. Catching sight of the two ladies, he cried with a gesture of pleased surprise: 'What luck! Allow me, Baroness and Mademoiselle Jeanne, to introduce your neighbour, Monsieur le Vicomte de Lamare.'

The Viscount bowed, saying that he had long wanted to make the ladies' acquaintance, and he went on talking with the easy assurance of a gentleman used to polite society. He had one of those smiling faces that women dream of but all men dislike. His dark curly hair surmounted an unlined, sun-tanned forehead, and two thick bushy eyebrows as regular as if they had been drawn with a brush gave soft depth to his dark eyes, whose whites were tinged with blue.

Long thick eyelashes lent his glance that passionate eloquence which excites the proud society lady in the drawing-room and makes the peasant girl in a bonnet with a basket on her arm turn round in the street. The languishing charm of his eyes suggested depth of thought and lent importance to every word. His thick, close, glossy beard concealed a rather prominent jaw. They separated after the usual polite commonplaces.

Two days later Monsieur de Lamare paid his first call. He arrived as they were trying a rustic bench that had been set up that very morning under the tall plane tree in front of the drawing-room windows. The Baron wanted another under the linden to balance it, but Mama, who hated symmetry, refused. The Viscount, when asked his opinion, agreed with the Baroness. Then he talked about the countryside, which he declared 'very picturesque'; in his solitary walks he had discovered 'many very attractive spots'. From time to time he caught Jeanne's eye as if by accident and this momentary glance, quickly averted, made a strong impression on her, indicating tender admiration and awakened interest.

Monsieur de Lamare's father, who had died the year before, happened to have known a great friend of Monsieur des Curtaux, the Baroness's father; and the discovery of this acquaintance started an interminable conversation about marriages, dates, and family connexions. The Baroness performed prodigies of memory, recalling family pedigrees and making her way without ever losing herself through the complicated genealogical labyrinth.

'Tell me, Viscount, have you ever heard mention of the Saunoys of Varfleur? The eldest son, Gontran, married a Mademoiselle de la Roche-Aubert, who was connected with the Crisanges. Now Monsieur de Crisange was a great friend of my father, and he must have known your father too.'

'Yes, Madame. It was that Monsieur de Crisange who emigrated, wasn't it? His son went bankrupt.'

'Yes, that's the man. He had proposed to my aunt after her husband's death – he was the Comte d'Eretry – but she would have nothing to do with him, because he took snuff. By the way, do you know what happened to the Villoises? They left Touraine about 1813, because they had lost their money, and settled in the Auvergne, and I never heard any more of them.'

'I believe, Madame, that the old Marquis died as a result of a fall from his horse, leaving one daughter married to an Englishman and the other to somebody called Bassolle, a business-man said to be wealthy, who had seduced her.'

These childhood memories of names heard in the conversation of their parents were recalled, for the marriages of these noble families assumed in their minds the importance of great public events. They spoke of people they had never seen as if they knew them well, and people in other districts spoke of them in the same way; they all felt themselves acquaintances, almost friends and connexions, simply because they belonged to the same class and the same caste by virtue of their common blue blood.

The Baron, who was by nature unsociable and alienated by education from the beliefs and prejudices of the people of his world, hardly even knew the families in the district; he questioned the Viscount about them.

'Oh, there aren't many of the nobility round here,' replied Monsieur de Lamare, in the same tone of voice in which he would have said that there were not many rabbits on the hills; and he gave details.

In the immediate neighbourhood there were only three families, the Marquis de Coutelier, the head of the Normandy nobility, the Vicomte and Vicomtesse de Briseville, well born but keeping very much to themselves, and finally the Comte de Fourville, a sort of bogy-man, who was supposed to be killing his wife with misery and who spent all his time hunting from his mansion of La Vrillette, which was built on a lake. A few *nouveaux riches,* who only mixed with each other, had bought estates here and there; the Viscount knew none of them.

As he took his leave, his last glance was for Jeanne, as if he was addressing a special good-bye, more cordial and more tender, to her.

The Baroness pronounced him charming, such a gentleman.

'Yes, he certainly knows his manners,' replied Papa.

The following week he was invited to dinner and after that he came regularly. He usually arrived about four o'clock in the afternoon and joined Mama in 'her drive', giving her his arm, while she took 'her exercise'. When Jeanne was not out, she supported the Baroness on the other side, and the three of them strolled slowly up and down the straight path, going back and forth again and again. He hardly said anything to the girl, but his eyes, like black velvet, often caught hers, which were like blue agate. More than once they both went down to Yport with the Baron. One evening, when they found themselves on the beach, old Lastique accosted them, and without taking his pipe out of his mouth – its absence would have been more surprising than the disappearance of his nose – he said : 'Seein' as the wind be in this quarter, Sir, us might go to Étretat tomorrow and back quite easy.'

Jeanne clapped her hands : 'Oh, Papa, could we go?'

The Baron turned to Monsieur de Lamare : 'Would you care to come with us? We could have lunch there.' And the trip was fixed up on the spot.

Jeanne was up with the sun. She waited for her father, who took longer to dress and they set off on foot through the dew, first crossing the common, then the wood, which echoed with the song of birds. They found the Viscount and old Lastique sitting on a winch. Two other sailors helped to get them off; pushing with their shoulders against the planking of the hull, they exerted all their strength and the boat moved slowly over the shingle ledge. Lastique slipped rollers of greased wood under the keel, and then, climbing on board, chanted in his drawling voice: 'Heave ho! Heave ho!' to give the men the time. When it reached the shelving slope, the boat suddenly gathered speed and slid over the rounded pebbles with a sound of tearing linen, but it stopped dead where the wavelets were breaking in foam, and they all took their seats on the thwarts. Then the two sailors, who had remained behind, got the boat afloat. A steady light breeze from the open sea was skimming over the water, just wrinkling its surface. The sail was hoisted and bellied out and the boat gathered way, gently rocked by the waves.

First they went straight out to sea. In front the sky curved down to mingle with the ocean on the horizon; on the landward side the tall steep cliff cast a dense shadow at its foot, pierced here and there by sunlight reflected from the patches of grass. Away astern brown sails were coming out from the whitewashed jetty of Fécamp, and ahead an oddly shaped rock, bulging out and pierced with holes, looked rather like a monstrous elephant plunging its trunk into the sea; it was the Little Gate of Étretat.

Jeanne, gripping the gunwale with one hand and slightly dazed by the rocking of the boat, was gazing into the distance; she felt that there were only three really beautiful things in creation: light, space, and water. No one spoke; old Lastique, holding the tiller and the sheet, took a little drink at intervals straight from a bottle hidden under his seat and went on all the time smoking the stump of his pipe, which never seemed to go out; from it issued a thin thread of blue smoke and another similar one came from the corner of his mouth. No one ever saw him re-light the clay bowl, which was blacker than ebony, or refill it. Sometimes he took it from his mouth with one hand and from the same corner from which the smoke came he spat out a long jet of brown saliva.

The Baron up in the bows kept an eye on the sail and acted as crew. Jeanne and the Viscount found themselves side by side, both slightly embarrassed. Some mysterious power was always making them both raise their eyes at the same moment, so that they met as if impelled by some affinity of feeling; for there was already established between them that subtle, undefined tenderness so quickly born between a young couple, when the boy is not plain and the girl is pretty. They were glad to be near one another, perhaps because each was thinking of the other.

The sun was climbing the sky, as if to get a better view of the sea stretching below, but with a sort of coy modesty it veiled its beams in a thin mist. It was a transparent fog, quite low, gilded by the rays which hid nothing but softened the outlines of the distance. The orb of the sun melted this shining cloud with darting shafts, and as it reached its full heat the fog evaporated and disappeared and the sea as smooth as ice shimmered in the light. Deeply moved, Jeanne murmured: 'How lovely it is!'

'Yes, it is lovely,' replied the Viscount. The tranquil beauty of the morning raised an echo in both their hearts.

Suddenly they sighted the long jetties of Étretat, like the two legs of a cliff striding out into the sea, high enough to shelter ships, with a sharp needle of white rock rising up at the end of the first one. They made land and while the Baron, who had jumped out first, kept the boat from drifting away by pulling on a hawser, the Viscount carried Jeanne ashore to prevent her getting her feet wet. Then the two of them made their way up the hard shingle slope side by side, both excited by their brief embrace. Suddenly they heard old Lastique say to the Baron: 'It do seem to me they'd make a pretty couple anyways.'

They had an excellent lunch at a little inn near the beach. The sea, muting alike voices and thoughts, had checked conversation earlier, but at the meal they became talkative, chattering like schoolboys on holiday. They all roared with laughter again and again at the most ordinary incidents. As old Lastique sat down at table, he carefully hid his pipe, still smoking, in his beret, and everyone laughed. A fly settled several times on his nose, no doubt attracted by its redness, and when he chased it away with a hand too slow to catch it, it took up a position on a muslin curtain, already much stained by its sisters, as if to keep an eye on the sailor's fiery proboscis, for it soon took off again to return to its former landing-ground. Every descent of the insect provoked an outburst of merriment, and when the old man, annoyed by the tickle, murmured : 'It's a damned obstinate creature!' Jeanne and the Viscount laughed till they cried, twisting and choking with their napkins to their lips to stifle their guffaws.

When they had finished their coffee, Jeanne said: 'Shall we take a stroll?' The Viscount immediately got up but the Baron preferred to enjoy a siesta on the beach in the sun : 'You go off, children; you'll find me here in an hour.'

They made their way straight between the few cottages of the village, and after passing a small country-house more like a large farm they found themselves in an open valley stretching in front of them. The rocking of the boat had sapped their energy, upsetting their normal balance, and the fresh salt air had given them an appetite; then their lunch had satisfied them and their amusement had relaxed them. They now experienced a crazy longing to career over the country. Jeanne felt a buzzing in her ears, overwhelmed by a flood of new sensations. The sun was blazing overhead. On the slopes bordering the road the ripe harvest was drooping as if weighed down by the heat. Grasshoppers as thick as blades of grass were singing themselves hoarse, their shrill deafening note rising from the wheat, barley, and gorse on the slopes. No other sound was audible in the torrid heat, and the blue sky shimmered with a yellow tinge as if on the point of turning red like iron too close to a fire.

Seeing a small wood further on to the right, they went to it. There was a narrow path shut in between two banks under tall trees, which kept the sun off. A sort of chill from decaying vegetation greeted them as they walked, the damp which makes the skin shiver and penetrates the lungs. The grass had withered from lack of light and air but the ground was carpeted with moss. They walked on: 'Look, we might sit down there,' she said. Two old trees had died and through the hole in the ceiling of foliage a beam of sunlight penetrated and warmed the earth, waking into life the seeds of grass, dandelions, and creepers and bringing out a cloud of little white flowers and spindly foxgloves. Butterflies, bees and fat hornets, big gnats like the skeletons of flies, swarms of winged insects, pink spotted ladybirds, devil's coach-horses, some with flashes of green, others horned, crowded the warm patch of sun that pierced the chilly shade of the thick foliage. They sat down with their heads in the shade and their feet in the sun, watching the teeming life of tiny creatures brought out by a ray of sun, and Jeanne, deeply moved by the sight, kept repeating: 'This is real happiness! What a wonderful place the country is! I sometimes wish I was a gnat or a butterfly, so that I could hide in the flowers.'

They talked about themselves, their life and their tastes in the low intimate tone proper to confidences. He said that he was tired of smart society and weary of his futile existence; there was such a sameness about everything, there was nothing genuine, nothing sincere in it. Smart society! She would certainly like to know it, but she was convinced in advance that it could not compare with country life. The closer they came in their hearts, the more punctiliously they called each other 'Monsieur le Vicomte' and 'Mademoiselle', but the more their eyes met and smiled, the closer a new bond of affection seemed to unite them, an interest in a thousand things of which they had never thought before.

Then they went back, but the Baron had gone off on foot to the Chambre-aux-Demoiselles, a cave high up on the cliff face, and they waited for him at the inn. He did not return till five o'clock in the afternoon after a long walk along the coast.

Presently they boarded the boat again. It moved smoothly on an even keel with a following wind, hardly seeming to advance. The warm breeze blew in gentle gusts and made the sail now belly out, now fall slack against the mast. The thick water seemed dead and the sun having exhausted its heat in its journey across the sky was slowly westering towards the horizon.

The peace of the sea silenced every tongue. At last Jeanne said: 'I *should* like to travel!'

'Yes,' replied the Viscount, 'but it's no fun travelling alone; there must be at least two to share impressions.'

She thought for a moment: 'Yes, that's true, but I like walking by myself.'

Fixing his eyes on her face, he remarked: 'Dreams too can be shared.'

She lowered her eyes; was it a suggestion that they might share their dreams? Perhaps it was. She was gazing at the horizon as if anxious to pierce beyond it, and speaking slowly she said: 'I should like to travel in Italy ... and in Greece ... yes, in Greece and in Corsica ... Corsica must be so wild and so beautiful.'

He preferred Switzerland with its chalets and lakes. She went on: 'No, I like countries which are either quite new like Corsica, or very old and full of memories like Greece. It must be thrilling to find traces of a nation whose history one has known since childhood and to see the places where great events occurred.'

The Viscount, less romantically inclined, declared: 'England has a powerful attraction for me; one can learn a lot there.'

Then they went all over the globe from the poles to the equator, discussing what each country had to offer and going into ecstasies over the imagined scenery and the strange habits of life of people like the Chinese and the Lapps; but in the end they agreed that the most beautiful country in the world was France, with its temperate climate not too hot in summer and mild in winter, its fertile soil, its green forests, its broad navigable rivers, and its cultivation of the fine arts, unparalleled elsewhere except in the great age of Athens.

After that they fell silent. The sun seemed to turn to blood as it set; a broad trail of light like a dazzling high-road ran from the ocean's edge up to the wake of the boat. The last whispers of the breeze died away leaving a flat calm and the sail, now motionless, was blood-red. An all-embracing peace swallowed up the whole of space, silencing the strife of the elements, while the sea, heaving up its gleaming belly heavenwards in an arch, looked like a monstrous bride awaiting the descent of her fiery lover; he was hastening his downward path, flushed by his longing for their embrace. At last he was united with

33

her and she gradually swallowed him up. Then a quick gust of cold air from the horizon ruffled the breast of the water, as if the sun's orb, now beneath the sea, had heaved a sigh of contentment to the world.

After this a brief twilight with twinkling stars spread over the world. Old Lastique took the oars and they noticed that the sea was phosphorescent. Jeanne and the Viscount sat side by side and watched the boat's gleaming wake. Their minds were a blank; they were just looking round, breathing the evening air in blissful content. Jeanne had one hand resting on the thwart, and one of her companion's fingers touched it as if by accident; she did not move her hand, surprised and happy, her emotions stirred by the light touch.

When she reached home in the evening and went up to her room, she felt strangely excited and so upset that the slightest thing moved her to tears. Catching sight of her clock she thought of the little bee as beating like a kindred heart; it would be the witness of her whole life, accompanying all her joys and sorrows with its quick regular tick, and she stopped the pendulum to print a kiss on the little creature's gilded wings – she would have kissed anything. She remembered that she had hidden one of her childhood's old dolls at the back of a drawer and at the sight of it she experienced the joy one feels on meeting a beloved friend; pressing it tightly to her breast she printed passionate kisses on its painted cheeks and curly tow wig, and, still holding it in her arms, she went on dreaming. Was *he* really the husband promised by a thousand whispering voices, thrown in her way by a divinely beneficent providence? Was *he* really the man made for her, to whom her life would be devoted? Were they the two beings predestined to be united in a lifelong embrace which would give birth to *Love*? She did not yet feel those thrills of her whole being, those wild ecstasies and deep-seated disturbances which she imagined were the essence of passion. But she thought she was beginning to love him, for the mere thought of him sometimes made her quite faint and he was never far from her mind. His presence made her heart beat faster and she blushed or went pale when she met his eye and trembled at the sound of his voice. That night she hardly slept. As the days went on, the disturbing urge to

34

love dominated her thoughts more and more. She was always consulting her heart as well as daisies, clouds and coins tossed in the air.

One evening her father said: 'Make yourself beautiful to-morrow!'

'Why, Papa?'

'That's a secret,' he replied.

When she came down next morning, looking charming in a light summer frock, she found the drawing-room table covered with boxes of sweets and a huge bouquet on a chair. A van drove into the yard with the name 'Lerat, Confectioner, Fécamp; Wedding Breakfasts'. Ludivine, with the help of an errand-boy, took from the boot at the back a number of flat baskets which smelt good.

The Vicomte de Lamare appeared. His tight-fitting trousers were strapped under his smart patent-leather boots, which emphasized the smallness of his feet. His long tight-waisted frock-coat showed the lace frill of his shirt-front, and a fine stock which went several times round his neck made him hold his fine dark head high with an air of grave distinction. He was a changed man, for an unusual get-up gives the best-known face a new look.

Jeanne looked at him in amazement as if she had never seen him before; he was the perfect type of the noble lord from head to foot.

'Well, my dear, are you ready?' and he bowed with a smile.

'What is it?' she stammered. 'What's it all about?'

'You'll find out all in good time!' said the Baron.

The barouche drove up to the door. Madame Adélaïde came down from her room in her smartest frock, supported by Rosalie, who seemed so impressed by Monsieur de Lamare's elegance that Papa whispered: 'Look, Viscount! You've made a conquest!' He blushed up to the ears, pretending not to hear, and picking up the largest bouquet offered it to Jeanne; she took it, still more astonished. The four of them got into the carriage, and Ludivine the cook, who had brought out a cup of cold soup to keep up the Baroness's strength, exclaimed: 'It's just like a wedding, Madame!'

They alighted on the outskirts of Yport, and as they walked

35

through the village, the fishermen in their best clothes with the creases still visible came out of their houses, took off their hats to shake hands with the Baron, and fell in behind the party as if behind a procession. The Viscount with Jeanne on his arm led the way. They stopped in front of the church. The large silver cross was brought out, held erect by a choir-boy, who was followed by another in a red cassock and a white surplice carrying a holy-water stoup with a sprinkler in it. Behind them came three old cantors, one of them lame, and behind them the player on the serpent, followed by the priest, his prominent paunch thrusting forward his gold-embroidered stole which was crossed over it. He greeted them with a smile and a nod; then, with eyes half-closed and lips moving in prayer and his biretta pulled down over his forehead, he followed his surpliced staff, as they went down to the sea.

On the beach a crowd was waiting round a new garlanded boat. Its mast, sail, and rigging were decorated with long ribbons fluttering in the breeze, and its name 'Jeanne' in gold letters was visible on the stern.

Old Lastique, the owner of the boat, which had been built at the Baron's expense, advanced to meet the procession. All the men took off their hats in one simultaneous movement and the line of pious women, their heads draped with broad black kerchiefs which fell down to their shoulders in folds, knelt down in a ring at the sight of the cross. The priest stood between the two choir-boys at one end of the boat, while at the other end the three old cantors, in their soiled white surplices with unshaven chins, solemnly keeping their eyes on their chant-books, sang their words at the top of their voices slightly out of tune in the clear morning air. Every time they paused for breath the player on the serpent came in with his booming solo and his small grey eyes sank into the hollows of his cheeks, which were puffed out by his blowing; even the skin of his forehead seemed to have become loose from the bone, so vigorously was he blowing his instrument.

The clear calm sea seemed part of the reverent congregation at the boat's christening, hardly moving, just gently caressing the shingle with tiny wavelets no bigger than a finger. Great white gulls with wings spread flew past in long curves in the blue sky, soaring away and returning to circle over the kneeling crowd, as if anxious to get a good view of the proceedings. But after five minutes the singing came to an end with a fortissimo Amen, and the priest mumbled in his throaty voice a few Latin words, of which only the sonorous terminations were distinguishable. After that he walked all round the boat sprinkling it with holy-water, before beginning to murmur prayers, standing close to the planking of the hull and facing the god-parents, who were motionless hand in hand. Showing no sign of emotion, the young man looked like a tailor's dummy of the well-dressed man of fashion, but the girl, strangled with sudden feeling and almost fainting, began to tremble so violently that her teeth chattered. The dream that had been haunting her for some time had suddenly been translated into reality by a kind of hallucination.

The word 'wedding' had been spoken, and the priest was there giving the blessing and a surpliced choir singing the psalms. Surely she was the bride. Were not her fingers twitching nervously? Surely the beating of her heart driving the blood through her veins must have found its way to the heart of the man by her side. Did he understand, did he guess, was he like her possessed by the intoxication of love? She suddenly realized that he was squeezing her hand, gently at first, then more tightly till it hurt; and without any change of expression, so that no one noticed anything, he said, she was certain of it, he said quite distinctly: 'Oh, Jeanne, if you were willing, this might be our betrothal !'

She bent her head very slowly, which perhaps meant 'Yes'; and the priest, who was still sprinkling holy-water, let a few drops fall on their fingers.

Now it was all over and the women rose from their knees. There was a stampede to get back. The cross in the choir-boy's hands had lost its dignity; it was in a hurry, rocking from right to left, tilted forward, ready to fall on its nose. The priest, having finished his prayers, trotted along behind; the cantors and the serpent disappeared down an alley in order to get rid of their vestments quicker, and the sailors hurried away in twos and threes. The same thought, like the smell of cooking, quickened their steps, made them dribble at the mouth and penetrated to their stomachs, making their bowels rumble.

At the Poplars a good lunch was waiting for them all. A long trestle-table had been put up under the apple-trees. In the middle the Baroness had next to her the two priests from Yport and the Poplars; opposite, the Baron had the mayor on one side and on the other the latter's wife, a scraggy peasant already elderly, who was continually bowing all round; she had a narrow face framed in her broad Normandy coif, the face of a white-crested hen, with round eyes which always expressed surprise; she ate in quick little mouthfuls as if she were pecking at her plate.

Jeanne, next to the godfather, was plunged in a sea of happiness; she saw nothing, thought of nothing, said nothing, her brain paralysed with joy.

Suddenly she asked: 'What is your Christian name?'

'Julien,' he replied; 'didn't you know?'

She did not answer, thinking: 'How often I shall repeat that name!'

When the meal was over, they left the courtyard to the villagers and went to the other side of the mansion. The Baroness started off to take 'her exercise' escorted by the two priests. Jeanne and Julien went into the shrubbery along the narrow bushy paths; suddenly, seizing her hand, he whispered: 'Tell me, Jeanne darling, will you be my wife?'

She bent her head and when he whispered: 'Do give me an answer, I beseech you,' she raised her eyes gently to his and he read her answer in her glance.

CHAPTER FOUR

ONE morning the Baron came into Jeanne's room before she was up, and sitting down on the foot of the bed he said : 'The Vicomte de Lamare has asked us for your hand.'

She felt like hiding her face under the sheets; her father went on : 'We promised to give him an answer later.'

She was panting, strangled with emotion. After a minute the Baron added with a smile : 'We didn't want to do anything without discussing it with you. Your mother and I have no objection to this marriage, but we do not wish to put any pressure on you. You are much better off than he is, but when it is a question of lifelong happiness, the consideration of money ought not to come in. He has no near relative living; so if you do marry him, he will come into our family as a son, whereas with someone else it would be a case of our daughter going among strangers. We like the young man; would you, I wonder?'

'Yes, Father, I would,' she stammered, blushing up to the ears.

'I suspected as much, young lady !' replied Papa, looking hard at her and smiling.

She lived all that day in a state of intoxication, not knowing what she was doing, picking up the wrong thing by mistake, and her legs trembled with weakness as if after a long walk. About six o'clock, as she was sitting under the plane tree with Mama, the Viscount appeared. He came towards them with no visible sign of emotion. When he reached them, he took the Baroness's fingers and kissed them; then, raising the girl's trembling hand, he printed on it a passionate kiss of love and gratitude.

Now began the blissful period of their engagement. They talked by themselves in the corners of the drawing-room or sitting on the bank at the bottom of the shrubbery facing the wild moor; sometimes they walked up and down 'Mama's drive', he speaking of the future and she keeping her eyes lowered to the Baroness's footprints.

The decision was taken, they were anxious not to waste time and it was agreed that the wedding should take place in six weeks on 15 August, and that the young couple should leave on their honeymoon immediately afterwards. When Jeanne was asked where she would like to go, she settled on Corsica, where they would have more privacy than in the towns of Italy. They awaited the moment of their marriage without undue impatience, wrapped in an atmosphere of delicious tenderness and enjoying to the full the exquisite pleasure of brief caresses and the pressure of fingers and passionate glances so long drawn out that their very souls seemed to melt into one another; and they were aware of a vague longing for yet more intimate embraces. They decided to invite no one to the wedding except the Baroness's sister, Aunt Lison, who lived as a paying guest at a convent in Versailles. On their father's death the Baroness had wanted to keep her sister with her, but the old maid, obsessed by the idea that she was a nuisance to everyone and merely a useless encumbrance, had taken refuge in one of those religious houses which let out rooms to those unfortunate people who are left alone in the world. From time to time she came to stay with her family for two or three months.

She was a short, silent, unobtrusive woman, only appearing at meal-times and then retiring to her room, where she remained closeted all day. She had a friendly manner and was beginning to feel her age, though she was only forty-two. Her eyes were soft and sad and she had never counted for anything in the family. As a child no one had ever kissed her, for she was neither pretty nor noisy; she was like a shadow or some familiar object, a living piece of furniture that one sees every day without noticing it. Her sister, who had a recognized position in the family mansion, considered her a failure and a nonentity. She was treated with a free-and-easy familiarity, which concealed a sort of affectionate contempt. Her name was Lise, a name which seemed to embarrass her by its suggestion of sprightly youth. When it became obvious that she was not the marrying type and would probably never marry, they took to calling her Lison instead of Lise. Since Jeanne's birth she had been Aunt Lison, a humble relation, neat and extraordinarily shy even with her sister and brother-in-law, who were fond of her but with a distant chilly affection inspired by instinctive pity and natural kindliness.

Sometimes when the Baroness was talking about the events of her childhood now long past, she would say to fix the date: 'It was at the time of Lison's accident.' Nothing more was ever said; the accident was wrapped in mystery.

One evening Lise, who was twenty at the time, had thrown herself into a pond, no one knew why. Nothing in her life or behaviour had given any reason to anticipate this act of madness. She had been dragged out half dead, and her parents, raising their arms in indignation instead of trying to discover the mysterious motive for her act, merely referred to it as 'her accident', just as they spoke of the accident to the horse Coco, which had broken a leg in a rut and had had to be destroyed.

Since then Lise, later Lison, had been considered weak in the head, and the mild contempt which she had inspired in her parents spread to everyone round her. Jeanne with a child's instinctive insight left her alone; she never went up to give her a kiss in bed and never entered her room. The maid Rosalie, who did the little needed to look after her room, seemed to be the only person who even knew where it was. When Aunt Lison entered the dining-room for lunch, the child by habit went up to her to be kissed and that was all. If anyone wanted to speak to her, a servant was sent to fetch her, and if she could not be found, no one worried, no one even gave her a thought. It would never have occurred to anyone to say: 'Come to think of it, I haven't seen Lison this morning.' She had made no place for herself; she was one of those people who remain strangers even to their relations, like unexplored country, whose death leaves no gap, no void in a house and who are unable to enter into the life and interests or the affection of those around them. When anyone referred to Aunt Lison, the words made so to speak no impression on anyone's mind; it was as if the coffee-pot or the sugar-basin had been mentioned.

She always walked quietly with short tripping steps, making no noise and never bumping into anything; she seemed to communicate even to inanimate things the property of noiselessness.

41

Her hands seemed made of cotton-wool, so lightly and delicately did she handle whatever she touched.

She arrived about the middle of July, in a great state of excitement at the thought of the marriage. With her she brought a number of presents, which as coming from her were hardly noticed. By the day after her arrival no one knew that she was there. But her heart was bursting with powerful emotions and her eyes were continually fixed on the engaged couple. She busied herself over the trousseau with amazing energy and feverish activity, working in her room like a dressmaker's assistant all by herself. She was always showing the Baroness handkerchiefs which she had hemmed herself and napkins with embroidered initials, inquiring anxiously: 'Is it all right like that, Adélaïde?' And Mama with a cursory glance replied: 'Don't take so much trouble over the thing, poor Lison.'

One evening towards the end of the month, after an oppressively hot day, the moon rose on one of those warm clear nights which disturb and thrill the heart with excitement and awaken all its romantic secrets. The gentle breeze from the fields found its way into the quiet drawing-room. The Baroness and her husband were playing cards casually in the bright circle of light cast by the lamp-shade, Aunt Lison was sitting between them knitting, and the young couple were looking out over the moon-lit garden with their elbows on the window-sill.

The linden and the plane cast a shadow across the broad expanse of lawn, which stretched beyond it in the dim light to the dark shrubbery. Irresistibly attracted by the peaceful calm of the night and the hazy sheen of the trees and shrubs, Jeanne turned to her parents: 'Papa, we're going to take a stroll out there in front of the house.'

'All right, children! Go along!' replied the Baron without stopping his game. They went out and began to walk slowly across the moon-lit lawn to the little shrubbery on the far side. It was now getting late, but they did not think of going in. The Baroness was tired and wanted to go up to bed. 'We must call the lovers in,' she said. The Baron glanced across the moon-lit garden, where the two shadows were wandering slowly.

'Oh, let them be!' he said. 'Lison will wait up for them, won't you, Lison?' The old maid raised her sad eyes: 'Of course

I'll wait for them,' she replied in her shy voice. Papa helped the Baroness out of her chair and being tired himself after the hot day said: 'I'm going to bed too,' and left the drawing-room with his wife.

Then Aunt Lison got up in her turn and leaving her knitting unfinished with her wool and her long needles on the arm of her chair, she went and leant with her elbows on the window-sill and looked out into the night.

The young couple were still strolling across the lawn from the shrubbery to the terrace and back again. They were holding hands and not speaking, as if their minds had left their bodies and melted into the poetry rising from the earth in visible form. Jeanne suddenly noticed the old lady's figure silhouetted against the lamp-light. 'Look!' she cried, 'Aunt Lison is watching us!' They walked on slowly, dreaming, loving each other, but the dew had fallen on the grass and the freshness of the night air made them shiver. 'Let's go in,' she said, and they went indoors.

When they reached the drawing-room, Aunt Lison had gone back to her knitting; she was bending over her work and her skinny fingers were trembling as if she was very tired. Jeanne went up to her: 'Aunt, we're going up to bed now.' The old lady looked up at her and her eyes were red as if she had been crying. The lovers took no notice, but the young man suddenly saw that the girl's thin shoes were soaking wet, and he asked with tender solicitude: 'Aren't your darling little feet cold?'

Suddenly the aunt's fingers trembled so violently that she dropped her work and the ball of wool rolled away over the floor, and quickly hiding her face in her hands she burst into convulsive sobs. The young couple looked at her in amazement without moving; then Jeanne, thoroughly upset, fell on her knees and put her arms round her, repeating: 'What's the matter, Aunt Lison? What's the matter?'

The poor woman, stammering, her voice choked with sobs and her body twisted with misery, replied: 'It was when he asked you "Aren't your darling little feet cold?" . . . No one has ever asked me a question like that . . . never . . . never.'

With a mixture of surprise and pity Jeanne wanted to laugh at the idea of any man making love to Lison, and the Viscount turned round to conceal his amusement. But the old lady got up quickly, leaving the wool on the floor and her knitting on the arm-chair, and dashed upstairs in the dark, groping her way to her room. Left alone, the lovers looked at each other amused but touched, and Jeanne murmured : 'Poor Auntie !'

'She must be a bit mad this evening,' was Julien's comment.

They were holding hands, unable to separate, and very gently they exchanged their first kiss in front of the empty chair Aunt Lison had just left. Next morning they had almost forgotten the old lady's tears.

The fortnight before the wedding found Jeanne in a calm, peaceful state of mind, as if she was tired of soft emotions, and she had not much time to think on the morning of the great day itself; she was conscious only of a great void in all her body as if her flesh, her blood and her bones had melted under her skin, and when she touched anything her fingers trembled. She did not recover her self-possession till she was in the chancel of the church and the wedding service was in progress.

Married! So she was married! Everything, every movement, what she had done that morning, seemed just a dream. It was one of those moments when all around us is strange; even gestures take on a new meaning and the regular procession of the hours is broken. She was in a state of dazed bewilderment; the evening before there had been no change in the normal routine of her days; it was only that the realization of the hopes of her life was in sight, almost within reach. She had gone to sleep a girl and woken up a woman. At last she had cleared the barrier which seems to hide the future with all the joy and happiness of our dreams; a door had opened before her and her expectations were on the point of fulfilment.

The service ended and they went into the almost empty vestry, for no guests had been invited; then they came out again. When they appeared at the church door, a loud crash made the bride jump and the Baroness cry out; it was a volley of shots fired by the villagers and it continued all the way to the Poplars. Light refreshments had been served for the family, their private chaplain and the priest from Yport, the bridegroom and the witnesses who had been chosen from the leading farmers of the neighbourhood. After that they strolled round the garden to wait for the wedding breakfast. The

Baron, the Baroness, Aunt Lison, the mayor, and the Abbé Picot took 'Mama's drive', while the other priest strode up and down the path opposite reading his breviary. From the other side of the house the noisy gaiety of the peasants was audible; they were drinking cider under the apple-trees. All the villagers from the neighbourhood in their Sunday best crowded the courtyard, where the boys and girls were chasing each other.

Jeanne and Julien made their way through the shrubbery and climbed the bank, where they looked out over the sea in silence. It was rather chilly for the middle of August; there was a northerly wind and the sun was shining in a cloudless sky. The young couple, turning to the right across the common in search of shade, made for the winding wooded valley which ran down towards Yport. Reaching the copse, where they were out of the wind, they left the road and took a narrow path through the undergrowth, where they could hardly stand upright. Soon Jeanne felt an arm placed gently round her waist. She did not speak; her heart was beating and she had difficulty in breathing. The low branches combed their hair and they often had to lower their heads to get through. She touched a leaf and saw two ladybirds like two tiny red shells clinging to the under side. Plucking up her courage, she said guilelessly: 'Look! A married couple!'

Julien brushed her ear with his lips, saying: 'Tonight you will be my wife.' Although she had learnt the facts of life from living in the country, she still only thought of the romantic aspect of love and was surprised. His wife? Wasn't she that already?

Then he began to print little quick kisses on her temples and neck, where the first hairs started to curl. Startled by these kisses, the first which she had ever received from a man, she instinctively averted her head to avoid a caress which nevertheless entranced her. But suddenly they found themselves at the edge of the wood. She stopped, surprised at finding herself so far from the house. What would people think? 'Let's go back,' she said.

He took his arm from her waist and, as they both turned round, they found themselves facing each other, so close that they could feel each other's breath, and they gazed at each other with one of those steady penetrating glances in which two hearts seem to melt into one. They sought to pierce to the very soul behind their eyes and reach the unknown abysses of their being, plumbing their depths with wordless, obstinate questioning. What would they be to each other? What would the life that they were beginning be like? What had they to give each other, what joy, what happiness, what disillusions in the long indissoluble bond of matrimony? They both felt that they did not really know each other yet.

Suddenly Julien, putting both his hands on his wife's shoulders, kissed her full on the mouth, a passionate kiss such as she had never received before. It pierced into her, making its way into her veins, into the very marrow of her bones; it gave her such a mysterious shock that she pushed Julien violently with both hands and nearly fell backwards.

'Let's go back! Let's go back!' she stammered.

He did not answer, but he took her hands and kept them clasped in his. Not a word was spoken till they reached the house. The rest of the afternoon dragged, till they sat down to dinner at dusk. The meal was plain and short, quite unlike the usual Normandy custom. The guests were seized with a sort of embarrassment; only the two priests, the mayor and the four specially invited farmers showed something of the coarse conviviality normal at weddings. If the laughter seemed to be dying down, a joke from the mayor rekindled it. It was getting on for nine o'clock and they were waiting for their coffee; outside under the apple-trees in the front courtyard country-dancing was starting and through the open windows they had a good view of the festivities; lanterns suspended from the branches cast a greenish-grey light on the foliage. Country boys and girls were jumping about, whistling a wild dance tune to a thin accompaniment from two violins and a clarinet perched up on a kitchen table on trestles. At times the noisy singing of the rustics entirely drowned the instruments, and their music dominated by the loud harsh voices seemed to be falling from the sky in tatters with short trills of scattered notes.

Two great barrels surrounded by blazing torches provided the guests with liquid refreshment. Two maids were kept busy washing glasses and bowls in a bucket before holding them still dripping under the spigots, from which spouted the red stream of the wine and the golden stream of the neat cider, while the thirsty dancers, the older men quietly and the girls dripping with perspiration, crowded round with hands outstretched in turn to get hold of any vessel and gulp down with heads thrown back the drink of their choice. Bread and butter, cheese and sausages were laid out on the table, and each villager from time to time took a mouthful. Under the bright ceiling of the leaves this innocent, noisy gaiety made the staid guests in the hall long to join the dancing and swill down draughts from the huge casks, eating a slice of bread and butter with a raw onion. The mayor beating time with his knife exclaimed : 'My goodness! How well it's all going! It might be Pantaloon's wedding feast!'

A ripple of stifled laughter greeted his words, but the Abbé Picot, as the natural enemy of all civil authority, retorted : 'You mean the Marriage at Cana in Galilee.'

But the other did not accept the rebuke : 'No, Abbé, I mean what I say. When I say "Pantaloon", I mean "Pantaloon".'

They got up and retired to the drawing-room, and presently went out to mingle with the crowd that was enjoying itself thoroughly. Soon the invited guests left. The Baron and the Baroness were having a difference of opinion in whispers. Madame Adélaïde, more out of breath than usual, was apparently refusing something that her husband had asked; at last she said almost aloud: 'No, dear, I can't; I shouldn't know how to do it.'

Then Papa, leaving her quickly, went up to Jeanne : 'Will you come for a little stroll with me, my girl?'

'Certainly, Papa, if you like,' she replied, quite touched, and they went out.

Outside the door facing the sea a sharp gust of wind caught them, one of those chilly summer winds, the forerunners of autumn. Clouds were scudding across the sky, hiding and then revealing the stars again. The Baron took his daughter's arm, gently pressing her hand, and they walked on for a few minutes in silence; he seemed hesitant and worried. At last he took the plunge: 'Darling, I've got a difficult task to perform. It really ought to be your mother's but, as she refuses

47

to do it, it falls on me. I don't know how much you have learnt about the facts of life. That is one of those secrets carefully hidden from children, especially girls, whose minds must be kept pure and entirely innocent up to the moment when we entrust them to the arms of the man who will guard their happiness. It is for him to lift the veil that has hidden the tender secret of life. But if any suspicion has entered their minds, they often revolt before the coarse reality behind their dreams. Wounded in their soul, and sometimes even in their body, they refuse to their husband what law, both natural and man-made, grants to him as an absolute right. I cannot tell you more, darling, but never forget that you belong entirely to your husband.'

What did she really know? What did she guess? She was trembling, overcome by an aching, shattering melancholy of painful anticipation.

They returned to the house, where a surprise awaited them in the drawing-room. Madame Adélaïde was sobbing on Julien's breast; her tears, noisy tears which seemed to issue from the bellows of a forge, were coming from her nose, her mouth, and her eyes at the same time, and the young man in speechless embarrassment was supporting the heavy woman, who had collapsed in his arms as she was entrusting her beloved, her darling, her adored daughter to his care.

The Baron hurried in. 'Oh! don't let's have a scene, *please*!' he cried, and taking his wife's arm he made her sit down in an arm-chair, while she dried her eyes. Then turning to Jeanne he said: 'Come, dear, give your mother a kiss and run off to bed.'

On the verge of tears too she quickly kissed her parents and fled.

Aunt Lison had already gone to her room and the Baron and his wife were left alone with Julien. All three were in such a state of embarrassment that they could not find words; the two men were standing in their evening clothes with a blank stare and Madame Adélaïde was collapsed on her chair with the aftermath of her sobs still in her throat. The tension was becoming unbearable and the Baron began to talk about the honeymoon trip that was to start in a few days.

In her room Jeanne let Rosalie, who was in floods of tears, undress her. The maid could not control her hands, she could not find the ribbons or the pins and seemed more upset than her mistress, but Jeanne hardly noticed the girl's state; she felt that she had entered a new world, some unknown planet entirely different from anything she had known and loved; everything in her life and thoughts was upset. This strange question occurred to her: did she love her husband? He suddenly appeared a stranger whom she hardly knew. Three months earlier she had not been aware of his existence; now she was his wife. What did it all mean? Why should one fall into marriage so quickly, as into an abyss suddenly yawning before one's feet? Putting on her nightdress she slid into bed; the chill of the sheets made her shiver and increased the feeling of cold loneliness and sadness, which had been weighing upon her heart for the last two hours.

Rosalie fled from the room, still sobbing, and Jeanne waited. She waited anxiously with a beating heart for this mysterious something, which she had guessed and of which her father had spoken in vague terms, this strange revelation of the great secret of love. She heard no footsteps on the stairs, but someone gave three taps on the door. She started nervously and did not answer; the taps were repeated and then the lock grated. She hid her head under the bed-clothes, as if a burglar had broken into the room. There was a faint creaking of shoes on the floor and suddenly there was a touch on the bed. She gave a nervous start and uttered a low cry, and raising her head she saw Julien in front of her, looking at her and smiling.

'Oh, what a fright you gave me!' she said.

'So you weren't expecting me?' he replied.

She made no answer. He was in full evening dress, with his serious handsome face, and she felt dreadfully ashamed to be lying in bed before this immaculate young man.

They did not know what to say or what to do; they dared not even look at each other at this critical decisive moment, on which depends the inward happiness of a lifetime. He was perhaps vaguely conscious of the possible dangers of this struggle; he would need complete self-control and cunning tenderness, if he was not to shock the refined modesty of a virgin soul brought up on romantic dreams with infinite delicacy. Presently he took her hand gently and kissed it, and kneeling down by the bed as if before an altar he whispered: 'Will you love me?'

Suddenly recovering herself, she raised her head from the lace-fringed pillow and smiled: 'I love you already, my dear!'

He took her tapering finger-tips in his mouth and in a voice strangled by this gag he said: 'Will you prove that you love me?'

She replied, worried again, not knowing what he meant but remembering her father's words: 'I am all yours, my dear.'

He covered her wrist with moist kisses, and getting up slowly he bent his face down close to hers, which she tried to hide. Suddenly throwing one arm across the bed he grasped his wife through the sheets, and slipping the other arm under the pillow he lifted it up with her head upon it and asked in a low whisper: 'Then you will make just a little room for me by your side?'

With an instinctive shrinking she stammered: 'Oh, not yet, *please*!'

He seemed disappointed and hurt, and went on in a pleading tone but more sharply: 'Why not? We shall have to come to that in the end!'

She resented his words but with obedient resignation she repeated: 'I am all yours, my dear.'

He disappeared quickly into his dressing-room and she heard him distinctly moving about, the rustle of his clothes as he undressed, the clink of the money in his pockets, his shoes dropped on the floor one after the other; suddenly, clad only in drawers and socks, he darted across the bedroom to put his watch on the chimney-piece. Then he ran back into his dressing-room, where he moved about for some time longer. Jeanne turned over quickly shutting her eyes, when she sensed his approach.

When she felt a cold hairy leg thrust down against hers, she gave a sudden start as if to throw herself out of bed, and with her face in her hands ready to cry out in terrified astonishment she snuggled desperately down to the bottom of the bed. He immediately put his arms round her, although she had her back to him, and printed passionate kisses on her neck, the lace frill of her nightcap and the embroidered collar of her night-dress. She lay quite still, frozen by a horrible anxiety, as she felt a strong hand groping for her breast behind her elbows. She was fighting for breath, terrified by this brutal touch; she wanted to escape, run to the other end of the house and shut herself up somewhere away from this man.

He was now lying quite still and she felt the warmth of his body on her back. Her fear melted away and she suddenly thought that she had only to turn over to kiss him. At last he appeared to lose patience and said sadly : 'So you don't want to be my little wife !'

'But I *am* your little wife !' she murmured through her fingers.

'No, dear ! Look here, don't make a fool of me !' he replied rather crossly.

She was quite upset by his irritable tone and turned quickly to him to beg his pardon. Then he clasped her tightly to him as if consumed by a devouring thirst for her, covering her face and neck with a shower of quick, hard, wild kisses, dazing her with caresses. She had unclasped her hands and lay making no response to his advances, not knowing what she was doing or what he was doing, incapable of thought. Suddenly she felt a sharp pain and began to groan, writhing in his arms, while he roughly consummated the marriage.

What happened next? She remembered nothing. She had lost all power of thought; she seemed to recall that he had printed on her lips little kisses of gratitude. He must have talked to her and she must have replied. After that he made more advances, which she repulsed in terror; and as she struggled, she felt on her breast the prickly hair she had felt before on her leg, and recoiled in revulsion. At last, tired of vain attempts to excite her, he lay quietly on his back. She was thinking with despair in her heart, in the disillusion of an intoxication which she had dreamed so different, of anticipated pleasure now destroyed and a happiness now gone for ever; she said to herself : 'So that's what he calls being his wife ! That's all there is to it !'

She lay for a long while, her eyes wandering over the tapestry on the wall with its ancient love-story.

As Julien had fallen silent and did not move, she slowly turned her head towards him and saw that he was asleep. He was asleep! She could not believe her eyes, feeling despised and more insulted by this sleep than by his roughness; she was being treated like a common harlot. How could he sleep on a night like this? What had passed between them was nothing unusual for him! She would rather have been beaten, raped again, bruised by his clumsy caresses till she lost consciousness. She lay on her side without moving, pressing close to him, listening to his gentle breathing, which was sometimes almost a snore.

Day broke, first faint, then white, then pink, then bright. Julien opened his eyes, yawned and stretched; smiling at his wife, he asked: 'Did you sleep well, darling?'

She noticed that his tone was now affectionate, and amazed she replied: 'Oh yes! And you?'

'Yes, I had an excellent night,' he replied.

Turning over towards her, he kissed her and began to talk of this and that. He outlined his plans for the future with emphasis on the need for economy; the word occurred more than once and surprised Jeanne. She listened without taking in the meaning of his words, and looked at him, dreaming of many things which really made no impression on her mind.

Eight o'clock struck. 'Come,' he said, 'we must get up; we should make ourselves ridiculous, if we stayed in bed too long,' and he got out of bed first. When he was dressed, he helped her politely with her clothes in various little ways, not letting her call Rosalie. Just as they were going down, he stopped her: 'Look! When we are alone, we can call each other "darling", but before your parents, we had better wait a bit. It will be quite all right, when we get back from our honeymoon.'

She did not appear till breakfast was on the table, and the day passed as usual, just as if nothing had been changed. There was merely an extra man in the house.

CHAPTER FIVE

Four days later the travelling coach arrived to take them to Marseilles. After the misery of the first night Jeanne had got used to Julien's touch, his kisses and tender embraces, though her revulsion from their more intimate relations remained. She found him attractive and loved him, and her lightheartedness and gaiety returned. The farewells were short and cheerful, only the Baroness showing traces of emotion. As the coach was about to start, she thrust a large purse, as heavy as lead, into the girl's hand: 'That's for your little extravagances as a bride!' she said.

Jeanne pocketed it and the horses moved off. Towards evening Julien asked: 'How much was there in that purse your mother gave you?'

She had forgotten all about it and turned it out on her lap. A stream of gold fell out, two thousand francs; she clapped her hands: 'I shall buy all sorts of absurd things!' she said, replacing the coins in the purse.

After a week's travelling in intense heat they reached Marseilles, and the following day the *King Louis*, a small steamer which ran to Naples via Ajaccio, took them off for Corsica.

Corsica with its *maquis*, its bandits, its mountains, Napoleon's birth-place! Jeanne seemed to be travelling out of the real world into dreamland, wide awake. Standing on deck side by side, they watched the cliffs of Provence slipping by. The calm sea, brilliantly blue, as if congealed and stiffened by the sun's rays, stretched away to the horizon under a sky that was almost too blue.

'Do you remember our sail in old Lastique's boat?'

For an answer he kissed her lightly on the ear. The steamer's paddle-wheels churned up the water, breaking its heavy slumber, and astern a long line of foam, a broad white trail where the water broke into bubbles like champagne, prolonged the wake in a straight line as far as the eye could see.

Suddenly, only a few fathoms ahead, a huge fish, a dolphin, leapt out of the water, then dived in again head first and disappeared. Jeanne uttered a cry in sudden fright, throwing herself into Julien's arms, and laughing at her terror watched anxiously for the creature's reappearance. After a few seconds it shot up again like a clockwork toy, and then fell back, only to come up once more. Soon there were two of them, then three, then six; they seemed to be gambolling round the boat, as if escorting a giant brother, a great wooden fish with iron fins. They passed the boat to port and came back to starboard and, now all together, now singly as if in a game, shot up, pursuing each other in great curving leaps, and then plunged in again in single file. Jeanne clapped her hands, wriggling with excitement at each appearance of these huge agile swimmers; her heart leapt like them in a wild, childish ecstasy. Suddenly they were gone; once again they were visible far off towards the open sea. After that they were seen no more and Jeanne felt a twinge of regret at their departure.

Evening came on, a calm bright evening with a clear sky and happy tranquillity. Not a breath stirred in the air or on the sea; and this infinite restfulness of ocean and sky spread to their souls undisturbed by any breath of anxiety. The sun was setting slowly away to the south in the direction of Africa, below the horizon, Africa, that tropical continent whose heat seemed to be reaching them already. But a sort of cool caress, that was not even a light breeze, stroked their faces when the sun had disappeared.

They did not want to go down to their cabin, to which all the unpleasant smells of a steamer penetrated, and they both lay down on deck side by side, wrapped in their coats. Julien went to sleep at once, but Jeanne kept her eyes open, excited by the unknown future before her. The monotonous throb of the paddle-wheels lulled her and she watched the legions of stars overhead, so clear with their points of light twinkling like bubbles in the cloudless southern sky.

Towards dawn she dozed off, only to be wakened by noises and voices; it was the sailors tidying up the boat and singing as they worked. She shook her husband who was still sound asleep, and they got up. She inhaled with rapture the salty tang of the mist, which made its way down to her finger-tips. There was sea all round, but away ahead was something grey, still misty in the dawn light, something like a mass of isolated needles of cloud, which appeared to be resting on the water. Presently the view cleared and the outlines were silhouetted against the brightening sky, a long range of sharp peaks, strangely shaped; it was Corsica, veiled in a light haze. Then the sun rose behind the hills, showing up the jagged crests with dark shadows; soon all the summits were lit up, while the rest of the country was enveloped in mist.

The Captain, a short, squat, old man with a sun-tanned face, shrivelled and toughened by the strong salt sea-winds, appeared on deck and in a voice rendered hoarse by thirty years of giving orders and strained by shouting through gales, he said to Jeanne: 'Do you smell the Old Lady over there?'

She *was* conscious of a powerful, strange scent of vegetation and aromatic plants. The Captain continued: 'It's Corsica that smells like that; she has her own special smell, like a beautiful woman. I've been away twenty years, but I should recognize it five miles out to sea. I belong there. *He*, far away in St Helena, he's always talking about that smell, they say. He's a member of my clan,' and taking off his cap he saluted Corsica, and saluted far away across the ocean the imprisoned Emperor, his clansman. Jeanne was so moved that she almost burst into tears.

Then the Captain, pointing to the horizon, said: 'Look! The Bloody Ones!' Julien was standing beside his wife with his arm round her waist and they looked out to identify the object indicated. At last they caught sight of some rocks shaped like pyramids, which the steamer presently rounded to make its way into a broad calm bay fringed with high peaks, whose lower slopes seemed covered with moss. The Captain pointed to the stretch of green: 'That's the *maquis*.' As they advanced, the ring of mountains closed in behind the boat, as it steamed slowly up the blue bay, which was so clear that in places the bottom was visible. There were some small Italian craft at anchor in the harbour, and four or five boats came out and circled round the *King Louis* to take off the passengers.

Julien, who was collecting their luggage, whispered to his wife: 'One franc is enough as a tip for the steward, isn't it?'

For the past week he had been asking the same question, which she always resented, and she replied with a hint of impatience: 'When one isn't sure if a tip is enough, one always gives too much.'

He was continually having arguments with butlers and waiters, cab-drivers and everyone who had anything to sell, and when he had beaten them down by quibbling, he would rub his hands and say to Jeanne: 'I don't like being fleeced!' Whenever she saw a bill being presented, she was terrified, sure in advance of the criticisms he would make of each item; she was humiliated by his haggling and blushed to the roots of her hair at the contemptuous glances of the servants, who followed her husband with their eyes, holding his inadequate tip in their hands. He had another argument with the boatman who landed them; the first tree she saw was a palm!

They booked a room at a big empty hotel at one corner of the vast square and ordered lunch. After dessert, just as Jeanne was getting up to stroll round the town, Julien, taking her in his arms, murmured tenderly in her ear: 'Shall we lie down for a bit now, darling?'

She stopped in surprise: 'Lie down? But I'm not a bit tired.'

He gave her a hug: 'I want you, don't you understand? It's two days since ...'

She reddened with shame, stammering: 'Oh, now? What would people say? How could you dare ask for a bedroom in broad daylight? Oh, Julien, *please*!'

But he interrupted: 'I don't care what the hotel people say or think. You'll see how little that affects me,' and he rang the bell. She said nothing but lowered her eyes in a state of mental and physical revolt against her husband's extravagant demands; her duty of obedience disgusted her and she felt humiliated; it was something bestial and degrading, in fact an obscenity. Her passion had not yet been awakened and her husband was now treating her as if she shared his desire.

When the valet answered the bell, Julien asked him to show them to their room. The man, a typical Corsican with hair up to the eyes, did not understand and said that the room would be got ready for the night. Losing patience, Julien explained: 'No, we want it now. We are tired after our voyage and we want to lie down.' At that a smile ruffled the valet's beard and Jeanne would have liked to run away.

When they came down an hour later, she dared not face the people she met, convinced that they would snigger and whisper behind her back. She felt a grudge against Julien in her heart for not understanding her and having no refined modesty and instinctive delicacy. She felt as it were a veil, a barrier between herself and him, realizing for the first time that two people can never understand each other's deepest feelings and thoughts. They may walk side by side and sometimes embrace, but they remain apart and the moral being of each one is eternally isolated all through life.

They stayed for three days in the little town nestling at the head of the blue gulf, hot as a furnace behind its curtain of mountains, which never let a breath of wind reach it. The details of the trip were arranged and in order not to be defeated by any difficulties on the way, they decided to hire horses. So they took two small wild-eyed Corsican stallions, scraggy but untiring, and set off one morning at daybreak. A guide accompanied them on a mule with their provisions, for inns are unknown in this wild country. Their route followed the coastline and then plunged into a short valley in the direction of the main range. They often crossed torrent beds now almost dry. A trickle of water still flowed under the stones, gurgling faintly like some hidden creature.

The bare countryside seemed entirely uncultivated. The hillsides were covered with long grass parched yellow by the summer heat. From time to time they met a peasant from the mountains either on foot or on a pony or astride a grey donkey no bigger than a dog. They all carried on their backs a loaded gun, a rusty old weapon but formidable in their hands. The sharp scent of the aromatic plants with which the island is carpeted made the air heavy as their path climbed gently through the long glades that pierced the hills.

The pink and blue granite peaks lent the vast landscape the tints of fairyland; on the lower slopes forests of tall chestnuts looked only like green shrubs, dwarfed by the giant undulations of the earth all over the island. From time to time the guide pointed towards the beetling crags and mentioned a name; Jeanne and Julien looked but could see nothing. At last they would catch sight of something grey like a stone-fall from the crest; it was a granite hamlet stuck there, clinging like a bird's nest, almost invisible against the vast mountain side.

The long distance at a walking pace was affecting Jeanne's nerves.

'Let's move a bit faster,' she said and spurred her horse. Then, not hearing her husband galloping near her, she turned and burst out laughing when she saw him coming up, pale, clinging to the animal's mane, bobbing up and down in a ridiculous way. Even his good looks, the picture he presented of the perfect knight, made his poor horsemanship and his panic the more laughable. After that they continued at a gentle trot. Their path now took them between two interminable stretches of bush which draped the hill-sides like a mantle.

It was the *maquis*, the impenetrable *maquis*, made up of ilex, juniper, arbutus, mastic-trees, buckthorn, heather, laurustinus, myrtle, and box-trees, knotted together in one dense mass by interlacing clematis like disordered hair, gigantic bracken, honeysuckle, cistus, rosemary, lavender, and brambles, which draped the slopes with an inextricable tangle of vegetation. By this time they were getting hungry; the guide caught up with them and led them to one of those delightful springs so common in hilly country, a thin trickle of ice-cold water issuing from a small round hole in the rock and running to where the tip of a chestnut leaf had been placed by a passer-by to convey the tiny runlet to his mouth. Jeanne was so blissfully happy that she had difficulty in preventing herself from uttering cries of joy.

They continued on their way and began to lose height as they followed the bend of the Gulf of Sagone. Towards evening they rode through the Greek village of Cargèse, founded long ago by a colony of refugees who had been driven out of their own country. Tall, handsome girls with narrow hips, long hands and a slim figure, remarkably graceful, were crowding round a well-head. When Julien shouted 'Good evening!', sing-song voices replied in the melodious dialect of this isolated district.

When they reached Piana, they had to seek hospitality as in the Middle Ages, in regions far from civilization. Jeanne was quivering with excitement, while she waited for the door at which Julien had knocked to open. Yes ! This was the real thing, travelling in a virgin country, where everything was a surprise ! They happened to have hit upon the house of a young couple, who received them as the patriarchs must have received the guest sent by God. They had a straw mattress to sleep on in the tumbledown old house with worm-eaten beams, which, devoured by great deathwatch beetles, groaned and sighed like living creatures.

They went on at dawn and presently paused in front of a forest, a regular forest of ruddy granite, carved by time and pitted by the wind and sea-fog into needles, pillars, towers, and all manner of strange shapes. Rising to the height of a thousand feet, these amazing rocks, slender, rounded, twisted, hooked, mis-shapen, unexpected, fantastic, resembled trees, plants, animals, men, monks in cassocks, horned devils, gigantic birds, a monstrous brood, a nightmare army, petrified by the whim of some eccentric god.

Jeanne had stopped talking, strangely moved, and took Julien's hand and pressed it, overcome before the beauty of nature by the need to love. Suddenly, emerging from this scene of confusion, they found themselves in another cove entirely hemmed in by a blood-red wall of crimson granite, the scarlet rocks being reflected in the blue sea.

'Oh ! Julien ... !' stammered Jeanne, unable to find words; her heart was melted by the beauty of the scene, her voice was strangled in her throat, and two big tears welled from her eyes. He looked at her in amazement, asking : 'What's the matter with you, darling ?'

She wiped her cheeks, smiled and said in a voice that trembled a little : 'It's nothing ... just nerves ... something got me. I'm so happy that the least thing unbalances me !'

He did not understand a woman's nervous reactions, the shocks felt by a highly-strung nature, which the slightest thing affects and excitement stirs like a catastrophe, and a subconscious feeling upsets completely and plunges into joy or despair. Her tears seemed absurd to him and with his whole attention fixed on the difficulties of the path he said : 'You had better keep your eyes on your horse.' The track got worse and worse, but they forced their way down to the level of the cove and then turned to the right to ascend the sombre Val d'Ota. The path looked like becoming still more difficult and Julien suggested walking. She asked for nothing better, delighted at the prospect of walking alone with him after her recent emotions. The guide went on ahead with the mule and the horses and they climbed slowly up the slope. Here there is a cleft right down the mountain from top to bottom and the path winds through this opening; it keeps to the bottom between two huge walls and a roaring torrent flows through the passage; the air is ice-cold and the granite is dark, while high above the patch of blue sky dazzles and stuns. A sudden noise made Jeanne start, as a huge bird darted out of a hole; it was an eagle. It spread its wings, which seemed to graze the two sides of the chasm as it soared upwards and disappeared.

Farther on the cleft straightens out and the path climbs in short zigzags between the steep sides. Jeanne, light-footed and carefree, walked in front, dislodging the pebbles under her feet, balancing fearlessly above the precipices. He followed, rather out of breath, with his eyes fixed on the ground for fear of dizziness. Suddenly the sun caught them and they felt as if they had emerged from hell. Feeling thirsty, they followed a trail of dampness over a waste of stones, which led them to a tiny spring channelled into a trough for the use of goatherds. A carpet of moss covered the ground around. Jeanne knelt down to drink and Julien followed her example.

As she was enjoying the coolness of the water, he seized her round the waist and tried to rob her of her place at the end of the wooden pipe; she resisted and a tug-of-war ensued, their lips meeting and pushing each other away. In the course of the struggle each of them in turn seized the end of the thin pipe and gripped it in their teeth to keep hold of it, and the stream of cold water, sucked in and checked in turn, was interrupted and then released, splashing faces, necks, clothes and hands; drops gleamed in their hair like pearls and their kisses were drowned in the flood. Suddenly Jeanne had a lover's inspiration. She filled her mouth with the liquid and distending her cheeks like a water-skin she conveyed to Julien that she wanted to quench his thirst lip to lip. He bent forward with his head back and his arms extended and drained at one gulp this spring of living flesh, which kindled the fire of desire in his heart.

Jeanne was leaning against him with unusual affection; her heart was pounding and her breast heaving; her eyes seemed softer as if soaked in water. 'Oh, Julien, I *do* love you!' she murmured in a low whisper. Drawing him to her, she turned over on her back and, blushing crimson with shame, hid her face in her hands. He threw himself on her in a passionate embrace. She was panting with nervous anticipation and suddenly she uttered a cry, as she was smitten by the stab of the passion she had invited.

They took a long time to reach the top of the rise, for she was still breathless with exhaustion; and they did not get to the house of Paoli Palabretti, a relative of their guide, at Évisa till evening. He was a tall man, slightly bent, with the depressed manner of a consumptive. He showed them to their room, a gloomy room with bare stone walls, but not too bad for a country where elegance is unknown. He was expressing his pleasure at welcoming them in his Corsican dialect, a mixture of French and Italian, when a shrill voice interrupted him and a short, dark woman with large black eyes, a sun-tanned face, a slim figure and teeth always showing in a fixed smile, rushed in, kissed Jeanne and shook Julien's hand, repeating: 'Good day, Madame! Good day, Sir! I hope you are quite well!'

She took their hats and wraps, tidying everything up with one hand, as she had the other arm in a sling; then she made them all go out, telling her husband to take them for a walk till dinner-time.

Monsieur Palabretti hastened to obey and took them round the village, walking between the young couple. He dragged his feet and his words, coughing a good deal and repeating after every paroxysm: 'It's the cold air of the Val that gets me in the chest.'

He led them along a narrow path under the towering chestnuts and suddenly stopped, saying in his drawling voice: 'It was just here that my cousin, Jean Rinaldi, was murdered by Mathieu Lori. Look, I was there close to Jean, when Mathieu appeared ten yards away. "Jean," he shouted, "don't go to Albertacci, don't go there or I'll kill you; I swear I will." I seized Jean's arm: "Don't go there, Jean; he means what he says." It was all over a girl they were both after, Paulina Sinacoupi. But Jean shouted: "I'm going, Mathieu, and you won't stop me." Then Mathieu levelled his gun and before I could aim mine he fired. Jean leapt with both feet in the air like a child with a skipping-rope; yes, Monsieur, and he fell right on top of me, knocking my gun out of my hands, so that it rolled away as far as that tall chestnut over there. Jean had his mouth wide open but he didn't say a word; he was dead.'

The young pair listened in amazement to this calm eye-witness account of the crime and Jeanne asked: 'And what about the murderer?'

After a long fit of coughing Paoli Palabretti replied: 'Oh, he escaped to the mountains, but my brother got him the year after. You know my brother, of course, Philippi Palabretti, the bandit.'

Jeanne shivered: 'Your brother, a bandit?'

A flash of pride showed in the placid Corsican's glance: 'Yes, Madame; my brother had quite a reputation; he had shot six gendarmes. He died with Nicolas Morali, when they were cornered at Niolo, after six days' fighting, when they were nearly dead of starvation.'

And he added in a tone of resignation: 'It's the custom of the country,' in the tone in which he said: 'It's the cold air of the Val that gets me in the chest.' Then they went back to dinner, and the little Corsican woman treated them as if she had known them for twenty years.

But Jeanne was worried; would she experience again in Julien's arms that mysterious outburst of sensual emotion which she had felt when lying on the moss by the spring? When they were alone in their room, she was afraid that she might remain unmoved by his kisses, but her doubts did not last long, and she had her first night of love.

Next morning, when it was time to start, she found it hard to leave this humble cottage, where she felt that a new happiness had been born for her. She drew her host's little wife to her room and, making it quite clear that she was not offering a tip, she insisted, getting quite worked up about it, on sending her from Paris on their return a memento of their visit, a memento to which she attached an almost superstitious importance. For a long while the young Corsican woman refused to accept anything, but she finally agreed: 'Very well!' she said, 'send me a small pistol, a very small one.'

Jeanne opened her eyes in surprise. The woman put her mouth close to her ear and whispered: 'It's to shoot my brother-in-law.'

And with a smile she undid the bandage round her injured arm and said, pointing to her round white forearm, which was pierced right through with a dagger wound now almost healed. 'If I hadn't been as strong as he was, he would have killed me. My husband isn't jealous; he knows he can trust me, and besides he's an invalid as you know, and that keeps him quiet. Anyway, I'm an honest woman, Madame, and a good wife, but my brother-in-law believes all the gossip. He's jealous for my husband's sake and he'll certainly try again. If he does, I shall have my little pistol and be quite calm, well able to get my own back.'

Jeanne promised to send her the weapon, kissed her new-found friend tenderly, and started off.

The rest of the trip was one long dream, an unending embrace, an intoxication of caresses. She saw nothing, neither the country nor the people nor the places where she stayed; she had eyes only for Julien. They murmured love's sweet nothings in each other's ears in charming baby-talk, inventing pretty nonsense names for the curves, bends, and creases of their bodies, where their lips loved to rest. As Jeanne always slept on her right side, her left breast was often exposed when she woke. Julien noticed this and christened it 'Mr Sleeper-out' and the other 'Mr Kiss-me-quick', because the pink tip of the nipple seemed more sensitive to kisses. The depression between the two was referred to as 'Mama's drive', because he was always stroking it up and down with his lips. Another more intimate path got the name of 'the Damascus road', a reminiscence of the Val d'Ota.

When they reached Bastia, the guide had to be paid off. Julien felt in his pockets, and not finding what he wanted he said to Jeanne: 'As you are not using the two thousand francs your mother gave you, give them to me to look after; they will be safer in my belt and I shan't have to change notes.'

And she handed him the purse. They went on to Leghorn,

visited Florence, Genoa, and the whole of the Corniche, and found themselves back at Marseilles one morning when the Mistral was blowing. Two months had passed since they had left the Poplars and it was now 15 October. Jeanne, chilled by the strong cold wind, which seemed to come from far-away Normandy, felt depressed. For some time Julien had appeared altered, tired, and indifferent, and she was frightened without knowing why. For four days she put off the return journey, unable to bring herself to leave the lovely sunshine of the South, where she had run through the whole gamut of happiness.

At last they set off. In Paris they were to make the purchases needed for their permanent establishment at the Poplars, and Jeanne was looking forward to taking back all sorts of treasures, thanks to Mama's present. But the first thing she thought of was the small pistol she had promised to the young Corsican woman at Évisa. The day after reaching Paris she said to Julien : 'Will you give me back Mother's money? I want to do some shopping.'

He turned to her crossly : 'How much do you want?'

She was surprised and stammered : 'But . . . what you like.'

He went on : 'Well, here are a hundred francs, but don't go and waste it.'

She didn't know what to say, tongue-tied and confused; finally she stammered : 'But I gave you the money to . . .'

He interrupted her : 'Quite so, but what difference does it make whether it's in your pocket or mine, since we now have a common purse? I'm not refusing you, am I? I'm giving you a hundred francs.'

She took the five gold pieces without a word, but she dared not ask for any more and only bought the pistol.

A week later they started on their return journey to the Poplars.

CHAPTER SIX

In front of the white boundary wall with its brick pillars the family and the servants were waiting for them. The post-chaise stopped and there were long embraces all round. Mama was crying and Jeanne, deeply moved, wiped away two tears; Papa walked nervously up and down. While their luggage was being unloaded, the young couple gave an account of their travels in front of the drawing-room fire. Jeanne was never at a loss for words and in half an hour the whole story had been told except perhaps for a few details forgotten in her haste. Jeanne then went up to unpack, helped by Rosalie, who was also much moved. When this was finished and her underclothes, frocks and dressing-table accessories had been put in their proper places, the little maid left her mistress and Jeanne sat down, rather tired. She wondered what to do next, looking for something to occupy her thoughts and keep her hands busy. She did not want to go downstairs again to join her mother, who was dozing; she thought of going for a walk, but the country looked so depressing that just gazing out of the window induced a feeling of melancholy.

Suddenly she realized that she had nothing to do and never would have anything. Her young days at the convent had been filled with thoughts of the future and crowded with dreams; the continual excitement of her hopes in those days had occupied the hours, so that she did not notice the passage of time. But hardly had she left those stern walls, where all her illusions had been born, when her expectations of love had been suddenly fulfilled. The man whom she had hoped for, met, fallen in love with and married in a few weeks, as one does in these cases of sudden impulse, had swept her into his arms without giving her time to think.

But now the magic reality of those first days was about to become the everyday reality, which closed the door upon those vague hopes and the delightful enigmas of the unknown. Yes, it was the end of expectation and she had nothing to do today or tomorrow or ever again. She was conscious of all this with a certain sense of disillusion, a fading of her dreams. She got up and pressed her face against the cold window, and after gazing for some time at the sky covered with dark clouds she made up her mind to go out.

Was it still the same countryside, the same grass, the same trees that had been there in May? What had become of the sun-drenched laughter of the leaves, the verdant poetry of the grass with the orange dandelions, the red poppies, the white daisies, and the fantastic yellow butterflies quivering as if on the end of wires? The intoxication of the air charged with life, scent, embryos of fertility was no more.

The avenues, soaked by the heavy autumn rains, stretched away, thickly carpeted with dead leaves under the shivering skeletons of the almost bare poplars. The slender branches quivered in the wind with a remnant of foliage still clinging to them, ready to drop. Continually, all day long, like incessant depressing rain, these last leaves, now yellow like small gold coins, dropped off and fluttered about in eddies before coming to the ground. She walked as far as the shrubbery; it was as cheerless as a death-chamber. The walls of greenery, separating and masking the pleasant little winding paths, were no longer there; the thick shrubs, once a delicate tracery of interlacing twigs, rubbed their bare branches against each other, and the rustle of the dry falling leaves, blown about and piled up here and there by the wind, was like the melancholy sigh of a dying man.

Tiny birds fluttered from branch to branch, twittering faintly in search of shelter from the cold. But protected by the thick curtain of elms from the sea-wind, the linden and the plane, still decked with their summer finery, seemed clothed, the one in red velvet, the other in orange silk, tinted by the first cold according to their different saps.

Jeanne walked slowly up and down Mama's drive on the side of the Couillards' farm. Something was weighing on her mind, a presentiment of the long drawn out boredom of the new life in front of her. Then she sat down on the bank where Julien had first spoken to her of love, and she stayed there dreaming, her mind a blank and her thoughts paralysed; she would have liked to go to bed and sleep in order to escape from the sadness of the day. Suddenly she caught sight of a gull flying across the sky caught in a gust of wind, and she remembered the eagle which she had seen far away in Corsica in the sombre Val d'Ota. She felt the sharp shock caused by the recollection of happiness that has passed away; she saw again the radiant beauty of the island, with its wild scents, its sun which ripens oranges and citrons, its pink mountain tops, its blue gulfs and its ravines with their roaring torrents. But the damp dour country round her, with the dismal shedding of the leaves and the dark clouds scudding before the wind, plunged her into such a depth of depression that she had to go back to the house to avoid bursting into tears.

Mama in a state of torpor was dozing in front of the fire; accustomed to the dullness of her life, she was no longer aware of it. Papa and Julien had gone for a walk to discuss business. Darkness came on, shrouding in gloom the huge drawing-room, which was only lit up here and there by the glimmer of the fire. Outside there was still just enough daylight left to enable one to see through the windows nature's autumn sadness and the grey sky, which looked as if it too was muddy.

Presently the Baron appeared, followed by Julien. As soon as he entered the dingy room, he rang the bell, calling out: 'Quick! Quick! Lights! It's miserable here!' and sat down in front of the fire. While his wet boots were steaming close to the flames and the mud on his soles dropped off as it dried, he rubbed his hands cheerfully: 'I'm sure it's going to freeze,' he said; 'the sky is clearing in the north. The moon is full this evening; it's going to freeze hard tonight,' and turning to his daughter he went on: 'Well, little one, are you glad to be back in your own country, in your own house, with your old parents?'

This simple question upset Jeanne; she flung herself into her father's arms with tears in her eyes and kissed him nervously as if she had done something wrong; for in spite of genuine efforts to appear cheerful she was feeling ready to faint with sadness. But she remembered all the happiness which she had anticipated from being with her parents again at home, and she could not understand the coldness which had chilled her affection. It was as if, when one has been thinking a great deal about absent friends and lost the habit of seeing them round one every day, one experienced on meeting them again a check to one's affection, until the bonds of a common life were re-established.

Dinner was a tedious meal. No one spoke; Julien seemed to have forgotten his wife. Afterwards in the drawing-room, in front of the fire, facing Mama, who was sound asleep, she let herself doze; and once, woken up by the voices of the men who were having an argument, she asked herself, as she tried to rouse her thoughts, if she was going to become a prey to that dismal lethargy which is the result of a monotonous routine. The flames in the fire-place, dying down and ruddy in the twilight, were livening up and beginning to crackle. They cast sudden bright flashes on the faded tapestry of the armchairs, on the fox and the stork, the melancholy heron and the ant.

The Baron came across with a smile, and spreading his hands to the blazing logs he cried: 'Ha ha! The fire's doing well tonight; that means frost, my dears, yes, frost!' Then, laying his hand on Jeanne's shoulder and pointing to the fire: 'Look, my girl,' he said, 'that's the best thing in the world, the fire-side in the bosom of one's family! There's nothing like it! But what about going to bed, children? You must be dead tired.'

Back in her room Jeanne wondered how it could be that the return to the same place which she believed she loved could be so different on two separate occasions. Why did she feel as if she had been beaten? Why did this house, this beloved country, everything that before had made her heart bound, now seem so terribly depressing?

Suddenly her clock caught her eye; the little bee was still ticking from left to right and right to left with the same unceasing movement above the enamel flowers. An outburst of affection gripped her and she was moved to tears in front of this mechanical toy, which seemed alive and told her the time, throbbing like a beating heart. She had certainly not been so moved when she kissed her father and mother; the heart has its mysteries beyond the reach of reason.

For the first time since her marriage she was alone in bed. Julien, alleging that he was tired, was sleeping in another room; they had agreed that each should have his own room. She was a long time going to sleep; it felt strange not to have a body pressing against her. She had got out of the habit of sleeping alone and was kept awake by the vicious north wind tearing at the roof. In the morning she was woken up by a blood-red light on her bed; the window-panes, blurred with hoarfrost, were crimson as if the whole sky was on fire. Wrapping herself in a thick dressing-gown, she ran to the window and opened it. An icy wind, fresh and biting, blew into the room, stinging her face with a chill that made her eyes run; and in a deep red sky a huge crimson sun, bloated like a drunkard's face, was rising behind the trees. The ground, covered with white frost, still hard and dry, rang under the feet of the farm workers. In this one night all the branches of the poplars that still had leaves had been stripped, and on the far side of the common the long greenish line of the waves appeared, streaked with trails of white; the plane and the linden were rapidly losing their foliage in the squalls. At every gust of the icy wind, eddying leaves, loosened by the sudden frost, swirled to the ground like flocks of birds taking flight. Jeanne dressed and for something to do went to visit the farmers.

The Martins all raised their hands in greeting and Madame Martin kissed her on both cheeks; after that she had to drink a glass of cherry-brandy. From there she went on to the other farm. The Couillards also raised their hands; the wife gave her a peck on the ear and she had to swallow a glass of cassis. Then she went back to lunch. The day passed exactly like the day before, only it was cold instead of damp. The other days of the week were just like the first two; and all the weeks of the month were just like the first. Gradually, however, her longing for distant lands faded. Habit spread over her life a layer of resignation like the chalky deposit left on the ground by certain kinds of water; and a faint interest in the thousand trivialities of everyday life and care for the simple unimportant duties of the house was reborn in her heart. She developed a kind of meditative melancholy, a vague disillusion with life. What had gone wrong with her? What did she really want? She had no idea. She had everything she needed in the world; she no longer thirsted for pleasure and she had no dreams of possible happiness. Anyhow what was happiness? Like the old drawing-room arm-chairs, faded with age, everything was losing its brightness in her eyes, everything was growing dim, blurred into a dismal sameness.

Her relations with Julien had completely changed; he was an entirely different man since their return from their honeymoon, like an actor who has finished his part and resumed his ordinary life. He scarcely noticed her; he hardly spoke. Every trace of love had disappeared and it was only rarely that he came to her room at night. He had assumed control of the family finances and the running of the house; he checked the leases, dunned the peasants, and cut down expenses. Now that he was playing the part of the gentleman-farmer he had lost all the polish and elegance which he had had during the engagement. He now always wore, though it was badly stained, an old velvet shooting-jacket which he had come across in a wardrobe of his young days; with the carelessness of one who no longer needs to render himself attractive, he had given up shaving, so that a long, badly trimmed beard made him incredibly ugly. He no longer attended to his hands and after every meal he drank four or five glasses of brandy. Jeanne tried mild protests but he replied crossly: 'You had better leave me alone, hadn't you?' so that she risked no further comment.

She accepted the change in her husband to an extent that surprised herself. He had become a stranger, whose heart and thoughts were a closed book to her. She often thought about it, wondering why after meeting, falling in love and marrying in a sudden outburst of affection they now found themselves as much strangers as if they had never slept together. Why did this estrangement not cause her more pain? Was life like this? Had they made a mistake? Did the future hold nothing for her? If Julien had remained handsome, smart, elegant, attractive, would she have been more miserable?

It had been arranged that after New Year's Day the young couple would be left alone and Papa and Mama would return to their house in Rouen for several months. The whole winter the young couple would stay at the Poplars to get settled in, become used to the place where their whole life would be spent and grow fond of it. There were neighbours to whom Julien would introduce his wife, the Brisevilles, the Couteliers and the Fourvilles.

But the young couple could not begin their round of visits yet, because they had not been able to get the painter to come and change the armorial bearings on the carriage. The old family coach had actually been made over by the Baron to his son-in-law; and nothing in the world would have made Julien agree to appear at the great houses of the neighbourhood, if the coat-of-arms of the de Lamares had not been quartered with that of the Le Pertuis des Vauds. There was only one man anywhere around who specialized in heraldic painting. He was a painter from Bolbec called Bataille, who was sent for to all the great houses of Normandy to paint those precious coats-of-arms on carriage doors. At last, one morning in December, towards the end of lunch, a figure was seen to open the garden gate and make his way up the straight drive with a box on his back. It was Bataille.

He was shown into the hall and given a meal as if he were a gentleman; for his specialist skill, his continual relations with the aristocracy of the county and his knowledge of heraldry with its age-old techniques and emblems had made him into a living heraldic figure, whose hand was shaken by all the nobility. Drawing paper and a pencil were produced and, while he was eating, the Baron and Julien sketched the quartering of their shields. The Baroness, always thrilled by these things, made suggestions and Jeanne herself entered into the discussion, as if some mysterious interest had suddenly been aroused in her. Bataille, while going on with his lunch, put forward his ideas, sometimes picking up a pencil to illustrate a suggestion; he quoted examples and described all the carriages of the neighbourhood. In fact there was something in his ideas, even in his voice, which breathed an atmosphere of nobility. He was a short man, with close-cropped grey hair and hands stained with paint and smelling of turpentine. In the past, such was the gossip, he had been mixed up in an unsavoury affair, but the consideration which he enjoyed among the titled families had long since cleansed the stain.

As soon as he had finished his coffee, he was taken to the

coach-house and the oilcloth covering the carriage removed. Bataille examined it, gravely discussing the exact size of the design which he thought necessary for the suggested bearing; after that and after further consideration he set to work. In spite of the cold the Baroness had a chair brought out, so that she could watch the painting. Presently she sent for a foot-warmer, as her feet were getting frozen. She talked quietly to the painter all the time, asking questions about marriages of which she was ignorant, about recent births and deaths, completing from his information the genealogical trees which she treasured in her memory.

Julien stayed by his mother-in-law, sitting astride a chair. He smoked his pipe, spitting from time to time and listening to the conversation, keeping his eye fixed on the visible representation of his nobility. Presently old Simon, on his way to the kitchen-garden with his spade on his shoulder, stopped to look at the work in progress and, as the news of Bataille's arrival had got round to the two farms, it was not long before the two wives appeared. Standing one on each side of the Baroness they went into ecstasies, repeating: 'My word, them finicky things do need a bit of doing!'

The shields on the two doors could not be finished that day, but they were completed by eleven o'clock next morning. Everyone was there and the coach was pulled out to give a better view of the painting. It was perfect. Compliments were showered on Bataille, who left with his paint-box on his back. The Baron and his wife, Jeanne and Julien were unanimous that the painter was a man of real ability, who in other circumstances would certainly have become an artist.

In the interests of economy Julien had introduced several reforms. The old coachman had now become the gardener, the Viscount taking it on himself to drive. But as there had to be someone to hold the horses when the family alighted, he had turned a young cowherd named Marius into a groom. Finally, in order to have horses for the carriage, he inserted a special clause into the lease of the Couillards and Martins, by which the two farmers were bound each to supply a horse one day every month on a date fixed by him, in return for which service they were freed from the obligation to provide chickens.

Accordingly one day, when the Couillards brought a big chestnut screw and the Martins a small white pony, the two animals were harnessed side by side, and Marius, swamped in an ancient livery coat of old Simon's, led the turn-out up to the front door of the mansion. Julien, smartened up and throwing out his chest, had recovered something of his former elegance, but his untrimmed beard gave him a common appearance. He examined the harness, the carriage, and the boy-groom and passed them as satisfactory, the newly painted armorial bearings being the only thing in which he was really interested.

The Baroness, who had come down from her room on her husband's arm, climbed in with difficulty and sat down propped up with cushions at her back; and then Jeanne appeared. First she was amused by the two ill-matched horses; the white pony, she said, must be the chestnut's grandchild. A moment later she caught sight of Marius with his face almost completely hidden by the top-hat with a cockade, which was only kept in place by his nose, and his hands buried in the depths of his sleeves; the skirts of the long livery coat hid both his legs like a petticoat, from which protruded his feet shod in huge clogs. When she saw him bending his head back in order to see and raising his knees at every step as if he was wading through a stream, fussing about like a blind man to carry out his orders, his whole body swathed and shrouded in his absurdly large clothes, she was quite overcome and could not control her laughter.

The Baron turned round and saw the bewildered little man; unable to resist the infection he burst out laughing and, hardly articulate, called out to his wife: 'Look ... at Mar ... Marius! What a figure of fun! My God, what a figure of fun!'

Then the Baroness, who had leant out of the window to look, was shaken by such a convulsion of merriment that the whole carriage jolted up and down on its springs, as if it was bumping over a rough road. But Julien, pale with anger, asked: 'What's the matter with you all, laughing like that? You must be mad.'

Jeanne, quite out of control and convulsed with laughter which she could not stifle, sat down on one of the terrace steps, where she was joined by the Baron. Inside the carriage outbursts of sneezing accompanied by clucking sounds suggested that the

Baroness was choking. Suddenly Marius's long coat began to heave; no doubt he realized how he looked, for he was roaring with laughter himself inside his head-gear.

Julien dashed forward in exasperation and with a clout over the ear knocked the huge hat off the boy's head, so that it rolled away on the grass.

Turning to his father-in-law, he stammered in a voice trembling with anger: 'I hardly think you have any cause to laugh. We shouldn't be where we are, if you hadn't wasted your fortune and thrown away your substance. Whose fault is it that you're ruined?'

All their mirth was frozen and stopped dead; no one spoke. Jeanne, on the verge of tears, got in with her mother, the Baron sat down facing the two ladies and Julien took his place on the box, after hoisting up beside him the boy, who was sobbing with a swollen face.

It was a long depressing drive; not a word was spoken in the carriage. They were all three glum and embarrassed, refusing to admit what was worrying them. They knew that they could talk of nothing else with this distressing obsession on their minds, and they preferred silence, so as not to touch on this painful subject.

At the uneven trot of the ill-matched horses the coach skirted the farmyards, scattering terrified black hens, which dived into the hedges and disappeared; it was sometimes followed by a baying Alsatian, which soon ran back to its house, its hair bristling, to turn round and bark after the carriage. A boy in muddy clogs, with lanky ill-controlled legs, who was passing with hands thrust deep into his pockets and his blue blouse bellying out behind him in the wind, stood aside to make room for the carriage and took off his hat awkwardly, showing his straight hair plastered down on his head. Between the farms was a stretch of common land with other scattered farms here and there in the distance.

At last they entered a long avenue of pines running back from the road. Deep muddy ruts made the coach roll from side to side, which brought little screams from Mama. At the end of the avenue there was a closed white garden-gate; Marius ran to open it and they drove round a vast lawn, till the circular drive brought them to a tall gloomy house with closed shutters.

The door in the centre suddenly opened and an old crippled butler in a red and black striped waistcoat, partly covered by his apron, made his way in a slow zigzag course down the terrace steps. He took the visitors' names and showed them into a very large drawing-room, where with some difficulty he opened the Venetian shutters, which were closed like the others. All the furniture was covered with dust-sheets and the clock and the candelabra were swathed in white linen covers. The air was musty with the mildew of age, chilly and damp, and it seemed to pierce the lungs, the heart and the skin with melancholy.

They all sat down and waited. Footsteps could be heard in the passage above, indicating unwonted bustle. The owners of the mansion, caught unawares, were changing hurriedly. There was a long pause and a bell rang several times. Footsteps came down one staircase and went up another. The Baroness, chilled by the piercing cold, could not stop sneezing and Julien walked up and down; Jeanne remained in a state of depression, sitting by her mother's side, while the Baron stood with lowered head leaning against the marble chimney-piece.

At last one of the great doors opened to reveal the Vicomte and Vicomtesse de Briseville. They were both short, skinny, with a jerky walk, of uncertain age, pompous and nervous. The wife, in a flowered silk dress with a widow's cap and ribbons, spoke quickly in a shrill voice. The husband, in a tight formal frock-coat, bowed with bent knees. His nose, his eyes, his prominent teeth, his hair, which looked as if it was plastered with grease, and his smart formal attire, all had the gloss of things of which great care is taken.

After the first welcome and the commonplaces of neighbourly politeness conversation flagged. Pointless compliments were exchanged; the present happy relations would, they hoped, be maintained on both sides. Living in the country, it was always pleasant to see one's friends. The icy air of the drawing-room was getting into their bones and the Baroness was now coughing as well as sneezing. Then the Baron gave the signal for departure. The Brisevilles protested: 'What? So soon? Don't go yet!' But Jeanne had stood up in spite of signs from Julien, who considered the visit too short. An attempt was made to ring for the footman to have the coach brought round, but the bell was out of order; the butler bustled off, but returned to say that the horses had been put in the stable; so they had to wait.

Everyone did their best to make conversation. They talked of the rainy winter. Jeanne with uncontrollable shivers of discomfort asked what their hosts found to do all alone the whole year. The Brisevilles could not understand the question; they were always busy writing long letters to their noble relatives scattered all over France; they spent their days in unimportant chores, as formal in their relations with each other as with strangers and discussing the most trivial incidents in high-flown language. Under the lofty blackened ceiling of the unused drawing-room, which was always draped in dust-sheets, the man and the woman, so small, so neat, so correct, seemed to Jeanne museum pieces of an extinct nobility.

At last the carriage with its two ill-matched horses appeared in front of the windows, but Marius was nowhere to be found. Thinking that he would not be wanted before evening, he had no doubt gone off for a country walk. Julien told them angrily to send him back on foot; and after long good-byes on both sides they started home for the Poplars.

As soon as they were settled in the coach, Jeanne and her father, though unable to shake off the obsession of Julien's rudeness, recovered sufficiently to amuse themselves by parodying the Brisevilles' gestures and intonations. The Baron played the part of the man and Jeanne that of the woman, but the Baroness, whose respect for them was wounded, said: 'You're wrong to make fun of them; they are very well born and well connected.' Nothing more was said for a while, so as not to annoy Mama, but from time to time, in spite of everything, Papa and Jeanne went on with their game, catching each other's eye. He gave a dignified bow and said pompously: 'Your mansion at the Poplars must be very chilly, Madame, with the strong sea-wind raging every day.'

She, with a prim expression and simpering with a little wriggle of the head like a duck preening itself, replied: 'Oh, I have quite enough to do all the year round, Sir! You see, we have so many relatives to write to, and Monsieur de Briseville leaves everything to me; he is fully occupied with scholarly research; he and the Abbé Pelle are collaborating in a History of Religion in Normandy.'

The Baroness smiled good-humouredly, though still worried, and repeated: 'It's quite wrong to laugh at people of our own class like this.'

Suddenly the carriage stopped; Julien was shouting to someone behind. Jeanne and the Baron leant out of the window and saw a strange figure rolling along towards them. It was Marius, following the coach as fast as his legs would carry him; his progress was hampered by the fluttering skirts of his livery coat, and he was blinded by his hat which was continually falling off. He was waving his sleeves like the sails of a windmill, as he splashed through the great puddles, which he was trying desperately to cross, stumbling over the stones in the road, jigging up and down and jumping about, covered with mud. As soon as he caught up with the carriage, Julien leaned down, seized him by the collar and hoisted him up by his side; then letting go of the reins he set about him with his fists, pounding his hat, which was forced right down to the boy's shoulders, booming like a drum. Inside it the boy was screaming, trying to free himself and jump down from the box, while Julien, gripping him with one hand, kept on striking him with the other. Jeanne, thoroughly upset, cried: 'Oh! Papa, Papa!', and the Baroness, bursting with indignation, seized her husband's arm, crying: 'Oh, do stop him, Jacques!'

Suddenly the Baron, lowering the front window, shouted in a quivering voice: 'Have you nearly finished beating the poor child?'

Julien turned round in astonishment: 'But can't you see what a filthy mess the little wretch has made of his livery?'

The Baron thrust his head between them and cried: 'I can't help that; it's no excuse for being brutal.'

Julien lost his temper again: 'Be so good as to leave me alone; this is none of your business,' and he raised his hand again, but his father-in-law seized his arm and brought it down with such force that it hit the woodwork at the back of the seat, and he shouted: 'If you don't stop, I'll get out and make you stop!'

so loud that the Viscount calmed down and, shrugging his shoulders without a word, whipped up the horses and they went on at full speed. The two women, furiously angry, did not move and the Baroness's heart could be heard beating wildly.

At dinner Julien laid himself out to be more charming than usual, as if nothing had happened; Jeanne, her father and Madame Adélaïde, whose placid kindliness easily forgot any trouble, touched by his pleasantness, cheerfully let themselves go with that sense of well-being that convalescents feel, and when Jeanne mentioned the Brisevilles again, her husband joined in the fun, but added quickly: 'Anyhow they are gentlefolk.'

They paid no more visits, both being unwilling to raise the problem of Marius again; they decided merely to send New Year cards to the neighbours. They would wait to call for the warm weather in the spring. Christmas came, and they had the mayor and his wife and the priest to dinner, repeating the invitation for New Year's Day. These were the only distractions to break the monotony of their life. Papa and Mama were due to leave on 9 January. Jeanne wanted to keep them, but Julien was not anxious to do so, and the Baron, in face of his son-in-law's increasing coldness, ordered a post-chaise from Rouen.

The evening before they left, when their packing was finished, as it was a clear frosty night, Jeanne and her father decided to go down to Yport, where they had not been since her return from Corsica. They went through the wood, where she had walked on her wedding-day in intimate communion with the man whose helpmate she was to become for life, the wood where she had received her first kiss and felt the first shiver, the forerunner of sensual passion, which she was not to know till she felt it in its fullness in the wild Val d'Ota by the spring where they had drunk, mingling their kisses with water. The leaves and climbing plants had now gone; there was nothing but the rustle of the branches, the confused brittle murmur of bare branches in the winter.

They reached the little village, whose silent deserted streets still kept the smell of the sea and kelp and fish. Huge tarred nets were drying, hanging up in front of the doors or spread out on the shingle. The cold grey waves, breaking in foam with their ceaseless rumble, were beginning to recede with the ebbing tide and lay bare the greenish rocks at the foot of the cliff towards Fécamp. All along the beach the broad-beamed fishing-boats were lying on their sides, looking like great dead fishes. Evening was coming on and parties of fishermen were making for the breakwater, plodding along in their heavy sea-boots, with a woollen scarf round the throat, a bottle of brandy in one hand and the ship's lantern in the other. They spent a long time wandering round the smacks; with the slowness typical of Normandy the men were putting on board their nets, their buoys, a large round loaf, a pot of butter, and a bottle of proof spirit. Then after righting the boat they heaved it forward, so that it ran down the shingle slope with a grating sound, parted the fringe of foam and rose on the wave, and balanced for a moment on the crest, before spreading its brown wings and disappearing into the night with its tiny light at the mast-head.

The sailors' sturdy wives, their bony frames standing out under their thin clothes, who had stayed till the last fisherman had left, now returned to the sleeping village, disturbing the heavy slumber of the dark streets with their raucous voices. The Baron and Jeanne, standing still, watched as the fishermen disappeared into the night. These men went out every night, risking death to avoid starvation, and yet were so miserably poor that they could never afford meat to eat. The Baron was thrilled before the ocean: 'It's beautiful,' he murmured, 'but it's frightening. The sea with darkness falling, where so many lives are lost, is a wonderful thing, isn't it, Jeannette?'

She answered with a wry smile: 'It isn't as wonderful here as in the Mediterranean.'

Her father was indignant: 'The Mediterranean! That's only oil, sugar, and water, the blue of the wash-tub! Look at it here, how terrifying it is with its foaming crests. Think of all the men who have gone out over it and disappeared.'

Jeanne agreed with a sigh: 'Yes, perhaps you are right.'

But the word 'Mediterranean', which had risen to her lips, had again touched her heart and taken her thoughts back to those distant lands, the grave of her dreams.

Then father and daughter, instead of going back through the wood, took the road and climbed the hill slowly. They hardly spoke; both were sad at their coming separation. Here and there, as they walked alongside the ditches in front of the farms, the smell of crushed apples and the scent of fresh cider, which seems to pervade the whole countryside of Normandy at this time of year, hit them in the face, or else the strong whiff of the cowsheds and the warm, healthy reek of dung. A small window with a light in it at the end of a yard showed where the family lived. It seemed to Jeanne as if her heart was broadening, enabling her to grasp things unseen, and these little scattered lights in the fields suddenly gave her a keen sense of the isolation of all human beings, with everything to keep them apart and divide them, leading them far away from all the things that they might love; and with resignation in her tone she said : 'Life isn't really much fun.'

The Baron sighed : 'Well, what do you want to do? We can't change it.'

Next day Papa and Mama had gone and Jeanne and Julien were left alone.

CHAPTER SEVEN

It was at this time that cards became part of the young couple's life. Every day after lunch Julien, smoking his pipe and clearing his throat with brandy, of which he now drank six or eight glasses after every meal, played several games of Bezique with his wife. After that she went up to her room, sat down by the window and, while the rain beat on the panes and the wind made them rattle, she worked conscientiously, embroidering the frill of a petticoat. Sometimes, getting tired, she raised her eyes and gazed at the choppy grey sea in the distance, and after staring blankly for a few minutes resumed her work.

In fact she had nothing else to do. Julien had taken on the running of the house, in order to satisfy to the full his passion for authority and his itch for economy, which amounted to miserly stinginess; he never gave a tip and cut down the food to a bare minimum. Since she had been at the Poplars, Jeanne had ordered a small Normandy girdle-cake from the baker every day, but he cancelled the order as an extravagance and condemned her to toast.

To avoid explanations, arguments, and quarrels she made no comment; but she felt each new instance of her husband's niggardliness as another pinprick. Brought up in a family where money counted for nothing, it all seemed to her hateful and unworthy. How often had she heard Papa say to Mama : 'Money only exists to be spent !' But now Julien was always saying : 'Won't you ever learn not to throw money out of the window?' and whenever he had knocked a few pence off someone's wages or off a bill, he would say with a smile, as he pocketed the change : 'Little streams make big rivers !'

At times Jeanne went back to her dreaming. She would gradually stop sewing and, dropping her work with lack-lustre eyes, she would go back to one of her childhood's romantic dreams and lose herself in delightful adventures. But suddenly Julien's voice giving Simon an order roused her from these soothing reveries, and she went on with her patient sewing, saying to herself: 'That's all over and done with,' and a tear fell on the fingers holding the needle.

Rosalie too, who had always gone about her work singing cheerily, had changed; her chubby cheeks had lost their colour and were almost hollow and muddy. Jeanne often asked her if she felt ill, but the little maid always replied: 'No, Madame.' A little blood mounted to her cheeks and she hurried away. Instead of tripping about as before she now dragged her feet painfully and no longer worried about her appearance; she never bought things now from travelling salesmen, who showed her in vain their silk ribbons and corsets and different kinds of scent. The whole great house seemed dreary and lifeless, scarred with grey streaks by the rain.

At the end of January the snow came. Far away to the north great banks of cloud swept over the dark sea and white flakes began to fall. Then in the course of a single night the whole common was buried, and in the morning the trees were all draped in a mantle of frozen snow. Julien, in high boots and unshaved, spent his time on the far side of the shrubbery, hiding in the ditch separating it from the common, on the look-out for migrant birds. At intervals a shot broke the silence of the frozen fields, scaring flocks of black crows, which rose in circles from the tall trees. Jeanne in her boredom sometimes came down to the terrace, where the sounds of life reached her from the distance, echoing over the sleepy peace of the dreary grey flagstones. Then she heard nothing but the far-off boom of the waves and the faint, unceasing drip from the thin coating of frozen rain. The blanket of snow was rising all the time under the continuous fall of the thick light flakes.

On one of these white mornings Jeanne was sitting quietly, warming her feet at the fire in her room, while Rosalie, more changed every day, was making the bed slowly. Suddenly she heard a deep sigh behind her. Without looking round she asked: 'What's the matter?' The maid as usual replied: 'Nothing, Madame,' but her voice sounded choked and breathless. Jeanne was already thinking of something else, when she noticed that there was no sound of movement from the girl. She called her; there was dead silence. So, thinking that the maid had left the room, she shouted : 'Rosalie !' and was about to reach for the bell, when a deep groan quite close made her jump with a shiver of anxiety. The little maid, deathly pale with a drawn face, had collapsed on the floor with her legs stretched out in front of her, leaning back against the frame of the bed. Jeanne ran to her crying : 'What's the matter with you? What's the matter with you?'

The girl did not answer and did not move. She was looking at her mistress with wild eyes, gasping as if in the grip of some agonizing pain. Suddenly she tensed her whole body and slid down on her back, stifling a cry of distress with clenched teeth. Then under her skirt, which was stretched tight by her strain-ing thighs, something moved, and immediately a strange sound was audible, a throaty gurgle of strangled breathing, and there came a long-drawn mew like a cat, a faint wail of pain, the first moan of a new-born infant. In a flash Jeanne understood and ran to the staircase distraught, shouting : 'Julien ! Julien !'

He answered from downstairs : 'What do you want?'

She could hardly stammer : 'It's Rosalie ... she ...'

He dashed up, two steps at a time, and rushing into the room pulled up the girl's clothes to reveal a hideous little piece of flesh, shrivelled, whimpering, bent, clammy, writhing between two bare legs.

Standing up with an unpleasant look on his face, he hustled his terrified wife out of the room : 'This is no job for you; go away and send me Ludivine and old Simon.'

Trembling all over, Jeanne went down to the kitchen; then, not daring to go up again, she went to the drawing-room, where there had been no fire since her parents' departure, and waited anxiously for news. Presently she saw one of the men-servants running out, and five minutes later he returned with the widow Dentu, the local midwife. Presently there was a great bustle on the stairs, as if a stretcher were being carried down; and Julien came and told Jeanne that she could go up to her room again. She was shaking as if she had been present at a fatal accident. Sitting down in front of her fire, she asked : 'How is she?'

Julien, extremely preoccupied, was walking up and down nervously, apparently very angry. At first he said nothing, but after a few seconds he paused, saying: 'What do you propose to do with the girl?'

She did not understand and looked at her husband: 'What? What do you mean? I don't understand.'

Suddenly he raised his voice as if he was losing control of himself: 'Anyhow we can't keep an illegitimate child in the house.'

Jeanne did not know what to say, but after a long silence she ventured: 'Perhaps, my dear, we could put it out to nurse.'

He cut her short: 'And who is going to pay? You, I suppose.'

She pondered the problem for some time and at last she said: 'But the father will make himself responsible for the child. And if he marries Rosalie, there will be no further difficulty.'

Julien, losing patience and furiously angry, retorted: 'The father!... The father! Do you know who the father is? No, you don't! Well then?'

Jeanne with deep feeling broke in: 'But he surely won't leave the girl like this; it would be unforgivable. We'll discover his name and find him; he'll have to explain.'

Julien, now calmer, continued to walk up and down: 'But, my dear, she won't tell you his name – she won't tell you any more than me. And what if he doesn't want to have anything more to do with her, what then? Anyhow we can't keep an unmarried mother with her bastard in our house. Surely you can see that.'

Jeanne repeated obstinately: 'Then he's a cad, this fellow. But we must find out who he is and he will have us to deal with.'

Julien, getting red in the face, was still irritable: 'But ... meanwhile ...'

Not knowing what to say, she asked: 'Well, what do you suggest?'

He immediately settled the question: 'Oh, as far as I'm concerned, it's quite simple; I should give her a little money and tell her to go to hell with the little misery.'

But his wife, deeply shocked, reacted sharply: 'I will never stand for that. The girl is my foster-sister and we grew up together. Unfortunately she has made a slip, but I will never turn her out for that. If necessary, I will bring up the child.'

At this Julien exploded: 'And we shall get a fine reputation, we shall, with our name and connexions. Everyone will say that we are sheltering vice and harbouring prostitutes. Decent people won't set foot in the house. I don't know what you are thinking of – you must be mad.'

She kept her temper: 'I will never allow Rosalie to be turned out. If you refuse to keep her, my mother will take her back; and in the end we shall be bound to discover the name of the child's father.'

At that he went out of the room in a rage, banging the door and shouting: 'Women do get absurd ideas into their heads!'

After lunch Jeanne went up to the new mother's room. The little maid was lying motionless in bed with her eyes open, under the widow Dentu's watchful care, while the nurse rocked the new-born infant in her arms. At the sight of her mistress Rosalie began to sob, hiding her head under the sheets in utter despair. Jeanne tried to kiss her but she struggled to keep her face covered. The nurse however intervened and pulled back the bed-clothes; she did not resist but went on crying quietly.

There was a poor fire in the grate; it was cold and the child was crying. Jeanne dared not mention the infant for fear of causing another outburst; she held the girl's hand, repeating mechanically: 'It'll be all right! It'll be all right!'

The poor girl watched the nurse furtively, starting every time the baby cried. The aftermath of her distress kept her catching her breath with a convulsive sob, while the tears which she was trying to restrain made a gurgling sound in her throat. Jeanne kissed her again and whispered in her ear: 'We'll look after him well.' Then, as Rosalie's tears threatened to start again, she hurriedly left the room.

Every day she went back and every day Rosalie burst into tears at the sight of her mistress. The child was put out to nurse with a neighbour's wife. Julien was hardly on speaking terms with his wife, as if he still harboured a grudge against her for her refusal to get rid of the maid. One day he brought up the subject again, but Jeanne took a letter from her pocket from the Baroness asking that the girl should be sent to her immediately, if they were not keeping her on at the Poplars. Julien, furious at this, cried: 'Your mother is as mad as you are,' but he did not insist.

In a fortnight the young mother was able to get up and go on with her work. One morning Jeanne made her sit down and, holding her hands and looking hard at her, she said: 'Come now, dear, tell me everything.'

'What, Madame?' stammered Rosalie trembling.

'Whose is this child?'

At this the little maid broke down again and tried desperately to disengage her hands to hide her face. But Jeanne kissed her in spite of her efforts and attempted to console her: 'Of course, it's all very unfortunate, my dear, but many others have done the same thing. If the father marries you, people will forget all about it. We'll take him into service in the house with you.'

Rosalie continued to groan, as if she were being tortured, and from time to time made violent efforts to free herself and escape.

Jeanne went on: 'I quite understand that you are ashamed of yourself, but you can see that I'm not a bit angry and that I'm discussing the whole thing in a friendly spirit. If I ask the man's name, it's only for your good, for I can see from your being so upset that he is leaving you in the lurch, and I mean to stop that. Look, Julien will go and find him and we'll make him marry you; and as we shall keep both of you in the house, we'll see that he makes you happy.'

This time, with a great effort, Rosalie wrenched her hands from her mistress's hold and rushed out of the room like a mad woman.

That evening at dinner Jeanne said to Julien: 'I tried to get Rosalie to tell me the name of her seducer, but I failed; now it's up to you to try, so that we can compel the wretch to marry her.'

But Julien immediately lost his temper: 'Look here! I don't want to hear any more of this business. You insist on keeping the girl in the house: well, keep her, but don't worry me any more about it.'

Since the birth his temper seemed worse than before; now he never spoke to his wife without raising his voice, as if he were furiously angry; whereas she on the contrary kept hers low and behaved in a conciliatory manner to avoid argument. She often cried in bed at night. But in spite of his constant irritability her husband had resumed his amorous habits, which had been interrupted since their return, and three consecutive nights hardly ever passed without his coming to her bed.

Rosalie was soon quite well again and seemed more cheerful, but she was still nervous as if haunted by some undefined fear; and she ran away twice more, when Jeanne tried to question her. Julien, too, seemed less difficult, and Jeanne's hopes revived and she was more cheerful, though sometimes she was tormented by vague forebodings, which she kept to herself.

There was no sign of a thaw yet. For five weeks now a cloudless sky like blue crystal during the day and by night sparkling with stars, which looked like specks of rime in the bitter cold, stretched above the hard gleaming carpet of snow. The farms, isolated in their square yards behind their curtain of tall trees powdered with hoar-frost, seemed asleep in their white drapery. Neither men nor animals ventured out; it was only the cottage chimneys that showed by threads of smoke rising straight up in the freezing air that life was going on inside. The common, the hedges, the elms round the fenced areas, everything seemed dead, killed by the cold. From time to time trees were heard cracking, as if their wooden arms were breaking under the bark, and sometimes a big branch broke off and fell to the ground, the penetrating frost having hardened the sap and split the grain. Jeanne waited anxiously for the advent of the warm spring winds, blaming the terrible severity of the weather for all her torturing anxieties.

At times she could not eat and the mere sight of food made her feel sick; at times her pulse raced; at times the scanty meals which she did eat brought on the nausea of indigestion. The tension of her quivering nerves made her whole life one unceasing unbearable strain.

One evening the thermometer dropped still further, and Julien, shivering as he left the table – the dining-room was never adequately heated, as he was always trying to save wood – rubbed his hands, murmuring: 'It *will* be nice in bed together tonight, won't it, darling?'

He gave his cheery laugh of the old days as he spoke, and Jeanne threw her arms round his neck; but that evening she happened to be feeling so worried, so bruised, so unaccountably nervy, that kissing him full on the mouth she begged him in a whisper to let her sleep by herself; she explained in a few words : 'Please, dear, I'm not feeling well tonight. I shall be all right tomorrow, I'm sure.' He did not insist : 'Just as you like, my dear; if you aren't well, you must look after yourself,' and they changed the subject.

She went to bed early. Julien for once had the fire lit in his bedroom. When they told him that it was burning well, he kissed his wife on the forehead and went up. The cold seemed to have got into the whole house; even the walls, penetrated by the frost, were cracking, as if they were shivering; and Jeanne was shaking in bed. She got up twice to put more logs on the fire, and look for dresses, skirts and old clothes to pile on the bed. But she could not get warm; her feet were numb and shivers ran all the way up her calves to her thighs, making her fidget and turn over continually, quite unable to control her nerves. Soon her teeth began to chatter and her hands trembled; her heart, usually sluggish, was being violently and sometimes seemed to stop altogether, and she was panting as if her throat was choked. A ghastly anxiety gripped her mind, as the bitter cold penetrated to the very marrow of her bones. She had never experienced anything like this before; she had never felt so dead, so close to her last gasp. She thought : 'I'm going to die . . . I am dying.'

In a panic she jumped out of bed, rang for Rosalie, waited, rang again, waited again, shivering and chilled to the bone. The little maid showed no sign of coming; no doubt she was sound asleep in that first sleep which nothing disturbs. Losing her head, Jeanne started up the stairs with bare feet. She went up noiselessly, feeling her way, found the door and called : 'Rosalie !' Then she went in, bumped against the bed, passed her hands over it and realized that it was empty. It was empty and quite cold, as if no one had slept in it. In surprise she said to herself : 'Well, surely she can't have gone out on the spree on a night like this !' But as her heart suddenly got out of control and began to throb, choking her, she tottered downstairs again to wake Julien up. She dashed into his room, spurred on by the conviction that she was going to die and wanting to see him once more before losing consciousness.

By the light of the dying embers she saw Rosalie's head on the pillow by the side of her husband's. She uttered a loud cry and they both sat up. Dazed by the discovery, she stood still for a second, before running back to her own room; and as Julien cried desperately: 'Jeanne!' she was suddenly seized by an agonizing fear of seeing him, hearing his voice, having to listen to his lies and meet him face to face. She rushed out to the stairs and dashed down.

She was now running in the dark at the risk of falling down the stairs and breaking her bones on the flag-stones. But she went on, urged by a mad longing to get away, discover nothing and be alone. When she reached the bottom, she sat down on a step, still in her nightdress with bare feet, and stayed there unable to think.

Julien had jumped out of bed and was throwing on some clothes. She got up to escape from him. He was already on the way down, crying: 'Listen, Jeanne!' No, she would not listen, she would not let him touch her with the tips of his fingers! She rushed into the dining-room, as if pursued by a murderer. She wanted to find a way of escape, somewhere to hide, a dark corner, any place to avoid him. She hid under the table, but he was already opening the door with a light in his hand, repeating: 'Jeanne!', and she rushed off again like a hare and dashed into the kitchen, running round it twice like an animal at bay. Just as he was catching up with her, she suddenly opened the garden door and fled out into the country.

The icy touch of the snow, into which she often sank up to the knees, gave her the strength of desperation; she was not conscious of the cold, though she was undressed. She did not feel anything, the mental shock having numbed her body, and she ran on as white as the snow-covered ground. She went down the main drive, crossed the shrubbery, climbed over the ditch and went off across the common. There was no moon and the stars were twinkling like sparks of fire in the dark sky; but the flat plain was light, a dull white, frozen into immobility, a desert of silence.

Jeanne ran on, breathing easily, her mind a blank, unable to think. Suddenly she found herself at the top of the cliff; she stopped instinctively and crouched down, her thoughts and her will paralysed. In the dark abyss in front of her the invisible, silent sea exhaled the salty smell of seaweed at low tide. She stayed there a long time, her mind as frozen as her body, till a fit of trembling seized her and she shook all over like a sail filled with the wind. Her arms, her hands, her feet, under some overmastering force, were quivering and shaking in quick jerks. Suddenly she recovered consciousness and was able to think clearly though painfully.

Old memories flashed across her mind, the boat trip with Julien and old Lastique, their talk, the birth of her love, the christening of the boat; and she thought back to her dreams on the evening of his first visit to the Poplars. And now! And now! Her whole life was shattered, all joy was dead, all her expectations blasted; the ghastly future with all its tortures, his betrayal, her despair, rose up before her eyes. It would be better to die; then everything would be over and done with.

She heard a shout in the distance: 'This way! Here are her footprints! Quick! This way!'

It was Julien looking for her; but she would never see him again. At the bottom of the precipice in front of her she could hear a faint sound, the murmur of the waves breaking on the rocks. She struggled to her feet to throw herself down, and in a desperate farewell to life she moaned the last word of the dying, the last cry of the young soldier fatally wounded in battle: 'Mother!'

Suddenly the thought of Mama flashed across her mind; she saw her sobbing, she saw her father on his knees before her drowned body, and she felt the stab of their despair. Then she fell back limp on the snow and made no attempt to run away when Julien and old Simon, followed by Marius with a lantern, seized her by the arms and dragged her back from the edge of the precipice. She offered no resistance; she was incapable of movement. She was aware of being carried away, put to bed and later rubbed with hot cloths; after that she remembered nothing; she had lost consciousness.

Later a nightmare – was it a nightmare? – seized her. She

was in bed in her room; it was daylight, but she could not get up. Why? She had no idea. She heard a faint sound on the floor, a sort of scraping, scratching sound, and suddenly a mouse, a tiny grey mouse, darted over the bed-clothes. Another followed, and a third, which ran up to her breast with little hurrying steps. Jeanne was not frightened, but she wanted to catch the creature and stretched out her hand, but she could not get hold of it. Soon more mice, ten, twenty, hundreds, thousands of them appeared on all sides; they climbed the bed-posts, crawled all over the hangings, covering the whole bed, and presently made their way under the clothes. Jeanne felt their chilly touch on her skin, tickling her legs and climbing all over her body; she saw them flocking up from the foot of the bed right up to her throat, trying to get inside. She struggled, stretching out her hands to catch one, but she never succeeded. At last, losing patience, she tried to get out of bed, uttering cries, but she felt herself being held down in the grip of strong arms which prevented her moving, though she could see no one. She had no sense of time, but it must have lasted a very long time.

At last she woke up, tired and exhausted but quite calm. She felt weak and opened her eyes, and was not surprised to see her mother sitting in the room with a portly man whom she did not know. How old was she? She had no idea. She felt like a small child; moreover she could remember nothing. The gentleman cried: 'Look! She is recovering consciousness!' and Mama began to cry. The portly gentleman went on: 'Come! Calm yourself, Baroness! I promise you it will be all right now, but don't talk to her; let her sleep.'

Jeanne felt that she dozed for a long time, overcome by heavy drowsiness whenever she tried to think; and she gave up all attempt to remember anything, for she had a vague fear of the realities of life, which were awakening again in her brain.

Once, as she opened her eyes, she saw Julien, alone beside her, and suddenly everything came back to her, as if a curtain, which had hidden all her past life, had been drawn. She felt a stab of excruciating pain in her heart and wanted to escape. She threw back the clothes and jumped out of bed, but fell to the ground, as her legs were too weak to support her. Julien ran to her and she began to scream at him not to touch her. She was writhing and rolling about on the floor when the door opened and Aunt Lison hurried in with the widow Dentu, followed first by the Baron and then by Mama, out of breath and distraught.

They put her back to bed, and she immediately closed her eyes deliberately to avoid having to speak and to be able to think undisturbed. Her mother and her aunt looked after her and fussed round, asking: 'Can you hear us now, darling?' She pretended not to hear and did not answer. She was fully conscious that it was getting dark. Night came on and the nurse settled down by her, giving her something to drink at intervals. She took the drink in silence, but she did not go to sleep. Consecutive thought was difficult; she was always trying to recollect things which escaped her, as if there were gaps in her memory, blank empty voids, on which incidents had made no impression.

Gradually, after great efforts, everything came back to her and she recalled the past with grim determination. Mama, Aunt Lison, and the Baron had come back; so she must have been very ill. But what of Julien? What had he told them? Did her parents know the truth? And what of Rosalie? Where was she? And what was she herself to do now? What was she to do? She had a bright idea; she would go back with Papa and Mama to Rouen as before; she would be a widow, that was all. So she waited, listening to the talk round her, taking it all in without showing any sign, glad that she had recovered her reason, ready to wait and make her plans.

Finally one evening, finding herself alone with the Baroness, she called to her in a whisper: 'Mama!' She was surprised at the sound of her own voice; it was quite changed. The Baroness seized her hands: 'My dear, my darling Jeanne, do you know me, dearest?'

'Yes, Mama, but you mustn't cry! we've got a lot to talk about. Has Julien told you why I ran away in the snow?'

'Yes, dear, you had a very dangerous fever.'

'That is not the reason, Mama; I had the fever afterwards. Did he tell you what caused it and why I ran away?'

'No, darling.'

'It was because I found Rosalie in bed with him.'

The Baroness thought that she was still delirious and caressed her: 'Go to sleep, darling; control yourself and try to sleep.'

But Jeanne went on obstinately: 'I'm not delirious any longer, Mama; I'm not raving now, as I must have done lately. One night I didn't feel well and I went to look for Julien. Rosalie was in bed with him. The shock made me lose my reason and I ran out into the snow to throw myself over the cliff.'

But the Baroness repeated: 'Yes, darling, you were very ill.'

'That's not true, Mama. I did find Rosalie in bed with Julien and I won't stay with him any longer; I want to go back with you to Rouen as before.'

The Baroness, whom the doctor had told not to contradict Jeanne in anything, replied: 'Yes, darling.'

But Jeanne, losing patience, broke in: 'I see you don't believe me. Go and fetch Papa; he'll understand me in the end.'

So Mama got up with some difficulty, picked up her sticks and shuffled out of the room, returning a few minutes later on the Baron's arm. They sat down facing the bed and Jeanne began immediately. She told the whole story in a quiet faint voice but quite clearly; she recounted Julien's strange behaviour, his bullying, his miserliness, and finally his infidelity. By the end the Baron realized that she was perfectly sane, but he did not know what to think, what to do, what to suggest. He took her hand tenderly, as he used to do when he was telling her stories to send her to sleep: 'Listen, darling! We must be cautious and do nothing in a hurry. Try to put up with your husband, until we have made up our minds. Promise me you will do that.'

'Very well,' she murmured, 'but I mean to leave the house as soon as I'm well,' and she added in a whisper: 'Where is Rosalie now?'

'You won't see her again,' replied the Baron.

But she insisted: 'But where is she? I want to know.'

Then he admitted that she was still in the house, but said that she was leaving shortly.

On leaving the sick-room the Baron, very angry and deeply wounded in his paternal feelings, went to find Julien and said without preamble: 'Sir, I have come to ask for an explanation of your conduct with regard to my daughter. You have been unfaithful to her with her maid, which makes it twice as bad.'

But Julien played the innocent, passionately denied his guilt, swearing and calling God to witness. Anyhow what proof had they? Wasn't Jeanne insane? And hadn't she just had brain fever? Hadn't she run out into the snow one night delirious at the beginning of her illness? And it was just at the start of this attack, when she was running about the house almost naked, that she alleged that she had seen the maid in her husband's bed. He lost his temper, threatening legal proceedings and unable to control himself. The Baron in confusion made his excuses, begged pardon and offered in all sincerity to shake hands, an offer which Julien refused. When Jeanne heard her father's story, she kept her temper and replied: 'He is lying, but we shall establish the truth in the end.'

For two days she remained silent and introspective, thinking.

On the third morning she insisted again on seeing Rosalie, but the Baron refused to bring her up, declaring that she had left the house. But Jeanne pressed her point, repeating: 'Then she must be sent for, wherever she is.' She was already beginning to lose control when the doctor came in. They told him the whole story, so that he could decide what to do. But Jeanne suddenly burst into tears, her nerves overstrained, and almost shouted: 'I want to see Rosalie! I must see her!'

The doctor took her hand and said in a low voice: 'Calm yourself, Madame; violent emotion may have serious consequences, for you are pregnant.'

Staggered by this news, she was stunned, when suddenly she seemed to feel something stir inside her. After that she remained dumb, not listening to what was being said, wrapped in thought. That night she did not sleep, kept awake by this strange new idea that there was a child alive in her womb. She was worried by the thought that it was Julien's child and tortured by the fear that it might be like its father.

Next morning she sent for the Baron: 'Papa,' she said, 'I've made up my mind. I must know everything, especially now. You understand, I insist. You know that I mustn't be crossed in my present state. Listen! Go and fetch the priest. I shall need him here to prevent Rosalie lying. As soon as he arrives, bring him up to me and you stay downstairs with Mama. Be especially careful that Julien has no suspicion of his presence.'

An hour later the priest came in, even fatter than before and as short of breath as Mama. He sat down in an arm-chair near Jeanne with his prominent stomach resting between his knees. He began with a few jocular remarks, passing his check handkerchief over his forehead as usual : 'Well, Baroness, we're neither of us getting any thinner ! We make a good pair !' Then, turning to the bed, he went on : 'Well, well ! What is this they tell me? So we shall soon be having another christening, and it won't be a boat this time, ha, ha !' And he added seriously : 'It will be a son to fight for his country,' and after a pause. 'Unless indeed it is a future mother of a fine family, like you, Madame,' and he bowed.

The door at the end of the room opened and Rosalie, in tears and terribly upset, struggled to avoid coming in, clinging to the frame of the door, as the Baron pushed her forward. Losing patience, he thrust her into the room with a shove. Covering her face with her hands, she stood there sobbing. As soon as Jeanne saw her, she sat up in bed, whiter than the sheets, and the wild beating of her heart made the thin nightdress which clung to her body quiver. She was almost beyond speaking; at last in a voice trembling with emotion she stammered : 'I needn't ... I needn't ask you anything ... it's enough to see you like this ... to realize the shame you feel in front of me.'

After pausing for breath she continued : 'But I want to know everything ... everything. I have sent for the priest, so that it is like a confession for you, do you understand?'

Standing quite still, Rosalie was weeping noisily between her clenched hands. The Baron, getting more and more angry, seized her arms and pulled them apart, and pushing her down on her knees by the bed, he said : 'Now speak ... answer !'

She remained on her knees in the posture in which Mary Magdalene is always represented in art; her cap was awry, her apron on the floor and her face was once more covered with her hands which were now at last free again.

The priest began : 'Now, my daughter, listen to what is being said to you and answer. We don't want to be cruel to you but we want to know the truth.'

Jeanne, leaning over the edge of the bed, looked at her saying:
'It is perfectly true, isn't it, that you were in Julien's bed, when
I surprised the two of you?'

'Yes, Madame.'

At that the Baroness suddenly burst out into noisy choking
sobs, and her convulsive tears accompanied Rosalie's. Jeanne,
keeping her eyes fixed on the girl, continued: 'How long had
this been going on?'

Rosalie stammered: 'Ever since 'e come 'ere.'

Jeanne did not understand: 'Ever since he came here, you
say? Then that means . . . ever since . . . the spring?'

'Yes, Madame.'

'Ever since his first visit?'

'Yes, Madame.'

Jeanne, as if overwhelmed by all that she wanted to ask,
hurried on with her questioning: 'But how did it all happen?
How did he approach you? How did he trap you? What did
he say? Exactly when and how did you yield? How could
you give yourself to him?'

At last Rosalie, taking her hands from her face, eager now to
speak, said: ' 'Ow does I know? It were the first time 'e come to
dinner, 'e come to find me in my room. 'E'd 'idden in the attic.
I dursen't make a noise so as not to make a fuss. 'E come into
bed with me; I don't rightly know what I was a-doin' of that
night. 'E did what 'e wanted. I didn't say naught, 'cos I liked
'im.'

Jeanne uttered a cry: 'Then your . . . your child is . . . is his?'

'Yes, Madame.'

Nothing more was said, and nothing was heard except the
sobs of Rosalie and the Baroness.

Jeanne, quite overcome, felt her eyes filling with tears and
the drops ran noiselessly down her cheeks. So the maid's child
had the same father as hers! Her anger had evaporated and
she now only felt a sad deep despair, abysmal, devastating,
that would last for ever. At last she went on in a changed, shaking voice like a woman weeping: 'When we came back from
our honeymoon . . . when did all this begin again?'

'It was the first night 'e come,' stammered the little maid,
collapsed on the floor. Every word was a stab in Jeanne's heart.

So on the first night, the night of their return, the night that they had got back to the Poplars, he had left her for this girl. That was why he had let her sleep by herself!

Now she knew enough and wanted to hear no more. 'Clear out! Go away!' she shouted. As Rosalie did not move, Jeanne, exhausted, called to her father: 'Take her away out of my sight!' But the priest, who had not yet spoken to her, thought that the moment had come for his little sermon: 'What you have done, my daughter, is bad, very bad. God will not easily forgive you. Think of hell awaiting you, if you do not reform. Now that you have got a child, you must settle down. The Baroness no doubt will do something for you and we will find you a husband....' He would have gone on talking, but the Baron, seizing Rosalie by the shoulders, picked her up, dragged her to the door and threw her out into the passage like a bundle of clothes.

When he came back, paler than his daughter, the priest went on: 'You can't do anything about it. All the girls in the neighbourhood are like that. It's deplorable but one is powerless; one must make allowances for the weakness of nature. Girls never marry till they are pregnant, never, Madame,' and he added with a smile: 'You might call it a local custom!' He went on angrily: 'Even the children get mixed up in it. Last year I discovered two of my Sunday school kids at it in the cemetery. I told the parents and do you know what they said: "What can you expect, Sir? It isn't we as taught them all this dirt; we can't do anything about it." So you see, Sir, your maid is just like all the others.'

But the Baron, trembling under the nervous strain, interrupted him: 'She? I don't care about her; it's Julien who makes me wild. He has behaved like a blackguard and I'm going to take my daughter away.'

He was walking up and down, working himself up in his exasperation: 'It's scandalous the way he has betrayed my daughter, scandalous! The man is a wretch, a cad, a rotter, and I mean to tell him so. I'll box his ears and beat him unconscious!'

The priest was taking a leisurely pinch of snuff by the side of the Baroness, who was in tears, and he felt that it was time for him to make an effort to establish good relations between the Baron and Julien. So he went on: 'Come, Sir, let's be honest. He has behaved like most men. How many husbands do you know who are entirely faithful?' And he added with an arch smile: 'Look, Baron, I bet you amused yourself in your youth. Come now! Lay your hand on your heart, didn't you?' The Baron paused facing the priest, who continued: 'You were like all the rest. You may have had some little servant girl like this one in your arms, who knows? I tell you, all men are the same; but your wife hasn't been any less happy on that account, or less loved, has she?'

The Baron stood stock still, impressed by the priest's words. Of course it was perfectly true; he had done just the same thing himself, and as often as he could. He had not respected the marriage bed and, when they had been attractive, he had never hesitated to approach his wife's maids. Did this mean that he had behaved like a blackguard? Why then was he taking such a serious view of Julien's conduct, when it had never occurred to him that his own might have been disreputable? The Baroness, still out of breath after her sobbing, had the ghost of a smile on her lips at the memory of her husband's sprees, for she belonged to the romantic generation, quick to fall in love and quick to forgive, for whom flirtations are a part of life.

Jeanne collapsed, staring straight in front of her with arms relaxed, filled with gloomy thoughts. One phrase which Rosalie had used wounded her to the quick as she recalled it, piercing her heart like a drill, 'I didn't say naught, 'cos I liked 'im.' She had liked him too, that was the only reason why she had given herself to him chained for life, why she had sacrificed all other hopes, all her vague plans, all the unknown future. She had plunged into this marriage, this bottomless abyss, to come back to the surface in all this misery and grim despair, just because like Rosalie she had liked him.

The door burst open and Julien appeared with a wild look in his eyes. He had caught sight of Rosalie groaning on the stairs and he had come for an explanation; he realized that something was in the air and that the maid had probably talked. At the sight of the priest he stopped dead. In a voice that trembled but was controlled he asked: 'What's all this about? What's the matter?'

The Baron, who had been so violent before, dared not say anything, remembering the priest's words and fearing that his son-in-law might quote his own past behaviour. Mama was crying more bitterly, but Jeanne, supporting herself on her hands and gazing at the man who was causing her such acute suffering, gasped out: 'Now we know everything, we know all your unpardonable behaviour ... since the first day you came to the house.... It is true that this maid's child is yours like ... like mine ... they will be brothers.'

Overwhelmed by the agony of the thought, realized now for the first time, she fell back in bed in a paroxysm of tears. He stood there gasping, not knowing what to do.

The priest intervened again: 'We must pull ourselves together, dear lady, and not take on so; let's be reasonable.'

He got up and went to the bed-side and laid his hand on the desperate woman's forehead. This simple touch had a strangely soothing effect and her agitation suddenly calmed, as if the strong hand of the peasant priest, accustomed to granting absolution and dispensing comfort, had merely by its touch brought her some mysterious appeasement. Still standing by the bed the good soul went on: 'Madame, forgiveness is the duty of us all. A great misfortune has befallen you, but God in His mercy has given you a great happiness in compensation. It is in the name of your child that I beg you, I adjure you, to forgive Monsieur Julien's slip. The child will be a new bond between you, a guarantee of his fidelity in future. Can you remain alienated from the heart of a man whose seed you carry in your womb?'

She remained silent, crushed, aching, exhausted, too weak even to feel anger or grudge; her nerves seemed relaxed and gently disconnected, she was hardly alive. The Baroness, who was incapable of resentment and whose soul was unequal to any prolonged effort, murmured: 'Come now, Jeanne!'

The priest took the young man's hand and, drawing him to the bed, placed it in his wife's hand. He gave it a little pat as if to unite them for ever, and dropping his professional pulpit manner, he said cheerfully: 'Well, that's that! Believe me, it's all for the best.'

The two hands after a moment's contact were immediately

withdrawn. Julien, not daring to kiss Jeanne, touched the Baroness's forehead with his lips, turned round, took his father-in-law's arm without resistance, for the Baron was glad that things had been settled amicably, and they went out to smoke a cigar.

Then Jeanne dozed, exhausted, while the priest and Mama talked quietly in lowered voices. The Abbé went on explaining and developing his ideas, and the Baroness agreed with everything with a nod. Finally he said: 'So it's agreed; you give the girl the Barville farm, and I promise to find her a husband, a decent respectable fellow. Oh, with a property of 20,000 francs there will be no lack of candidates; the only difficulty will be the choice of one!'

The Baroness was now smiling happily; she had two tears which had stopped half-way down her cheeks, but their moist traces were now dry: 'It's all agreed,' she repeated. 'Barville is worth 20,000 francs at the lowest estimate; the property will be settled on the child, and the parents will have the enjoyment of it for their lifetime.'

The priest got up and shook hands with Mama: 'Don't worry, Baroness,' he said, 'don't worry! It's always the first step that is the trouble!'

On the way out he met Aunt Lison, who was coming to see the patient. She noticed nothing. Nothing was said to her, and as usual she found out nothing.

CHAPTER EIGHT

ROSALIE had left the house and Jeanne was going through the painful period of pregnancy. She felt no pleasure at the prospect of having a child; she was too unhappy. She waited for the birth without curiosity, still oppressed by fears of undefined troubles ahead. Spring had been slow to come. The bare trees were shivering in the wind, which was still chilly, but in the wet grass of the ditches, where the autumn leaves were rotting, yellow primroses were beginning to show. From all over the common, the farmyards and the soaking fields, there rose a damp smell of decaying vegetation and masses of little green shoots were springing up from the brown earth and shining in the sun.

A sturdy, heavily built woman, massive as a fortress, had taken Rosalie's place and supported the Baroness on her monotonous walks up and down her drive, where the trail left by her bad leg was always visible, damp and muddy. Papa used to give his arm to Jeanne, who had grown heavy and was in continual pain, while Aunt Lison, worried and fussing over the expected event, held her hand on the other side, intrigued by the mystery which she would never experience herself. They walked about for hours, hardly speaking, while Julien went out riding all over the country, having conceived a sudden passion for this pastime. Nothing occurred to disturb the even tenor of their lives. The Baron, his wife, and the Viscount paid a visit to the Fourvilles, whom Julien seemed to know quite well, no one understood how. Another formal call was exchanged with the Brisevilles, who remained shut up in their sleepy mansion.

One afternoon about four o'clock two people on horseback, a man and his wife, trotted into the courtyard in front of the house. Julien, quite excited, ran into Jeanne's room: 'Quick! Go down quick! Here are the Fourvilles! Say that I'm out but shall be back quite soon; I'm going to tidy myself up.'

Jeanne in surprise went down. A young woman, pale, pretty,

with a sad expression, wild eyes, and lustreless fair hair, which looked as though no ray of sun had ever stroked it, quietly introduced her husband, a sort of giant ogre with a flowing red moustache.

'We have met Monsieur de Lamare several times,' she added, 'and have heard from him that you are not well; so we did not put off coming to pay a quite informal neighbourly call. Besides, as you see, we are on horseback. Moreover the other day I had the pleasure of a visit from your mother and the Baron.'

She was completely at her ease talking, and her voice was friendly and refined. Jeanne was attracted, indeed fascinated, at first sight. 'Here's a real friend!' she thought. The Comte de Fourville on the contrary was like a bear that had got into a drawing-room. After taking a seat he put his hat down on the nearest chair, hesitated what to do with his hands before resting them first on his knees and then on the arms of his chair, and finally clasped his fingers together as if in prayer.

Suddenly Julien entered the room and Jeanne hardly recognized him, she was so surprised. He was quite the beau, smart and attractive, as in the days of their engagement. He shook the hairy paw of the Count, who seemed to wake up at his coming, and kissed the hand of the Countess, whose ivory cheek showed a faint flush of pink while her eyelids fluttered. He talked and was friendly as in the old days; his large eyes reflected affection and were soft again, and his hair, which had lately been stiff and had lacked shine, had recovered its brilliant waves thanks to brushing and scented oil.

As the Fourvilles were leaving, the Countess turned to him and said: 'My dear Viscount, would you care to come for a ride on Thursday?' And while he bowed, murmuring: 'I should love to, Madame,' she took Jeanne's hand and in her clear soft voice said with a pleasant smile: 'As soon as you are well again, we'll all three of us career over the countryside; it will be delightful. Will you promise?'

With a natural gesture she picked up the train of her habit and sprang into the saddle with the lightness of a bird, while her husband after a clumsy bow lumbered on to his great Normandy mare, where he balanced like a centaur.

When they were out of sight round the bend at the gate,

Julien, who seemed in high spirits, cried: 'What charming people! Knowing them will be a great asset to us.'

Jeanne, pleased for some undefined reason, replied: 'The little Countess is adorable; I know I'm going to be very fond of her, but the husband is a pretty rough type. Where did you get to know them?'

He rubbed his hands cheerily: 'I met them by chance at the Brisevilles'. The husband is a bit of a rough diamond; he's mad on hunting, but he's very well born.' That evening dinner was almost merry, as if some mysterious happiness had entered the house.

Nothing else happened till the last days of July. One Tuesday evening as they were sitting under the plane tree round a wooden table with two liqueur glasses and a decanter of brandy on it, Jeanne suddenly uttered a groan and turning very pale pressed both hands to her sides. A sharp shooting pain ran through her, but immediately ceased. Ten minutes later however, another spasm, which lasted longer but was less acute, shot through her. She had great difficulty in getting back to the house, almost carried by her husband and father. The short distance from the plane tree to her room seemed interminable; and she groaned involuntarily, wanting to stop again and again, weighed down by the crushing burden in her womb.

Her time was not yet up, the birth not being expected till September. But as they were afraid that something was wrong, a carriage was harnessed and old Simon went off at full speed to fetch the doctor. He arrived about midnight and immediately recognized the symptoms of a premature delivery. In bed the pains eased somewhat, but Jeanne was in the grip of an unbearable depression, the complete collapse of her resistance, a kind of presentiment of the mysterious hand of death. It was one of those moments when death passes so close that its icy breath freezes the heart.

Her room was full of people. Mama was sobbing, collapsed in her arm-chair; the Baron was fussing about, fetching and carrying, asking the doctor questions, not knowing what he was doing. Julien was pacing the room, looking worried but really quite unmoved, and the widow Dentu was standing at the foot of the bed with an expressionless face, the face of a woman of experience, whom nothing surprises. Hospital nurse, midwife, watcher of the dead, she was used to receiving those coming into the world, hearing their first cry, giving them their first wash, wrapping them in their first baby-clothes, and listening with the same unruffled calm to their last words, the death-rattle in the throat, the last shiver of the dying; she also bathed the bodies, sponging the shrunken limbs with vinegar and wrapping them in the shroud. In this way she had developed unshakeable self-control in face of all the accidents of birth and death.

The cook Ludivine and Aunt Lison kept discreetly out of sight by the door of the lobby. At intervals a low moan came from the sick-bed. For two hours the crisis seemed likely to be delayed; but about dawn the pains suddenly began again violently and were soon unbearable, and uncontrollable cries issued from Jeanne's clenched teeth. She was thinking all the time of Rosalie, who had suffered so little and hardly groaned at all, whose bastard child had been born without these agonizing pains.

In her dark anguished soul she was continually making comparisons between herself and Rosalie; she cursed God, whom until now she had considered just. Now she rebelled against the criminal favouritism of fate and the baseless lies of those who preach righteousness and decency. At times her pains became so agonizing that she could not think; she had lost all power, all vitality, all consciousness except of suffering.

In the short intervals between the spasms she could not take her eyes off Julien, and another agony, an agony of mind, gripped her, as she remembered the day when the maid had collapsed at the foot of this very bed with the child between her legs, the brother of the infant who was now inflicting such cruel torture on her. She recalled with dreadful clarity her husband's every gesture, every look, as he had stood before the girl stretched on the floor; and now, as if his thoughts had been written in every movement, she read in them the same indifference towards her as towards the other girl, the same lack of interest, the same unconcern of the egoist, to whom the name of father means nothing.

Suddenly she was convulsed with an excruciating spasm so

agonizing that she thought: 'I'm going to die – I am dying.' A wild revolt, an impulse to curse overwhelmed her, an exasperated hatred of the man who was responsible and of the infant who was killing her. She tensed her whole body in a last effort to throw off her crippling burden. Then her womb seemed to discharge and her pains ceased.

The nurse and the doctor were leaning over her and she felt their hands. They picked up something and soon the stifled sound that she had heard before made her start; a low cry of pain like the faint mew of a cat found its way into her heart and soul, into the whole of her poor tortured body, and she unconsciously tried to stretch out her arms. She felt a thrill of joy, an urge towards a new happiness. In a flash she was saved, soothed, happy as she had never been. Her heart and her body were alive again, she knew that she was a mother.

She asked to see the child. He had no hair and no nails, having been born prematurely; but when she saw the little mite move, open his mouth and wail, when she touched this puny imp with his ugly wrinkled face but alive, she was overwhelmed with a flood of joy; she knew that she was saved, armoured against despair, that she had in this child something to love, something that would fill her whole life.

From that day she had no thought but for the child. She had suddenly become the perfect mother, her devotion increased by the disillusionment of her love and the disappointment of her hopes. She always insisted on having the cot by her bed, and as soon as she was able to get up she spent whole days sitting in the window rocking the light cradle. She was even jealous of the wet-nurse and, when the infant was thirsty and stretched out his arms towards her swollen breast with its bluish veins and seized the wrinkled brown nipple with greedy lips, she glared pale and trembling at the sturdy placid peasant woman; she would have liked to snatch her son from her arms, strike her, scratch the breast at which he was drinking so greedily.

She insisted on embroidering with her own hand the finest baby-clothes of the most ornate elegance for his adornment. He was always wrapped up in a cloud of lace with a magnificent bonnet on his head; she could talk of nothing else and interrupted conversation to exhibit a napkin or a bib or a beautifully worked ribbon. She heard nothing that was being said round her and went into ecstasies over the pieces of linen, which she turned over and over in her raised hands in order to see better; and suddenly she would ask: 'Do you think he'll look nice in that?' The Baron and Mama smiled at her loving enthusiasm, but Julien, whose habits were being interfered with and whose dominant position in the house was undermined by the advent of this noisy all-powerful tyrant, unconsciously jealous of this scrap of a man who was filching his place, was always repeating with angry impatience: 'She does get a bit boring with the little brat, doesn't she?'

She was soon so obsessed by this passion that she spent her nights by the cot watching the child asleep. As she was wearing herself out with this morbid maternal solicitude and was having no rest herself, she grew weak and thin and began to cough; so the doctor ordered the child to be taken away from her. She was furious and begged and prayed, but her prayers went unheeded and the infant was put to sleep in the nurse's room.

But every night the mother got up and went bare-foot to put her ear to the key-hole to satisfy herself that he was sleeping quietly, that he wasn't awake and didn't want anything. She was discovered there one night by Julien, who had come in late after dining at the Fourvilles', and after that she was locked in her room to force her to stay in bed.

The baptism took place about the end of August; the Baron was godfather and Aunt Lison godmother, and the child was christened Pierre Simon Paul, Paul to be the name for everyday use. At the beginning of September Aunt Lison left the house, her absence being as little noticed as her presence had been.

One evening after dinner the Abbé appeared; he seemed embarrassed as if he had some secret to communicate. After some desultory conversation he asked the Baroness and her husband to grant him a few minutes in private. The three of them went out slowly and walked down to the bottom of the drive talking excitedly, while Julien, left alone with Jeanne, was surprised and worried, puzzled by this mystery. When the priest left, he insisted on going with him and they disappeared in the direction of the church, from which the angelus was ringing. It was fresh, almost cold, and the others went in early.

They were all dozing, when Julien suddenly came in, red in the face and looking cross. From the door, taking no notice of Jeanne's presence, he shouted to his parents-in-law : 'My God ! You must both be daft, throwing away 20,000 francs on that strumpet !'

They were so dumbfounded that they did not reply. He went on, bellowing with anger : 'This is raving madness ! You'll leave us stony broke !'

The Baron, recovering himself, tried to stop him : 'Silence ! Remember you are in your wife's presence.'

But he was stamping with rage : 'I don't care a damn ! She knows all about it anyhow; she's the loser.'

Jeanne gazed at him in astonishment, not understanding, and stammered : 'What's all the fuss about?'

Then Julien turned to her and called her to witness as a partner defrauded of a hoped-for profit. He told her in a few words of the plot to marry off Rosalie with the Barville farm worth 20,000 francs as a dowry. He repeated : 'But your parents are crazy, my dear, they ought to be shut up ! 20,000 francs ! 20,000 francs ! They are insane – 20,000 francs for a bastard !'

Jeanne listened unmoved, without anger; she was surprised at her own calmness, but she was now interested in nothing except her child. The Baron was choking, unable to find a word. Finally he burst out, stamping his foot and shouting :

'Think what you're saying; it's really disgusting ! Whose fault is it that this unmarried mother has got to be given a dowry? Whose is the child? I suppose you would have thrown it over.'

Julien, surprised by the Baron's violence, stared at him and went on calmly : '1,500 francs would have been quite enough. All the girls round here have children before they marry. It doesn't matter who the father is; whereas by giving her one of your farms worth 20,000 francs, quite apart from the loss inflicted on us, you are publishing abroad what has happened. You ought at least to have thought of our name and position.'

He spoke sternly like a man confident in the justice of his case and the logic of his argument. The Baron, upset by this unexpected opposition, stood tongue-tied. Thereupon Julien, sensing his advantage, explained his plan : 'Fortunately nothing has been settled yet. I know the boy who is to marry her. He's a decent fellow and he'll be reasonable. I'll be responsible for the arrangements.'

With that he left the room, fearing no doubt to prolong the discussion and pleased at the silence which greeted his words and which he took to signify agreement.

As soon as he had gone, the Baron, shocked and simmering with anger, cried: 'This really is too much!'

But Jeanne, looking up at her father's disgruntled expression, suddenly burst out laughing; it was the frank natural laugh of the old days at some joke. "Papa! Papa!" she repeated. 'Did you hear the tone of voice in which he said "20,000 francs"?' And Mama, who was always as quick to smile as to cry, thought of her son-in-law's irritation, his expressions of indignation and his violent objection to allowing the girl he had seduced to be given money, which did not belong to him. She was glad too that Jeanne was taking the matter so calmly, and broke out into a wheezy laugh, which brought tears to her eyes. Then the Baron in his turn, caught by the infectious merriment, went off into a guffaw, and all three of them, as in the good old days, roared with laughter.

When they had recovered themselves, Jeanne voiced her surprise: 'It's odd; all this leaves me quite cold. I regard him as a complete stranger nowadays; I can't believe I'm his wife. I'm just amused by his lack . . . his lack of fine feeling.'

Without knowing exactly why, they kissed all round, still smiling happily.

Two days later, when Julien was out riding after lunch, a tall peasant boy between twenty and twenty-five, in a brand new blue blouse newly pressed, with puffed-out sleeves buttoned at the wrists, sneaked in through the garden gate, as if he had been lying in wait there since the morning, made his way along the Couillards' ditch, turned the corner of the house and stealthily approached the Baron and the two ladies, who were still sitting under the plane tree.

He had taken off his cap when he saw them, and advanced, bowing awkwardly. When he came within speaking distance, he stuttered: 'Your 'umble servant, Baron, Baroness and all!'

Then, as no one made any answer, he introduced himself: 'I

be Désiré Lecoq.' As the name meant nothing to them, the Baron asked : 'What do you want?' At this the boy, in hopeless confusion at the prospect of having to explain himself, stammered, lowering and raising his eyes in turn from the cap in his hand to the roof-top of the house : 'It were 'is Reverence what 'ad a word with me over this 'ere business ...' and he paused, afraid of compromising his interests by saying too much.

The Baron, puzzled, replied : 'What business? I don't understand.'

At that the boy, lowering his voice, took the plunge : 'It's this 'ere business of your maid ... Rosalie.'

Jeanne, who had guessed the truth, got up and went off with her baby in her arms, while the Baron said : 'Come and sit down here,' and he pointed to the chair which his daughter had left. The peasant sat down at once, murmuring : 'It's very good of you, Sir,' and he paused as if he had nothing more to say. After a rather long silence he at last made up his mind and raising his eyes to the blue sky he began : 'We be 'avin' very good weather for the time of year. It do be just what we wants for the seeds what 'as been sowed.' Then he stopped again.

The Baron, losing patience, plunged into the question drily without more ado : 'So it's you who are marrying Rosalie.'

The young man immediately got worried at this shock to his typical Norman caution and replied with decision in his tone, now on the defensive : 'That all depends, p'raps yes, p'raps no; it all depends.'

But the Baron was getting annoyed by all this beating about the bush : 'Good God! Give me a straight answer. Is that why you've come, yes or no? Are you marrying her or are you not?'

The boy hesitated, keeping his eyes on his feet : 'If it be what 'is Reverence said, I am 'avin' 'er. If it be what Monsieur Julien said, then I'm not 'avin' 'er.'

'What did Monsieur Julien say to you?'

'Monsieur Julien 'e did say as I would get 1,500 francs and 'is Reverence did say as I'd 'ave 20,000. I be willing to 'ave 'er for 20,000, but I ain't 'avin' 'er for 1,500.'

At this the Baroness in the depths of her arm-chair burst into little giggles at the peasant's obvious anxiety. The boy looked at her out of the corner of his eye, worried and not understanding her amusement, and waited.

The Baron, who disliked all this bargaining, cut it short: 'I told the priest that you should have the Barville farm for your life, and on your death it would revert to the child. It is worth 20,000 francs. I stand by my word. Do you accept? Yes or no?'

The young man smiled humbly, well satisfied and suddenly became talkative: 'Oh! if that be that, I agrees. That were the only trouble. When 'is Reverence spoke to me, I agreed straight-away, I did; and I were very glad to please you, Sir; it be well worth my while, I says to myself. If a fellow do something for a fellow, 'e do repay it and it be worth while. But Monsieur Julien 'e come to see me, and 'e say it were only 1,500 francs. I says to myself, I says "must find out", so I come 'ere. I doesn't want to argue; I trusted you, Sir, but I just wanted to make sure. Straight dealings make good friends, ain't that so, Sir ...?'

To stop him going on, the Baron said: 'When will you bring off the marriage?' At this the boy suddenly got shy and awkward again and at last said in a hesitating voice: 'Couldn't us 'ave a little bit of paper first?'

This time the Baron lost his temper: 'But good heavens! you'll have your marriage lines – that's the best contract you can have.'

But the peasant persisted: 'But meanwhile us might 'ave a scrap of paper – that don't never do no 'arm.'

The Baron got up to put an end to the argument: 'Answer yes or no straight away. If you don't want the deal any more, I've got another candidate.' The fear of a rival perturbed the crafty Norman. He made up his mind and held out his hand to the Baron, as he would have done after the sale of a cow: 'You put your 'and there, Sir, and the deal's settled. 'E be a real rotter who goes back on 'is bargain!'

The Baron shook hands warmly and shouted: 'Ludivine!' The cook's head appeared at the window. 'Bring us a bottle of wine!' They drank to the conclusion of the deal and the boy went off with a jaunty air. Julien was not told of the visit.

The contract was drawn up in complete secrecy, and after the banns had been put up the wedding took place one Monday morning. A neighbour's wife carried the baby to the church behind the bride and bridegroom as a guarantee of the property. No one in the neighbourhood was in the least surprised; indeed they envied Désiré Lecoq. He had been born with a silver spoon in his mouth, people said with a sly but quite good-natured smile. Julien made a terrible scene, which cut short the stay of his parents-in-law at the Poplars. Jeanne saw them go without too much regret, for Paul was now a source of inexhaustible happiness to her.

CHAPTER NINE

Now that Jeanne had quite recovered from her confinement, it was decided to return the Fourvilles' call and also to pay a formal visit to the mansion of the Marquis de Coutelier. Julien had just bought at an auction a new carriage, a phaeton, which needed only one horse, so that they could go out twice a month. One bright December day it was harnessed and after a two-hour drive across the plain of Normandy they descended a small valley, whose sides were wooded with the bottom under cultivation. Further on the sown fields were replaced by grassland and the grassland by a marsh, covered at this time of year with tall dry reeds, whose long leaves fluttered in the wind like yellow ribbons.

Suddenly, at a sharp bend in the valley, the mansion of La Vrillette came into sight, one side built against the wooded slope and the wall on the other side rising all its length out of the broad lake bounded by a tall pine wood, which clothed the far side of the valley. They had to cross an old drawbridge to reach a vast Louis XIII gateway to the court of honour, which led to an elegant mansion of the same period; this was framed in brick at each end by a turret with a slate roof. Julien explained to Jeanne all the points of the house with an expert's architectural knowledge. He did the honours at length, going into ecstasies over its beauties: 'Just look at that gateway! What a wonderful thing to have a house like this! The other façade rises out of the lake with a royal terrace, which goes right down to the water, and at the bottom of the steps there are always four boats moored, two for the Count and two for the Countess. Down there on the right, where you see that curtain of poplars, is the end of the lake; that is where the river which runs down to Fécamp starts. The whole district swarms with wild-fowl. The Count loves shooting all round. It is the perfect home for a member of the nobility.'

The front door opened and the pale Countess came out to

greet the visitors with a smile; she was wearing a dress with a long train, like the mistress of a castle in a bygone age. She was the lovely Lady of the Lake, perfectly fitted for this noble house.

The drawing-room had eight windows, four of which opened on the lake and the sombre pine wood running up the hill exactly opposite. The dark green foliage made the lake look deep and stern and sad, and when there was a wind the moaning of the trees sounded like the voice of the marsh. The Countess took both Jeanne's hands as if they had been childhood friends, and made her sit down, seating herself close by on a low chair, while Julien, whose manners had been refurbished during the last five months, chatted and smiled in a pleasant, friendly way.

The Countess and he talked of their rides. She made fun of his method of mounting, calling him Sir Hop-and-go-one, and as a joke he christened her the Amazon Queen. A shot fired under the windows made Jeanne utter a little cry; it was the Count who had killed a teal. His wife immediately called to him. They heard the splash of oars and the bump of a boat against the stone terrace, and he came in, a huge figure in gumboots, followed by two dripping dogs, red-haired like himself, which lay down on the rug by the door. He seemed more at ease in his own house and delighted to see the visitors. He had the fire made up and madeira and biscuits brought in. Suddenly he cried: 'But of course you'll stay to dinner.' Jeanne, thinking as usual of her child, refused; but he pressed the invitation, and when she still tried to get out of it, Julien made a sharp gesture of impatience. She was afraid of provoking a return of his irritable quarrelsome temper and, although she hated the idea of not seeing Paul again till next morning, she accepted.

They spent a delightful afternoon. First they went to look at the springs, which gushed out at the foot of a moss-covered rock into a clear basin, that was always bubbling like boiling water; after that they went for a row along regular paths cut through the forest of dry reeds. The Count did the rowing, sitting between his two dogs, who sniffed with their noses to the wind, and at each stroke he lifted the heavy boat out of the water and drove it forward. Jeanne sometimes let her hand trail in the cold water, enjoying the fresh chill, which ran from her fingertips to her heart. In the stern Julien and the Countess, wrapped up in shawls, were smiling with the permanent smile of the blissfully happy.

Evening came on with long chilly gusts from the north, which blew over the wilting rushes. The sun had sunk behind the pines and the red sky, dotted with strangely shaped little crimson clouds, made one shiver just to look at it. They returned to the drawing-room, where a huge fire was blazing. A feeling of well-being and good cheer warmed the heart as one entered. The Count in high spirits picked up his wife in his powerful arms and, lifting her up like a child to his mouth, gave her two resounding kisses on the cheeks, the picture of simple happiness.

Jeanne smiled at the kindly giant, whose moustache had won him the reputation of a bogy man, and thought : 'How entirely wrong people are every day about everybody!' Then looking round involuntarily at Julien, she saw him standing in the doorway as white as a sheet, with his eyes on the Count, and going up to him : 'What's the matter?' she whispered, 'are you ill?'

He replied angrily : 'Nothing. Leave me alone. I just felt cold.'

When they went into the dining-room, the Count asked leave to let his dogs in; and they came in at once and sat down on their tails to the right and left of their master. He kept giving them scraps of food and stroking their silky ears, while the dogs stretched out their heads and wagged their tails, supremely happy.

After dinner, as Jeanne and Julien were preparing to leave, Monsieur de Fourville kept them to show them some fishing by torchlight. He settled them on the terrace above the lake, and climbed into his boat followed by a servant with a cast-net and a lighted torch.

It was a clear chilly night with brilliant stars. The torch shed strange trails of fire on the surface of the water and flashes of light danced over the reeds and lit up the curtain of pines. Suddenly, as the boat veered, a huge fantastic shadow, the shadow of a man, was cast on the bright edge of the wood. His head rose above the trees and faded away into the sky, and his feet sank into the lake. Presently the towering figure raised his arms as if to grasp the stars; those monstrous arms rose and fell, and a faint sound of water being flogged was audible. Then, as the boat veered gently again, the gigantic ghostly figure seemed to be running along the fringe of the wood lit up by the torch as it moved; soon the shadow sank out of sight below the horizon, and suddenly reappeared, smaller in size but clearer in outline, with its strange movements on the façade of the mansion, and the Count's deep voice shouted: 'Gilberte, I've caught eight!'

The splash of the oars in the water was audible again, and the huge shadow, now cast motionless on the wall, gradually diminished in height and width; its head seemed to be getting lower and its body shrinking, and when Monsieur de Fourville came up the steps of the terrace, still followed by the servant with the torch, the shadow had been reduced to his actual size and copied his gestures. He was carrying eight large fish wriggling in his net.

When Jeanne and Julien were driving home, wrapped in coats and rugs which they had been lent, Jeanne said almost involuntarily: 'What a good soul that giant is!' Julien, who was driving, replied: 'Yes, but he's not always careful enough about how he behaves in society.'

A week later they paid a visit to the Couteliers, who were considered the leading noble house in the district. Their estate at Reminil was on the outskirts of the market-town of Cany. The new mansion, built under Louis XIV, was hidden in a magnificent park surrounded by a wall. On a hill the ruins of the old castle were visible. Liveried footmen showed the visitors into a splendid drawing-room. In the centre of the room was a sort of pillar supporting a huge cup of Sèvres porcelain, and on the plinth an autograph letter from the King, protected by a crystal-glass plate, invited the Marquis Léopold-Hervé-Joseph-Germer de Varneville, de Rollebosc de Coutelier, to accept this present from the King.

Jeanne and Julien were examining this royal gift when the Marquis and his wife entered the room. The lady's hair was powdered and she had the gracious manner proper to her position, but an air of condescension rendered her affected. The man, heavily built, with white hair brushed straight back, showed in his gestures, his voice and his whole bearing an arrogance which proclaimed his position. They were the slaves of good form; their thoughts, their feelings, and their words were always stilted. They monopolized the conversation with a casual smile, not waiting for an answer. They always seemed to be carrying out the formalities of the obligation imposed by their birth of receiving politely the lesser nobility of the neighbourhood. Jeanne and Julien, tongue-tied, did their best to be pleasant, embarrassed at having to stay but unable to leave. However, the Marquise herself put an end to the visit quite easily and naturally, terminating the conversation with the air of a queen graciously closing an audience. On the way home Julien said : 'If you don't mind, we won't go there very often; the Fourvilles are enough for me.' Jeanne agreed.

December passed slowly, the dark month, the black abyss at the end of the year. Their cloistered existence of the previous year began again. But Jeanne was not bored, being fully taken up with Paul, at whom Julien looked askance, fidgety and worried. Often when his mother was cuddling him in her arms and caressing him with tender maternal affection, she would hold him out to the father, saying : 'Do give him a kiss! One would think you didn't love him !' With an air of disgust he would just touch the infant's smooth forehead with his lips, bending his body outwards in a circle so as to avoid the little clenched hands that were never still. Then he drew back quickly as if with a feeling of repugnance.

The mayor, the doctor and the priest came to dinner from time to time, and sometimes it was the Fourvilles, with whom their intimacy was increasing. The Count appeared to worship Paul. Whenever he was in the house, he kept the child on his knee, often for the whole afternoon. He handled him gently with his huge hands, tickling the tip of the little nose with the end of his long moustache and kissing him with a mother's passionate affection. The fact that his marriage was barren was a perpetual source of bitter regret. March was cloudless, dry and warm. The Comtesse Gilberte spoke again of the rides which all four of them meant to have together. After the boredom of the long evenings, the long nights and the monotony of the long days which were all the same, Jeanne gladly agreed to these plans. For a week she amused herself sewing her habit.

Then the rides began; they always went in pairs, the Countess and Julien in front and the Count and Jeanne a hundred yards behind. The latter couple talked quietly like old friends, for the honesty of their minds and the simplicity of their hearts had brought them close together. The pair in front often spoke in low voices, but sometimes burst into loud laughter, suddenly looking at each other as if their eyes had things to convey which their lips did not utter; and they would go off at a gallop, impelled by a desire to get away by themselves a long, long way from anyone. At times Gilberte seemed to become irritable and her shrill voice was borne on the wind to the ears of those behind. On these occasions the Count would smile and say to Jeanne: 'I'm afraid my wife's manners aren't always perfect!'

One evening on the ride home, as the Countess was exciting her mare, first giving it the spur, then pulling it up with a jerk, they heard Julien say several times: 'Take care! You must take care or she'll run away with you.'

She replied: 'So much the worse for me! But it's none of your business,' in a voice so clear and harsh that the words echoed over the countryside, as if they had been caught up in the air. The animal reared and lashed out, foaming at the mouth. Suddenly the Count shouted at the top of his powerful voice: 'Do be careful, Gilberte!' But as if in defiance, in one of those attacks of uncontrollable nervous irritation to which women are subject, she brought down her hunting-crop with a brutal crack between the horse's ears, so that it reared up violently, beating the air with its forelegs, and as it came down it made a great bound forward and bolted over the plain at full gallop.

First it crossed a meadow and dashed on over the ploughed fields, raising clouds of thick damp earth and travelling so fast that one could hardly distinguish horse from rider. Julien, dumbfounded, stayed where he was, calling desperately: 'Madame! Madame!' But the Count with a grunt bent forward over the withers of his powerful mount, urging it on with an effort of his whole body. He started it off at such a pace, exciting it, sweeping it on, maddening it with voice and hand and spur, that the giant rider seemed to be gripping the animal between his legs and lifting it off the ground. They went at an incredible speed, galloping straight ahead; and in the distance Jeanne saw the silhouettes of the woman and her husband receding, growing smaller and smaller, fading till they disappeared out of sight, as one sees two birds sink below the horizon pursuing each other.

Julien came up to his wife at a walking pace, murmuring crossly: 'I think she's quite mad today,' and the two of them went off after their friends, who were now hidden from view by the rolling country. After a quarter of an hour they caught sight of them coming back and presently they met. The Count, red in the face and perspiring freely, was smiling cheerfully, completely master of the situation; he was holding his wife's mount in his powerful grasp. She was pale, with a worried look on her contorted features, and was supporting herself on her husband's shoulder, as if about to faint. That day Jeanne realized how much her husband loved his wife.

During the following month the Countess was more cheerful than ever before; she came to the Poplars more often and was always laughing and kissing Jeanne with outbursts of affection. It was as if some mysterious ecstasy had come into her life. Her husband, apparently equally happy, never took his eyes off her and was always trying to touch her hand or her dress, as if his love had doubled. One evening he said to Jeanne: 'We are blissfully happy now; Gilberte has never been so loving; she is never irritable or angry. I feel that she loves me; till now I've never been sure.'

Julien too seemed changed, more cheerful, more controlled, as if the friendship between the two families had brought peace and happiness to both.

That year spring was unusually early and warm. From the mild mornings to the hot evenings the sun made the whole earth blossom. All the seeds came up together in a swift thrustful flowering, one of those quick up-rushes of sap, nature's passion of rebirth, which sometimes occurs in lucky years and makes one think that the rejuvenation of the world is at hand. Jeanne was vaguely troubled by this ferment of life; she would suddenly be overcome in front of a tiny flower in the grass with a delicious melancholy and would spend hours idly dreaming. Tender memories of the early days of her love came back to her, not that she felt any renewal of her love for Julien – that was finished and done with for ever – but under the caress of the breeze her senses were penetrated by the scents of spring and as it were excited by an unseen invitation to love. She enjoyed solitude and liked lying in the warm sun, abandoning herself to vague, placid, pleasurable sensations, which did not awaken conscious thought.

One morning as she was dozing in this way, a picture suddenly flashed across her mind, the picture of a little sun-drenched opening in the dark foliage of the copse near Étretat. It was there that for the first time she had felt her body thrill at the touch of the young man who had loved her in those days; it was there that he had first put into timid words the longing of his heart. It was there too that for the first time the bright future of her hopes had seemed to be a reality; and she wanted to see the wood again, make a sort of sentimental superstitious pilgrimage, as if a return to this spot was bound to change the course of her life.

Julien had ridden off at dawn, she did not know where. She had the Martins' small white pony, which she sometimes rode now, saddled, and started out. It was one of those windless days, when nothing stirs anywhere, not a blade of grass, not a leaf. All power of movement seems to have disappeared for ever, as if the wind was dead; even the insects seem asleep. A burning, sovereign peace came down imperceptibly from the sun in a golden vapour, and Jeanne rode at a walking pace, soothed and happy. From time to time she raised her eyes to look at a tiny white cloud, no bigger than a piece of cotton-wool, a wisp of vapour in the air, floating as if forgotten in the expanse of blue sky. She made her way by the valley which runs down to the sea between the two arched cliffs called the Gates of Étretat, and very slowly entered the copse. The sunlight was pouring through the leaves which were still thin. She searched for the spot, wandering along the narrow paths, but without finding it.

Suddenly, as she crossed a long drive, she saw right at the far end two saddle-horses tethered to a tree, and immediately recognized them as belonging to Gilberte and Julien. She was beginning to feel lonely and was glad at this unexpected meeting; so she put her horse to the trot. When she reached the two animals, which were standing patiently as if accustomed to long waits, she called, but there was no answer. A woman's glove and two crops were lying on the trampled grass. So they must be sitting down there and at some distance from the horses. She waited for a quarter of an hour, then twenty minutes, in surprise, wondering what they could be doing.

She had dismounted and was leaning against a tree quite still, when two little birds came down in the grass quite close to her, not seeing her. One of them hopped about, fussing round the other, fluttering with wings spread, bobbing its head and chirping, and suddenly they mated. Jeanne was surprised, as though she had known nothing about the mating of animals; she thought : 'Of course, it's spring.'

Then another thought flashed across her mind, a suspicion. She looked again at the glove, the crops and the two horses; and she remounted hurriedly with an irresistible urge to get away. She galloped all the way back to the Poplars. Her thoughts were busy, reasoning the matter out, recalling the facts, putting two and two together. How was it that she had not guessed earlier what was happening? How was it that she had noticed nothing? How was it that she had not understood Julien's frequent absences and the reason for the resumption of his smartness and the recovery of his good temper? She also recalled Gilberte's nervous brusqueness, her exaggerated caresses, and more recently the state of happiness in which she had been living and which gave the Count such pleasure.

She slowed down her horse to a walk; she wanted to think quietly and the pace distracted her thoughts. After the first shock she had calmed down, feeling no jealousy or hatred, only a profound contempt. She hardly gave a thought to Julien; nothing in him surprised her any longer. But the double treachery of the Countess, her friend, disgusted her. Everyone in the world was a traitor, a liar, a deceiver, and tears came into her eyes. One sometimes weeps over one's illusions with as much bitterness as over a death. She determined, however, to feign ignorance, to close her eyes to the emotions of the moment and love only Paul and her parents, merely tolerating everyone else with a placid face.

As soon as she reached the house, she fell upon her son, carried him up to her room and kissed him passionately for an hour without stopping. Julien came back to dinner, charming and smiling, eager to make himself pleasant. 'Aren't Papa and Mama coming to stay this year?' he asked. She was so grateful for his tact that she almost forgave him her discovery in the wood. She suddenly wanted the two people she loved best after Paul so badly, that she spent the whole evening writing to them urging them to come soon. They wrote back that they would come on 20 May – it was then 7 May.

She awaited their arrival with growing impatience, as if quite apart from her natural affection she was aware of a fresh need for contact with these honest souls; she must be able to talk with complete frankness to decent folk, free from all taint, whose life and actions and thoughts and every wish had always been straightforward.

What she now felt was a kind of isolation of her own clear conscience in the midst of all these guilty souls; and although she quickly learnt to dissemble and welcomed the Countess with a smiling handshake, a feeling of emptiness and contempt for humanity was increasing and overwhelming her.

Every day trivial bits of local gossip increased her disgust and lowered her opinion of mankind. The Couillards' daughter had just had a child and was going to be married shortly; the Martins' maid, an orphan, was pregnant, so was a neighbour's daughter of fifteen, and a widow too, a poor lame dirty old thing, known as Ma Mudlark from her filthy unwashed condition. One heard every day of some new pregnancy or of the misconduct of some girl or married woman with children of her own or of some wealthy respected farmer. The warm spring seemed to be stirring up the sap in mankind as violently as in the plants. Jeanne's sensual impulses were dead and no longer worried her; her broken heart and romantic soul were only soothed by the warm fertilizing breath of spring and she lived in a world of fancy, excited but without passion, day-dreaming, dead to all the lusts of the flesh. With a feeling of revulsion, which amounted almost to hatred, she could not understand the foul bestiality of the world.

The mating of human beings now revolted her as something unnatural and, if she bore a grudge against Gilberte, it was not because she had stolen her husband, but merely because she had fallen into the world-wide mire. The Countess did not come

of peasant stock, among whom the lower instincts are dominant. How could she have sunk so low as to give herself up to
the lusts of the flesh?

On the very day of her parents' arrival Julien revived her re-
pulsion by telling her jokingly as something quite natural and
amusing that the baker had heard a noise in his oven the day
before, which was not a day on which he baked, and thinking
to catch a cat on the prowl had actually caught his wife, 'who
wasn't using the oven to bake bread'.

He added : 'The baker stopped up the ventilation hole and
they were nearly suffocated inside. It was the little child of the
baker's wife who told the neighbours, as he had seen his mother
getting in with the blacksmith.'

Julien laughed, repeating : 'It's love-bread they make for us
these days, these practical jokers ! It's worthy of La Fontaine's
Fables !'

Jeanne refused to touch the bread.

When the post-chaise drew up on the terrace and the Baron's
cheery face appeared at the window, his daughter's heart and
soul were stirred by deep emotion, an overwhelming rush of
affection, such as she had never felt before. But she was staggered and almost fainted, when she saw Mama. In those six
winter months the Baroness had aged ten years. The bloated
cheeks, limp and drooping, were purple as if swollen with
blood; her eyes were dead and she could not walk unless supported under both arms. Her breathing, always difficult, was
now wheezy and so painful that it was positively disturbing to
be near her. The Baron, having seen her every day, was not
aware of her decline, and when she complained of the difficulty
of her breathing and her increasing weight, he used to reply :
'No, my dear; I've always known you like that.'

After taking them to their room Jeanne went to her own to
cry, she was so upset and distraught. Later she went to find her
father and throwing herself into his arms with her eyes still
full of tears cried : 'Oh ! how Mother has changed! What's the
matter with her? You must tell me !'

He was amazed and replied : 'You find her changed? Don't
be absurd, she hasn't. I've never left her and I'm sure she's all
right – she has always been like that.'

That evening Julien said to his wife: 'Your mother's in a pretty bad way. I think she's going downhill.'

When Jeanne burst into tears, he lost patience: 'Come, come! I'm not saying that she's finished. You always exaggerate things absurdly. She has changed, that's all; it's only natural at her age.'

After a week she thought no more about it, having grown used to her mother's altered appearance, perhaps repressing her fears, as one always represses or refuses to recognize worries and apprehensions, out of a kind of selfish instinct, a natural longing for peace of mind.

The Baroness, now unable to walk, only went out for half an hour a day; after one turn in 'her drive' she could not go another step and insisted on sitting down on 'her bench'; and when she could not complete even one turn, she would say: 'Let's stop here; my hypertrophy has got into my legs today.' She hardly ever laughed now, just smiling at things which would have made her roar with laughter the year before. But as her eyesight was still excellent, she spent whole days re-reading *Corinne* or Lamartine's *Meditations*; or she would ask for her 'relic drawer'; and having emptied out on her lap the old letters that were so precious to her, she put down the drawer on a chair by her side and replaced the 'relics' one by one after slowly perusing each one. When she was alone, quite alone, she even kissed certain of them, as one kisses the lock of hair of someone whom one once loved and who is now dead.

Sometimes Jeanne, coming into the room suddenly, found her weeping bitter tears and cried: 'What's the matter, Mama?'

And the Baroness with a deep sigh would answer: 'It's my "relics" that do this to me. The memory of things that were so good once but are no more is stirred; and there are people too, whom one had almost forgotten and suddenly remembers. One can almost see them and hear them, and that has a shattering effect. You'll experience the same thing later on yourself.'

When the Baron came in on these melancholy occasions, he murmured: 'Jeanne darling, if you take my advice, burn your letters, all of them, your Mother's, mine, all. There's nothing more depressing, when one is old, than reviving the memories of one's youth.'

But Jeanne preserved her letters and kept a box of 'relics', though she was an entirely different person from her mother, in obedience to an inherited instinct of romantic dreaming.

A few days later the Baron had to leave on business. The weather was perfect. Nights bright with stars followed windless evenings, clear evenings succeeded sunny days, and sunny days were ushered in by dazzling dawns. Mama was soon better and Jeanne, forgetting Julien's flirtation and Gilberte's betrayal, was almost completely happy. The countryside was full of flowers and scents, and the great calm expanse of the ocean shone in the sun from morning to night.

One afternoon Jeanne picked up Paul and went for a country walk; sometimes she looked at the child, sometimes at the grass dotted with flowers all along the edge of the road, moved almost to tears by the very completeness of her happiness. Every few minutes she kissed the infant, cuddling him passionately; then under the caress of some strong scent from the flowers she felt faint, overcome by a sense of blissful content. Later she dreamed of his future; what would he become? Sometimes she wanted him to be a great man, famous and powerful; sometimes she hoped that he would be undistinguished, always at her side, devoted, loving, with arms always open for Mama. When a mother's selfishness dominated her heart, she wanted him to be just her son, nothing more; but when reason controlled her affection, she had an ambition for him to become a figure in the great world outside.

She sat down on the edge of a ditch and gazed at him as if she had never seen him before. She realized with a shock of surprise that this tiny infant would grow up and walk firmly, that he would have a beard and bass voice. But someone was calling her from the distance; she looked up and saw Marius running towards her. She thought that some caller must be waiting for her and got up, annoyed at being disturbed. But the boy was running at full speed towards her and, as he got near, he shouted: 'Madame, the Baroness is took very ill!'

She felt as if a drop of icy water had run down her back and set off as fast as she could go for the house, distraught.

From a distance she saw a crowd of people under the plane tree; she rushed up and, when the circle opened, she saw her mother lying on the ground with her head supported on two pillows. Her face was quite black and her eyes shut, and there was no movement in her breast, which had been heaving for the last twenty years. The nurse seized the child from his mother's arms and carried him off. With wild eyes Jeanne kept asking: 'What has happened? How did she fall? Someone go and fetch the doctor.'

Turning round, she saw the priest, who had somehow got wind of what had happened; he offered to help and fussed round, turning up the sleeves of his cassock. But vinegar, eau-de-Cologne, and massage had no effect.

'We must get her undressed and put to bed,' said the priest.

Joseph Couillard from the farm was also there with old Simon and Ludivine. With the help of the Abbé Picot they tried to carry the Baroness in, but when they raised her, her head fell backwards and the piece of her dress which they had grasped was torn by her ponderous body, which was too heavy for them to move. Jeanne screamed with terror and the great limp body was laid down again on the ground. They had to bring an arm-chair from the drawing-room, and after lifting her into it they succeeded in moving her. They climbed the terrace a step at a time and then the stairs, and laid her on the bed in her room. As the cook was laboriously undressing her, the widow Dentu arrived just at the right moment, turning up suddenly like the priest, as if they had 'smelt death', as the servants put it.

Joseph Couillard galloped off to fetch the doctor, and as the priest was about to go for the holy oil, the nurse whispered in his ear: 'Don't worry, your Reverence. I'm a nurse and I know; she is dead.'

Jeanne, distracted, kept asking questions all the time; she did not know what to do, what to try, what treatment to give. The priest, to be safe, pronounced absolution. For two hours they waited beside the discoloured lifeless body. Jeanne, who had fallen on her knees, was sobbing, overcome by grief and anguish. When the door opened and the doctor came in, she thought that all would now be well and felt consoled and hopeful. She ran to him and stammered an account of all she knew of what had happened: 'She was taking her daily walk ... she was quite well ... very well in fact ... she had taken some soup and two eggs for lunch ... suddenly she fell down ... she was quite black in the face, as you see ... and she never moved again ... we tried everything to bring her round ... everything ...'

She stopped, struck dumb by the nurse's discreet gesture to the doctor conveying that all was over, that she was dead. But refusing to understand, Jeanne went on asking him: 'Is it serious? Do you consider it serious?'

At last he said: 'I am afraid it is ... it is all over. You must pull yourself together; you will need all your courage.'

With arms outspread Jeanne threw herself on her mother's body. At this moment Julien, who had just returned, came into the room. He stood there tongue-tied and worried, not uttering a sound and showing no outward sign of grief. He had been so completely taken by surprise that he had not had time to compose his features and put on a suitable expression of sorrow. 'I'm not surprised,' he murmured. 'I felt that the end was not far off.'

Taking out his handkerchief he wiped his eyes, knelt down, crossed himself, mumbling a few words, and then getting up he tried to raise his wife to her feet; but she was embracing the body and kissing it, almost lying on top of it. She had to be carried away, seeming quite out of her mind.

An hour later she was allowed back. There was no hope left. The room had been arranged as a mortuary chamber. Julien and the priest were talking in low voices near one of the windows. The widow Dentu, comfortably ensconced in an armchair, like one accustomed to vigils, who is quite at home in any house as soon as death has entered, was already dozing.

It was getting dark. The priest went up to Jeanne, took her hands and tried to comfort her, pouring into her disconsolate ears an unctuous flood of ecclesiastical eloquence; he spoke of the deceased with clerical eulogy, and with the affected sadness of a priest, to whom a dead body is a source of profit, offered to spend the night in prayer by the corpse. But Jeanne through her convulsive tears refused; she wanted to be left alone, quite alone, on this night of farewells. Julien came forward: 'But that is quite impossible; we will both stay here.' She shook her head, incapable of speech. At last with an effort she said: 'She is my Mother, *my* Mother; I want to watch by her alone.'

The doctor murmured: 'Let her do as she wishes; the nurse can stay in the next room.' The priest and Julien agreed, thinking of their beds. The Abbé Picot knelt down and said a prayer; after which he got up and went out saying: 'She was a saint,' in the tone in which he said 'Dominus vobiscum'.

Then the Viscount said in his ordinary tone of voice: 'Will you have something to eat?' Jeanne did not answer, not realizing that he was speaking to her. He went on: 'I think it would be good for you to take something to keep you going.' She replied with a dazed air: 'Send for Papa at once,' and he went out to send a man on horseback to Rouen. She remained plunged in silent grief, as if waiting for the opportunity of their last hour together to let loose the rising tide of sorrow and despair.

Darkness had come over the room, wrapping the body in shadow. The widow Dentu began to wander about, looking for invisible things and putting them in their proper places with a nurse's noiseless movements. Presently she lit two candles and put them gently on the night-table, which was covered with a white cloth near the head of the bed. Jeanne seemed to see nothing, feel nothing, take nothing in; she was just waiting to be alone. Julien came in again, having had dinner, and asked: 'Wouldn't you like something?' His wife shook her head. He sat down with an air of resignation rather than grief and did not speak. The three of them remained seated at some distance from each other, not moving. Occasionally the nurse snored a little as she dozed, and then woke up with a start. At last Julien got up and going up to Jeanne said: 'Would you like to be alone now?' She took his hand and with an instinctive outburst of gratitude cried: 'Oh, yes, do leave me alone.' He kissed her on the forehead, murmuring: 'I'll come and have a look at you from time to time,' and he went out of the room with the widow Dentu, who rolled her arm-chair into the next room.

Jeanne shut the door and went and opened both the windows wide, and felt on her face the warm caress of an evening during the hay-harvest; the grass on the lawn had been cut the day before and was lying ungathered in the moonlight. The pleasurable sensation hurt her, wounding her heart like a shaft of irony.

She returned to the bed-side, took one of her mother's cold limp hands and gazed at her. She was no longer bloated as at the moment of the attack; now she seemed to be sleeping more peacefully than ever before in her life, and the pale flicker of the candles in the breeze made the shadows shift continually over her face with lifelike movements as if she had actually moved.

Jeanne looked hard at her and a flood of memories of her early childhood came into her mind. She remembered Mama's visits to the convent parlour, the way she used to hold out the paper bag full of cakes, thousands of trivial details and actions, little kindnesses, words, intonations, familiar gestures, the wrinkles round her eyes when she laughed, her sigh of relief when she sat down out of breath. She stayed there looking at her in a sort of daze, repeating: 'She is dead,' and all the horror of the word was revealed to her. The body lying there, Mama, her beloved mother, Madame Adélaïde, was dead; could it be true? She would never move again, never speak again, never laugh again, never again sit at dinner opposite Papa, never say again 'Good morning, darling Jeanne!' She was dead. They would nail her down in a coffin and bury it – that would be the end; she would never be seen again. Was it possible? How could it be? Would she never have a mother again? This beloved familiar face, seen as soon as she had opened her eyes, loved as soon as she had opened her arms, the outlet for her affection, this unique being, a mother, more important to the heart than all the rest of the world, was gone. She had only a few hours left now to look at this face without movement, without thought; after that nothing, nothing, only a memory.

She fell down on her knees in an agony of despair, and with her hands clutching the sheet, which she twisted up, and her mouth pressed against the bed, she cried in heart-rending tones, stifled in the sheets and blankets: 'Oh! Mama, poor Mama, Mama!' But feeling that she was going mad, as she had been on the night when she had run out into the snow, she got up and ran to the window to refresh herself and get a breath of fresh air which did not come from the bed, from the dead body. The mown lawn, the trees, the common, the distant sea were asleep, silent and peaceful, lulled by the moon's soft caress.

Something of this restful calm entered into Jeanne's heart and she began to weep slow tears.

Then she came back to the bed-side and held Mama's hand, as if she were watching by a sick-bed. A large flying insect had got in, attracted by the candles; it was striking the walls like a ball from one end of the room to the other. Jeanne, distracted by its whirring flight, looked up to see it, but she could never catch anything but its flitting shadow on the white ceiling. Presently she heard it no more. Soon she noticed the faint tick of the clock and another low sound or rather an almost imperceptible hum. It was Mama's watch, which was still going, having been forgotten in the pocket of her dress, which had been thrown on a chair at the foot of the bed; and suddenly the link between the dead woman and this piece of mechanism, which was still going, revived the acute pain in Jeanne's heart. She looked at the time; it was only just half past ten, and suddenly a horrible fear gripped her at the prospect of spending the whole night there.

Other memories came back to her mind, memories of her own life, of Rosalie and Gilberte, the bitter disillusionments of her heart. There was nothing in the world except misery, sorrow, misfortune and death. Everything was deception and lying, everything was fraught with suffering and tears. Where was a little rest and happiness to be found? In another life no doubt. When the soul would be free from the prison of the flesh. The soul! And she began to dream of this insoluble mystery, following the theories of the poets, which other hypotheses equally vague immediately contradicted. Where was her mother's soul at this moment, the soul which had inhabited this body now incapable of movement and cold? Far away, perhaps, somewhere in space? But where? Dissolved like an invisible bird escaped from its cage? Was it called back to God? Or dispersed among new creations, mingling with the seeds of life destined for a new birth? Perhaps it was quite close, in this very room, fluttering round the body which it had just left. Suddenly she felt, or thought she felt, a breath as if a spirit had touched her. She was frightened, terribly frightened, too frightened to move or breathe or turn round and look behind her; her heart was beating wildly.

Now the invisible insect began to fly about again, hitting the walls as it whirled round. She shivered from head to foot, but recovering herself, when she realized that it was only the insect buzzing, she rose from her knees and turned round. Her eyes fell upon the bureau with the sphinxes' heads containing Mama's 'relics'. Suddenly she had the strange, fond idea that during this last vigil she would read, as she might have read some holy book, these old letters, which had been so much treasured by the dead woman. She felt that it would be carrying out a daughter's delicate, sacred duty and would give pleasure to Mama in another world.

There were old letters from her grandmother and grand-father, whom she had never known; she wanted to stretch out her arms to them over their daughter's body and be united with them on this night of mourning, as if they were suffering too, establishing a mysterious bond of love between them long dead, their daughter just passed away, and herself still alive in this world. She got up, opened the lid of the bureau and took from the little bottom drawer about ten small packets of papers yellow with age, neatly tied up and stowed away side by side. She put them all down on the bed on the Baroness's breast as a kind of sentimental refinement and began to read them. They were the ancient letters that one finds in old family writing-tables, letters breathing the spirit of past ages.

The first letter began 'My darling', another 'My beautiful grand-daughter'; soon it was 'Dear little one', 'My Pet', 'My beloved Daughter'; later 'My dear Child', 'Dear Adélaïde', 'My dear Daughter', according as they were addressed to the child, the girl, and later the young woman. They all reflected tender childlike affection with a thousand little intimate touches, the everyday important incidents of the home, so trivial to those who do not love: 'Father is down with flu', 'the maid Hortense has burnt her finger', 'Ratcatcher the cat has died', 'the pine on the right of the garden gate has been felled', 'Mother lost her prayer-book on the way back from church; she thinks it was stolen'.

Then there was talk about people whom Jeanne did not know, but whose names she vaguely remembered being mentioned long ago in her childhood days. These trivial details had a sentimental interest for Jeanne; they were revelations which allowed her to enter into her mother's past life, its secrets and its affections. She looked at the body lying there and began to read the letters aloud, as if to amuse or console the dead woman. The inert body seemed to be enjoying them. One by one she threw them down on the foot of the bed and thought she ought to place them in the coffin as one places flowers.

She untied another packet, which was in a strange hand. She began reading : 'I can't live without your kisses – I'm madly in love with you.'

That was all, there was no name. She turned the paper over, not understanding; it was certainly addressed to 'Madame la Baronne Le Perthuis des Vauds'.

So she opened the next : 'Come this evening as soon as he goes out; we shall have an hour. I worship you.' Another said : 'I have spent a night of delirium, wanting you so desperately. I felt your body in my arms, your lips on my mouth, your eyes gazing into mine, and I felt so mad that I wanted to throw myself out of the window at the thought that at that very moment you were by his side in bed and that he could do what he would with you.'

Jeanne, puzzled, still did not understand. What did it all mean? Who was it written to? For whom was it meant? Who was the writer of these words of love? She went on and found more passionate declarations, more assignations urging prudence, and always at the end the five words 'Above all burn this letter'. Finally she opened a formal note accepting an invitation to dinner signed 'Paul d'Ennemare', the man whom the Baron, when he spoke of him, always called 'poor old Paul', and whose wife had been the Baroness's best friend.

Now Jeanne felt a suspicion, which soon became a certainty, that her mother had had this man for a lover. Suddenly, quite overwhelmed, she hurled these vile letters away, as she would have thrown off some poisonous insect which had bitten her, and running to the window began to weep bitter tears with involuntary cries which tore her throat. Then in a state of complete collapse she crouched down at the foot of the wall, and hiding her face in her hands to stifle her groans, she sobbed in the depths of bottomless despair.

She might have stayed all night like this, but the sound of footsteps in the next room brought her to her feet with a bound. It might be her father, and all the letters were lying on the bed and on the floor; he had only to open one and he would know the whole ghastly truth. She dashed across the room and picked up all the faded old letters in handfuls, those of the grand-parents, those of the lover, those which she had not yet opened and those still tied up in the drawers of the bureau, and threw them in a heap into the fire-place. Then she took one of the candles from the night-table and set fire to the pile. A great blaze broke out, which lit up the room, the bed and the body with a bright dancing flame and cast the flickering shadow of the stiffened face and the outline of the swollen body under the shroud dark against the white curtain at the head of the bed.

When there was nothing left but a heap of ashes in the grate, she crossed the room and sat down by the open window, as if she no longer dared to stay by the body, and began to weep again with her face in her hands, groaning in her misery on a note of hopeless desolation: 'Oh, my poor Mama! Oh, my poor Mama!'

A painful thought came into her mind; suppose by some chance that Mama was not dead, suppose she were only sunk in a trance, suppose she suddenly got up and spoke. Would the knowledge of her secret love affair not lessen her own filial affection? Could she kiss her mother with the same sacred respect? Could she cherish the same religious love for her? No, that was impossible, and she was heart-broken at the thought.

The night was almost over and the stars were growing pale. It was the chilly hour before dawn and the moon low on the horizon was about to plunge into the sea, which gleamed with a pearly lustre. In a flash Jeanne recalled the night which she had spent at the window immediately after her return to the Poplars. How far away it all seemed, how changed every-thing was, how different the future was now! Suddenly the sky turned pink, a delicate joyous pink inviting love. She gazed at the radiant dawn, surprised as at some strange phenome-non; was it possible, she wondered, that in a world where such a sunrise could occur there should exist neither joy nor happiness?

A sound at the door made her start; it was Julien: 'Well,' he asked, 'I hope you are not too tired.'

'No,' she stammered, glad not to be alone any longer.

'Go and lie down now,' he said.

She gave her mother a slow kiss, a sad heart-broken kiss, and went to her room. The day was spent in the depressing preparation of the corpse. The Baron wept bitterly on his arrival that evening. The funeral was to take place next day. After she had pressed a last kiss on the cold lips and swathed the body in the grave-clothes and watched it being nailed down in the coffin, she left the room.

The invited guests began to arrive. Gilberte came first and fell into her friend's arms. From the windows carriages could be seen turning in at the gate and rolling up to the front door, and there was a buzz of conversation in the hall. Ladies in black, many of whom Jeanne did not know, made their way one by one into the mortuary chamber. The Marquise de Coutelier and the Vicomtesse de Briseville kissed Jeanne. Suddenly she saw Aunt Lison slip in behind her; she embraced her tenderly, which nearly made the old lady faint.

Julien entered in full mourning, very smart, fussing round, delighted at the number of guests. He asked his wife something he wanted to know, adding confidentially: 'All the nobility are here; it will be very useful to us.' And he went away, bowing gravely to the ladies.

Only Aunt Lison and the Comtesse Gilberte stayed with Jeanne during the funeral service. The Countess kept kissing her all the time, murmuring: 'My poor darling! My poor darling!'

When the Comte de Fourville came to fetch his wife, he was in tears himself as if he had lost his own mother.

CHAPTER TEN

THE days following the funeral were dreary; it is always a depressing period in a house, which seems empty owing to the absence of a familiar figure that has now gone for ever. Everything that the deceased handled every day brings back painful recollections. Memories crowd back every moment and wound the heart. There is her arm-chair, there is her sunshade left in the hall, that is her glass which the maid has not put away. In every room her things are lying about, her scissors, a glove, a book whose leaves are crumpled by fingers grown clumsy, a thousand trivial things that are painful because they recall a thousand little incidents. Her voice pursues one, one can hear her speaking, one would like to escape anywhere from the haunted house, but one has to remain, because others remain and also suffer. Jeanne too was still crushed under the weight of her discovery; the thought of it lay heavy on her heart, which was slow to recover from its wound. Her present loneliness was increased by this dreadful secret and her last hope had lost its last anchor.

A few days later Papa left; he needed new surroundings and a change of air; he had to escape from the black depression into which he was sinking deeper and deeper. The great house resumed its calm regular routine, being used to the periodical absences of its masters. Then Paul was taken ill; Jeanne lost her reason and for twelve days could not sleep and hardly ate.

He recovered, but she remained obsessed by the idea that he might die. What would she do then? What would become of her? Gradually the desire to have another child came into her mind. Soon she began to dream of it, possessed again by her former wish to see two children round her, a boy and a girl; before long it was an obsession. But since the affair of Rosalie she had lived apart from Julien. It seemed indeed impossible that in their present position they should come together again. Julien's love had been given elsewhere, she was sure of that;

and the mere thought of submitting to his caresses again filled her with loathing.

However, she would have resigned herself even to that, such was her longing for another child, but she did not see how their love-making could start again. She would have died of humiliation rather than let him guess her intention; and now he did not seem ever to think of her. Perhaps she would have given up the idea, but now every night she dreamt of a daughter; she saw her playing with Paul under the plane tree. Sometimes she felt an itch to get up and go and find her husband in his room without a word. Twice she had even slipped along to his door, but quickly turned back, her heart beating with shame.

The Baron had left and Mama was dead; so Jeanne had no one to consult, no one to whom she could confide her secret thoughts. At last she made up her mind to go and find the Abbé Picot and tell him under the seal of the confessional her difficult ideas for the future.

She arrived as he was reading his breviary in his little orchard garden.

After a few minutes of casual conversation she stammered, blushing : 'I want to make my confession, Father.'

He was dumbfounded and pushing up his spectacles to look at her he burst out laughing : 'But you can't have many grievous sins on your conscience !'

She didn't know what to say and went on : 'No, but I want to ask your advice on a matter so ... so ... painful that I dare not speak of it in the ordinary way.'

He at once changed his normal cheery attitude and put on his professional manner : 'Very well, my daughter; I will hear you in the confessional; come along.'

But she hesitated and stopped him, checked by a sort of scruple at broaching a shameful subject in the meditative peace of the empty church : 'Or else ... no, Father, I could tell you here what brings me, if you like. Look, let's go and sit down over there in your little arbour.'

They walked slowly across the garden. She was trying to find words to begin. They sat down and as if she was at confession she began : 'Father ...' then she hesitated and repeated : 'Father

'...' and stopped again, tongue-tied. He waited with his hands crossed over his stomach.

Seeing her embarrassment, he tried to encourage her: 'Well, my Daughter, one would think it was something that you dare not say; don't be frightened.'

At last she made up her mind like a coward plunging into danger: 'Father, I want to have another child.'

He was puzzled and said nothing. Then she explained, much worried and finding words with difficulty: 'I am alone in life now; my father and my husband don't get on; my mother is dead ... and ...' (she spoke almost in a whisper with a shiver) 'the other day I nearly lost my son. What would have become of me then?'

She paused and the puzzled priest looked at her: 'Come now, get to the point.'

'I want another child,' she repeated.

At that he smiled, accustomed to the coarse jokes of the peasants, who spoke quite freely before him, and with a sly nod he replied: 'Well, it seems to me that the matter is entirely in your own hands.'

She looked at him with her simple honest eyes and went on, stammering in her confusion: 'But ... but ... you realize that since the affair ... the affair with the maid ... my husband and I live ... we live quite apart.'

Accustomed to the promiscuity and unbridled sensuality of the countryside, this revelation amazed him; but suddenly the young woman's genuine longing flashed across his mind. He looked at her out of the corner of his eye, full of kindly sympathy for her distress: 'Yes, I quite understand; your widowhood weighs upon you. It is perfectly natural, all too natural.'

He began to smile again and with a country priest's natural outspokenness he tapped Jeanne's hand lightly, saying: 'It is allowed, indeed encouraged, by the Commandments: "Thou shalt not obey the prompting of the flesh save in marriage." You are a married woman, aren't you? You didn't marry in order to sow turnips!'

Now it was her turn not to understand the Abbé's implications, but as soon as she did realize what he meant, she blushed crimson, quite shocked and with tears in her eyes: 'Oh! Father, what are you saying? I swear ... I swear ...' and sobs choked her words.

He was surprised and tried to console her: 'Come, come! I didn't mean to hurt you. I was only speaking in jest; and there's no harm in that, provided one's intentions are good. But trust me, you can count on me; I'll see Monsieur Julien.'

She did not know what to say to that; she would have liked to refuse his intervention, which she feared might be clumsy and dangerous; but she did not dare, and she escaped after stammering: 'Thank you, Father.'

A week passed, during which she lived in a state of acute anxiety. At last, one evening after dinner, Julien looked strangely at her, his lips curling in a smile which she recognized from his old light-hearted days. His glance had even a touch of almost ironical gallantry and, as they were strolling afterwards in 'Mama's drive', he whispered in her ear: 'It seems we have made things up!'

She did not answer; she was looking on the ground at a sort of straight mark, almost invisible now that the grass had grown up; it was the trail of the Baroness's dragging foot, which was now disappearing as a memory fades. She felt her heart contract in a wave of sadness. Julien went on: 'I'm more than willing; I only thought you wouldn't like it.'

The sun was setting and the air was soft. A desire to weep overcame Jeanne; it was the longing of the heart to open towards the heart of a friend, a need to show affection and share sorrow. A sob rose in her throat, and opening her arms she fell on Julien's breast and burst into tears. He looked down in surprise on the top of her head, unable to see her face which was pressed against his chest. He thought that she still loved him and printed a perfunctory kiss on the nape of her neck. After that they went in without a word; he followed her to her room and they spent the night together.

Their former relations were resumed. He carried out his marital duties as if they were not displeasing, and she submitted to his embraces as a painful disgusting necessity, resolved to put an end to them for ever, as soon as she felt that she was pregnant again. But she soon noticed that his caresses were different now; they were perhaps more refined, but also less passionate. He behaved like a discreet lover, no longer like a satisfied husband. She was astonished and watched, and she soon realized that his embraces were checked before she could possibly have conceived.

Then one night, pressing her lips against his, she whispered: 'Why don't you give yourself wholly to me, as you used to do?'

'Well, of course,' he sneered, 'so that you shouldn't become pregnant.'

She started: 'Why, don't you want any more children?'

He was amazed at her words: 'What do you mean? Are you mad? Another child? No, I should think not indeed. One is more than enough to squall and keep everybody busy and cost money. Another child? No, thank you!'

She threw her arms round him, kissed him and did everything to rouse his passion, whispering: 'Oh, do give me another child, I implore you.'

But he lost his temper, as if her words were hurtful: 'You really are crazy; please don't give me any more of your folly.'

She said no more, but resolved to make him give her the happiness that she desired by a trick. She tried to prolong his embraces, simulating a mad passion, imprisoning him in her arms so that he could not escape, in affected ecstasy. She employed every trick, but he kept control and never once forgot himself. At last, tortured more and more by her wild longing and now ready for anything, she went back to the Abbé Picot.

He was just finishing his lunch, very red in the face, for he always had palpitations after eating. As soon as he saw her come in, he cried: 'Well, how goes it?' eager to know the result of his negotiations. Her mind now made up, she replied immediately without any modest reticence: 'My husband does not want any more children.'

The Abbé turned to her, his interest thoroughly aroused; with a priest's curiosity he was ready to probe the secrets of married life, which always make the confessional amusing: 'How does he show his unwillingness?' he asked.

In spite of her determination she found explanation difficult: 'But he . . . he . . . refuses to make me conceive.'

The Abbé understood; he knew all about these things. He put intimate questions of detail with the greedy appetite of one who normally fasts. Then he thought for a few moments, and in a calm voice, as if speaking of the prospect of a good harvest, he outlined a cunning plan of action, emphasizing each point: 'There is only one means, my Daughter; that is to make him believe that you are pregnant. Then he will not control himself and you really will conceive.'

She blushed up to the eyes, but ready for anything now she persisted: 'But ... but, if he does not believe me?'

The priest, who knew all the tricks to attract and hold a man, replied: 'Announce your pregnancy, tell everyone; in the end he will come to believe it himself.'

He added as if to absolve himself from the guilt of this trick: 'It is your right. Holy Church only permits marital relations between man and wife with a view to procreation.'

She followed this ingenious advice and a fortnight later she told Julien that she thought she was pregnant. He started in surprise: 'But that's impossible! It can't be true!'

She immediately gave the reasons for her belief, but he would not be convinced: 'Nonsense! You just wait a bit and you'll see.'

Every morning he asked: 'Well?' and she always replied: 'No, I'm not sure yet, but I shall be much surprised if I'm not pregnant.'

Now he began to be worried in his turn, angry and disappointed as much as astonished; he repeated: 'I don't understand it, I'm bothered if I do. I'll be hanged if I know how it happened!'

A month later she announced the news to all and sundry, except, by a kind of modest delicacy hard to explain, to the Comtesse Gilberte.

After his first misgivings Julien had not come near his wife again; now he accepted the position, though very much against the grain, and declared: 'Here at any rate is one who wasn't wanted,' and he began to return to his wife's bed.

The priest's expectations were exactly fulfilled; and she really became pregnant. In an ecstasy of delirious happiness she locked her bedroom door every night, registering a vow of life-long chastity with a feeling of profound gratitude to the vaguely conceived Deity whom she worshipped. Once again she was almost happy; she was herself surprised at the speed with which her grief at her mother's death had been assuaged. She had thought herself inconsolable and now in barely two months the wound was already beginning to heal; she only felt a tender melancholy spreading like a veil over her life. It seemed that nothing could ever happen to her; her children would grow up loving her and she would age in tranquil happiness, not worrying about her husband.

Towards the end of September the Abbé Picot paid a formal visit, in a new cassock with only one week's stains on it, to introduce his successor, the Abbé Tolbiac. He was a young priest, thin and very short, with an emphatic way of speaking, and his eyes, deep set with dark rings round them, indicated a forceful personality. The old priest had been appointed Dean of Goderville. Jeanne was genuinely sorry at his departure. The old fellow's kindly face was bound up with all the memories of her earlier days; he had married her, christened Paul, and buried her mother. She could not imagine Étouvent without the Abbé Picot's portly figure moving about in the farmyards, and she was fond of him, because he was a good soul without affectation. He did not seem to be looking forward to his promotion. He would say: 'It's a painful break, Countess; I've been eighteen years here. There's not much that is rewarding in the village, it's not much of a place. Religion doesn't mean much to the men, and the women, as you know, have no idea of decent behaviour. The girls only come to church to be married after a pilgrimage to Our Lady of Fertility, and orange-blossom doesn't count for much in these parts. But anyway I've been happy here.'

The new priest was showing signs of impatience and was very red in the face. He said sharply: 'Well, with me, things will be very different.' He looked just like a child in a temper, a slight figure, very thin, in a cassock which was already threadbare but clean.

The Abbé Picot with the sly glance characteristic of his lighter moments, replied: 'Look, Abbé, to stop this sort of thing you would have to keep your parishioners locked up, and even then it would be no good.'

The young priest answered curtly: 'We shall see.' The old priest replied, taking a pinch of snuff: 'Age will mellow you,

Abbé, and experience too; you will empty the church of your last faithful; that's all there is to it. Here in the country folk are believers but obstinate; so be careful. Look here, when I see a girl coming to church looking a bit heavy, I say to myself: "Here's a new parishioner she's bringing to me", and I try to get her married. You see, you'll never prevent them slipping up, but you can go and find the boy and prevent him throwing the mother over. Get them married, Abbé, and don't worry about anything else.'

The new priest replied rudely: 'We think differently; argument is useless.'

The Abbé Picot went on expressing regret at leaving the village, the view of the sea from the windows of his presbytery and the little bell-mouthed valleys, where he went to read his breviary, as he watched the boats passing in the distance. Then the two priests took their leave, the old man kissing Jeanne, who was on the verge of tears.

A week later the Abbé Tolbiac called again. He spoke of the reforms which he was introducing, as a prince might have done on his accession to the throne. He begged the Viscountess not to miss Mass on Sundays and to communicate on all the feast days.

'You and I,' he said, 'are the heads of the parish; we have to govern it and always set an example to be followed. In order to be powerful and respected, we must act together. If the church and the mansion go hand in hand, the cottage will fear us and obey.'

Jeanne's religion was entirely a matter of sentiment; she had the vague faith which a woman always keeps; and if she more or less carried out her religious obligations, it was mainly from the habit formed in her convent days, as the Baron's free-thinking philosophy had long since undermined her convictions. The Abbé Picot had been satisfied with the little that she could give him and never pressed her for more. But his successor, not having seen her in church the Sunday before, had come to ask the reason, disturbed and critical. She did not want a breach with the presbytery and gave the promises asked for, with the unexpressed intention of only being a regular attendant out of politeness for his first few weeks. But she gradually got into the habit of going to church and fell under the influence of this frail, upright, dominating personality. His mysticism appealed to her with its ecstasies and enthusiasms; he touched the chord of religious poetry latent in every woman's soul. His uncompromising austerity, his contempt for the world and its sensuality, his disgust at the prejudices of mankind, his love of God, his crude youthful inexperience, his stern language and his inflexible will, all represented to Jeanne the stuff of which martyrs are made; and she let herself be swayed, she who had suffered so much and been so disillusioned, by the iron fanaticism of this young man, God's minister. He led her to Christ for consolation, showing her how the pious gladness of religion would alleviate all her sorrows, and she knelt humbly in the confessional, feeling small and weak before this priest, who looked like a boy of fifteen.

But he was soon hated by the whole neighbourhood. The severity of his own rule of life was inflexible and he showed a relentless intolerance of the failings of others. One thing in particular aroused his indignant fury – love. He spoke of it from the pulpit with passion in the crude language usual with priests, letting loose on his peasant congregation thunderous denunciations of concupiscence. He quivered with rage, stamping his feet, carried away by the pictures called up in his ravings.

The young men and girls exchanged sly glances across the aisle, and the older peasants, who always like to regard love as a subject for jokes, voiced their disapproval of the young priest, as they went home to their farms after Mass by the side of their son in his blue smock and the farm-girl in her black shawl. The whole neighbourhood was simmering with revolt. People whispered to each other tales of his severity in the confessional and the excessive penances which he imposed, and when he obstinately refused absolution to girls whose chastity had been violated, jokes began to circulate on the subject. There were smiles at High Mass on festivals, when girls were seen to remain in their seats instead of communicating with the others.

Soon he began to spy on couples to prevent their meeting, like a keeper on the look-out for poachers. He followed them along the ditches, behind barns on moonlight nights and in the furze-bushes on the slopes of the little hills. Once he discovered a couple who did not remove their arms from each other's waists in his presence and went on kissing as they walked down a stony ravine; he shouted at them: 'Stop that, you mannerless boors!' The boy turned round and replied: 'Mind your own business, Sir; this is no affair of yours.' At this the priest picked up some pebbles and pelted them, as one pelts dogs. They ran away laughing. The following Sunday he denounced them by name from the pulpit. After that all the young men of the village gave up going to church.

The priest dined at the mansion every Thursday evening and often came during the week to talk to his penitent. She shared his enthusiasm, discussing metaphysics and plunging into the intricacies of medieval controversy. They walked up and down the Baroness's drive together, speaking of Christ and the Virgin and the Fathers of the Church as if they had known them personally. Now and then they stopped to discuss philosophical problems, which led them into the bypaths of mysticism. Jeanne lost herself in the arguments of the poets, which soared up into the heavens like rockets, while he with greater precision argued like a fanatical lawyer, eager to prove the squaring of the circle.

Julien treated the priest with great respect and was always saying: 'I like that man; he won't compromise.' He also went regularly to confession and communicated, always ready to set an example. He was now going nearly every day to the Fourvilles' mansion, hunting with the husband, who could not do without him, and riding with the wife in spite of rain and rough weather. The Count used to say: 'They're crazy about riding, but it's good for my wife.'

The Baron returned about the middle of November. He was changed, aged, lacking in vitality, plunged in the black depression which had mastered his mind. Suddenly the love binding him to his daughter seemed to have grown, as if the few months of dreary loneliness had increased his need for affection, support and tenderness. Jeanne did not tell him of her new interests, her intimacy with the Abbé Tolbiac and her religious fervour; but the first time that he saw the priest he instinctively took a strong dislike to him. When Jeanne asked him in the evening: 'What do you think of him?' he answered: 'That man is much too inquisitive; he will be a menace.' Later when he heard from

143

the villagers, with whom he was on friendly terms, of the young priest's severities, his high-handed behaviour and his attempt to suppress natural laws and instincts, his dislike burst out into hatred.

The Baron belonged to the old school of philosophers who worshipped Nature, and he was deeply affected by the sight of the mating of two animals. His devotion was given to a pantheistic Deity, and he reacted sharply against the Catholic image of a God with middle-class ideas, the temper of a Jesuit, and a tyrant's desire for vengeance. In his eyes such a God dwarfed the dimly understood mystery of creation, decreed by fate, limitless, all-powerful, the creation of life, light, the earth, thought, plants, rocks, man, the air, animals, stars, God, and insect life alike. Being creation, it creates and is stronger than any will, vaster than any reason; it produces without any object, unreasoning, endless, in every sense and every shape throughout infinite space, following the vagaries of chance and the proximity of the suns which warm the worlds. The power of creation contained in itself all seeds, all thought, and all life developed in it like flowers and fruit. Therefore for him reproduction was the great primary law, the sacred act, venerable and divine, which carried out the unrevealed, constant will of the Universal Being. So, going from farm to farm, he began a violent campaign against the intolerant priest who preached against life.

Jeanne, deeply grieved, prayed to the Lord and begged her father to stop, but he always replied: 'Such men must always be resisted; it is our right and our duty; they are not human,' and shaking his white locks he repeated: 'They are sub-human, they understand nothing, nothing at all; they live in a fatal dream, they are unnatural,' and he shouted the word 'unnatural' like a curse. The priest recognized an enemy in him, but, as he was anxious to remain in control of the mansion and its young mistress, he temporized, sure of ultimate victory.

He was obsessed by one fixed idea; he had discovered by accident the love affair of Julien and Gilberte and wanted to break it off at any price. One day he came to see Jeanne, and after a talk on mystical subjects he asked for her help in fighting and eliminating an evil in her own family in order to save two souls in danger. She did not understand and wanted to know more.

He replied: 'The hour is not yet come; I will see you again soon,' and he left abruptly.

Winter was drawing to its close, damp and warm, what they call a rotten winter in the country. The Abbé came a few days later and spoke in vague terms about one of those illicit connexions between two people who should be above suspicion. It was the duty of those who knew of such things to put a stop to them by any means. From this he went on to higher considerations, and taking Jeanne's hand he adjured her to open her eyes and help him.

This time she understood, but she did not answer, terrified at the prospect of trouble in the house, which was peaceful at the moment, and she pretended not to know what the Abbé meant. Then he hesitated no longer and spoke out frankly: 'I have a painful duty to perform, Countess, but I cannot do otherwise. My ministry forbids me to leave you in ignorance of something which it is in your power to prevent. I must tell you then that your husband has formed a criminal relationship with Madame de Fourville.'

She bent her head, resigned and overwhelmed. The priest went on: 'What do you propose to do about it?'

She stammered: 'What do you suggest that I should do?'

'Put a stop to this guilty passion,' he replied fiercely.

She began to weep, saying in heart-broken tones: 'But he has already been unfaithful to me with a maid. He won't listen to me, he has ceased to love me; he bullies me as soon as I show any inclination that does not suit him. What can I do?'

The priest, without replying directly, cried: 'Then you surrender, you resign yourself, you consent? The adulterer is under your roof and you tolerate him? The crime is being committed under your eyes and you turn away your head? Are you a wife, a Christian, a mother?'

She sobbed: 'What would you have me do?'

'Anything rather than allow this infamy to go on,' he replied, 'anything, I say. Leave him, quit this polluted house!'

She pleaded: 'But, Father, I have no money and I have not the courage now. Besides how can I leave him without proof? I have not even the legal right.'

The priest got up quivering with anger: 'That is the advice

of cowardice, Madame; I thought better of you. You do not deserve God's mercy.'

She fell on her knees: 'Oh! I beg of you, do not abandon me, give me your advice.'

He spoke sharply: 'Open the eyes of Monsieur de Fourville; it is for him to break off this connexion.'

At this thought terror seized her: 'But he would kill them, Father, and I should be responsible. I could never do that, never!'

At this the Abbé raised his hand in a wild rage as if to pronounce a curse: 'Then live on in your shame and guilt. You are more guilty than they; you are an accessory to your husband's crime. I have nothing more to do here.'

He left the house, trembling with anger. In desperation she followed him, ready to give in and prepared to promise, but he was still quivering with indignation, walking fast and angrily brandishing his umbrella, which was nearly as tall as its owner. He caught sight of Julien standing near the garden gate and superintending the lopping of the trees, and turned to the left across the Couillards' farm, repeating:

'Leave me, Madame, I have nothing more to say to you.'

Right on his path in the centre of the farmyard there was a crowd of children from the Couillards' and other near-by farms, gathered round the kennel of the bitch Mirza, looking at something with eager curiosity and concentrated silent attention. Among them, with his hands behind his back, the Baron was standing, also watching. He looked like a schoolmaster with his class, but, when he saw the priest, he moved away to avoid meeting him and having to greet him and speak. Jeanne in a tone of entreaty was saying: 'Leave me for a few days, Father, and then come back to the house and I'll tell you what I've been able to do and we'll talk it over.'

At that moment they reached the group of children and the priest went up to see what was interesting them so much. It was the bitch, who was giving birth to a litter. In front of the kennel there were five puppies crawling round their mother who was licking them gently, lying on her side, still in great pain. Just as the priest bent down to look, the mother in agony tensed her body and a sixth pup appeared. At that all the children shouted with joy and clapped their hands: 'There be another one! There be another one!' It was only a game to them, a perfectly innocent game; they regarded the birth just as they would have regarded apples falling off a tree.

At first the Abbé stood rooted to the spot; then in a fit of wild rage he raised his great umbrella and brought it down on the heads of the children with all his force. The children scattered and ran away as fast as they could, and he suddenly found himself facing the newly made mother, who tried to get up; but he did not give her time to rise to her feet, before completely losing control he began to beat her. Being on a chain she could not escape and groaned distressingly, as she struggled under the hail of blows. His umbrella broke and with bare hands he threw himself on the dog and trampled on her madly, pounding and crushing her. This made her give birth to a last pup, which was squeezed out of her by his grip. With a furious stamp of his heel he finished off the bleeding body, which was still quivering surrounded by the new-born puppies, whimpering and blind, which were crawling about already feeling for her teats.

Jeanne had run away, but the priest suddenly felt himself gripped by the collar; a box on the ear knocked off his clerical hat and the Baron in a blazing temper dragged him to the gate of the yard and hurled him out into the road. Turning round, the Baron saw his daughter on her knees sobbing with the puppies round her; she was picking them up in her skirt. He strode back to her, gesticulating and shouting: 'There you are! That's the man in the cassock for you! Now you realize the kind of man he is!'

The farmers had gathered round and everyone was looking at the disembowelled dog; Ma Couillard declared: 'Who'd 'ave ever thought anybody could be cruel like that?' But Jeanne had collected the puppies and insisted on looking after them. They tried to give them milk, but three died next day; then old Simon searched the countryside for a bitch with a litter. He could not find one, but he brought back a cat with kittens, insisting that she would do the job. So they drowned the three others and entrusted the last one to this alien foster-mother; she immediately adopted it and lying on her side offered it her teat. In order that the puppy should not exhaust its foster-mother, they weaned it a fortnight later and Jeanne undertook to bring it up herself on the bottle. She called it Toto, but the Baron insisted on changing the name to Murder.

The priest did not come back, but on the following Sunday he launched from the pulpit a flood of imprecations, curses, and threats against the mansion; the wound must be cauterized, he insisted, and he hurled anathemas against the Baron, who was only amused; he also made a veiled allusion, still timid, to Julien's new affair. The latter was furious, but fear of a serious scandal blunted the edge of his anger.

Later, in sermon after sermon, the Abbé went on threatening vengeance – the day of the Lord was drawing nigh, when all His enemies would be scattered. Julien wrote to the Archbishop in polite but forceful terms and the Abbé Tolbiac was threatened with disciplinary action and ceased his attacks. He was now often met taking long solitary walks, striding along with the air of one seeing visions. Gilberte and Julien were always coming across him in the course of their rides, sometimes as just a black speck far away in the distance on the edge of the common or on the top of the cliff, sometimes reading his breviary in some narrow valley which they were approaching; on these occasions they changed their direction to avoid him.

Spring had come and their thoughts again turned to love. Every day they were in each other's arms, now here, now there, in any kind of shelter which they found on their rides. As the leaves were not yet thick on the trees and the ground was damp, they could not penetrate into the undergrowth in the woods, as they could in the height of summer, and to hide their embraces they usually took advantage of a shepherd's hut on wheels, which had been left empty since the previous autumn on the top of the hill of Vaucotte. It had remained there abandoned, raised high on its wheels, five hundred yards back from the cliff just at the point where the steep incline down to the valley began. There they could not be surprised, as they had a view all over the country below, and they used to tether their horses to the shafts to wait till they tired of their love-making.

But one day, as they were leaving their refuge, they noticed the Abbé Tolbiac sitting almost hidden in the sea-rushes on the slope of the hill. 'We shall have to leave our horses in the ravine,' said Julien, 'they might be seen from a distance and give us away.'

After that they always tethered the animals in a fold of the valley full of brushwood. But one evening on their way back to La Vrillette, where they were to dine with the Count, they met the priest from Étouvent leaving the mansion. He stood aside to let them pass, bowing, but they turned their heads so as not to meet his gaze. They felt a twinge of anxiety but it did not last.

One afternoon Jeanne was reading by the fire on a very windy day at the beginning of May, when suddenly she saw the Comte de Fourville hurrying on foot towards the house so fast that she thought some accident must have happened. She hurried down to welcome him and when she met him she thought he had gone mad. On his head was a heavy fur cap, which he only wore at home, and he was wearing a hunting smock; he was so pale that his ginger moustache, which did not normally show up against his ruddy complexion, looked like a line of fire. His eyes were haggard and were rolling with a blank expression. 'My wife is here, isn't she?' he stammered.

Jeanne, losing her head, replied: 'No, I haven't seen her today.'

At that he collapsed on a chair, took off his cap and mopped his brow several times with a mechanical gesture; then, jumping to his feet, he took a step towards Jeanne with both hands outstretched and mouth open as if about to impart some bad news. But he stopped, looked hard at her, and speaking like one delirious said: 'But it's your husband ... so you too ...' and he rushed away in the direction of the sea. Jeanne ran after him, trying to stop him, calling to him, imploring, tortured with apprehension.

'So he knows everything,' she thought. 'What will he do now? Oh ! I do hope he doesn't find them !'

But she could not catch him up and he paid no heed to her cries. He went straight on without hesitation, sure of his direction. He crossed the dyke and reached the cliff, making his way through the furze with giant strides. Jeanne followed him with her eyes for a long time, standing on the tree-covered bank, but, when he disappeared, she went back to the house in an agony of apprehension. He had turned to the right, breaking into a run. The stormy sea was rising; great black clouds were rolling up at an incredible speed, one bank following another, and each one lashed the hill with a downpour of rain. The wind whistled and roared, flattened the grass and laid the growing crops, sweeping large white gulls like flakes of foam and carrying them far inland. A quick succession of squalls whipped the Count's face, drenched his cheeks and his moustache, and filled his ears with a roar and his heart with tumult. In front of him, down below, the deep gorge of the Valley of Vaucotte opened out. It was quite deserted except for a shepherd's hut near an empty sheep-pen; two horses were tethered to the shafts of the wheeled hut. In a storm like this what would anyone have to fear?

As soon as he sighted the horses, the Count lay down and presently crawled forward on hands and knees like some strange monster with his huge body stained with mud and his fur cap. He crept up to the isolated hut and hid under it so as not to be seen through the cracks in the wooden sides. At the sight of him the horses grew restive. He slowly cut the reins with a knife which he kept open in his hand. A sudden squall came up at this moment and the animals galloped away under the pelting hail, which beat on the sloping roof of the wooden hut, making it rock on its wheels. Then the Count, rising to his knees, glued his eye to the crack at the bottom of the door and looked in. He did not move; he seemed to be waiting. Some time passed; suddenly he got up, plastered with mud from head to foot. With a frantic gesture he pushed home the bolt, which fastened the pent-house door on the outside, and seizing the shafts he began to shake the hut as if he wanted to break it up. Then suddenly he harnessed himself and straining his whole body forward with a desperate effort he pulled, panting like a bull. He dragged the hut forward with its inmates towards the steep slope. They screamed from inside, banging with their fists against the planking, not knowing what was happening.

When he reached the brow of the incline, he let go of the light hut, which began to roll down the steep hill. It gained speed in its mad course, going faster and faster, jolting and bumping like a live thing, striking the ground with the shafts. An old tramp hiding in a ditch saw it leap over his head and heard the wild cries of the inmates of this wooden prison. Suddenly it lost a wheel torn off by a jolt; it collapsed on its side and began to roll over and over sideways like a ball, as a house uprooted on the top of a mountain would roll downhill. When it reached the edge of the last gully, it leapt into the air in a great curve and crashing down on the bottom burst open like an egg.

As soon as it had broken up on the stony ground, the old tramp who had seen it pass made his way slowly down through the reeds and with his peasant's caution, not daring to go near the disembowelled hut, went to the nearest farm to give news of the accident. People ran to the spot and in the débris they found two bodies, bruised and smashed and covered with blood. The man's forehead was split open and his whole face crushed. The woman's jaw was hanging down fractured by the shock; and their broken limbs were limp as if there were no bones left under the skin. But they were recognized and there was a great deal of talk about the cause of the accident. 'What ever was they doin' in this 'ere shanty?' asked a woman. The old tramp explained that they had apparently sheltered there from the storm and that the force of the wind must have capsized the hut and blown it down the hill. He told them that he had been on his way to take cover there himself, when he had seen the two horses tethered there and had realized that the place was already occupied. He smiled quite pleased with himself: 'Otherwise I'd 'ave been inside myself!'

A voice commented: 'Pity you wasn't!'

At that the old fellow lost his temper: 'Why be it a pity I be not dead? Because I be poor and they be rich? Look at 'em now!' and shivering, in rags, soaked to the skin, unwashed, with an unkempt beard and long hair flowing from under a shabby hat, he pointed to the bodies with the end of his crooked stick and declared: 'That do make us all the same, all equal!'

By this time other peasants had come up and were watching the scene, worried, with shifty eyes, frightened, self-centred, cowardly. There was a discussion as to what to do. In the hope of a reward it was decided to take the bodies to the two mansions, and two carts were harnessed. But a new difficulty arose; some wanted merely to put straw in the carts, others thought it more seemly to put mattresses. The woman who had spoken before shouted: 'But them mattresses, they'll get covered with blood and then they'll 'ave to be washed with bleachin'-powder.'

A portly farmer with a cheery smile replied: 'In that case they'll 'ave to pay for it; the more it costs us, the more they'll 'ave to shell out!'

This argument clinched matters, and the two carts with tall wheels and no springs started off at a trot, one to the right and the other to the left. At every bump and jolt the bodies of the two lovers, who were never to meet again, were tossed to and fro.

As soon as the Count had seen the hut well on its way down the steep slope, he had rushed away at top speed through the rain and the gale. He ran for several hours, taking short cuts, jumping over banks and breaking through hedges. He reached home about sunset somehow, he did not know how. The servants were waiting for him in a panic and told him that the two horses had just returned riderless, Julien's mount having followed the other. At that Monsieur de Fourville staggered and said in a broken voice: 'They must have had an accident in this ghastly weather. You must all go out and look for them.'

He went out again himself, but, as soon as he was out of sight, he hid among some rushes, keeping his eyes on the road, by which the woman whom he still loved passionately would soon return, dead or dying or perhaps crippled and disfigured for ever. Presently a cart passed with an unusual load. It stopped at the gate of the mansion and went in. It was what he was waiting for; it was *She*. But a paralysing anguish pinned him to the spot; he was afraid to know, terrified of the truth, and he stayed where he was like a hare in hiding, starting at every sound. He waited for an hour, perhaps two, but the cart did not come out again. He thought: 'My wife is dying,' and the idea of seeing her and meeting her eye filled him with such terror that he was suddenly afraid of being discovered in his hiding-place and having to go back and be present at her last moments, and he plunged into the depths of the wood. But suddenly he thought that perhaps she needed help, that there was no one to look after her, and he returned at full speed to the house. As he came in at the gate, he met a gardener and shouted:

'What news?' The man did not dare answer. Then de Four-ville, raising his voice, screamed: 'Is she dead?'

'Yes, Sir,' replied the servant.

He experienced a feeling of intense relief. A sudden peace calmed his blood, his muscles relaxed and he went up the ter-race steps firmly.

The other cart had reached the Poplars. Jeanne saw it in the distance and noticed the mattress; she guessed that a body lay upon it and realized the truth. Her emotion was overmastering and she fell to the ground in a dead faint. When she came to again, her father was holding her hand and chafing her temples with vinegar. He asked in a hesitant voice: 'You know ...' 'Yes, Papa,' she murmured. But when she tried to get up, she could not, she was in such pain. That very evening she was de-livered of a dead child, a girl.

She saw nothing of Julien's funeral; indeed she did not know that it had taken place. She was only aware after a day or two that Aunt Lison had come back and in the feverish nightmares that haunted her she tried obstinately to recall how long ago it was that the old lady had left the Poplars, at what date and under what circumstances, but she could not remember even in her lucid moments; she was only sure that she had seen her after Mama's death.

CHAPTER ELEVEN

For three months Jeanne was confined to her room, having become so weak and pale that she was thought, and even said, to be dying. But gradually she picked up; Papa and Aunt Lison were with her all the time, both of them having come to live at the Poplars. She had developed a nervous complaint from the shock and the least noise made her swoon; she fell into long fainting-fits from the most trivial causes. She had never asked for details of Julien's death. What did it matter to her? She knew enough. Everyone thought it had been an accident, but she was not deceived. She kept in her heart the secret of his adultery and the memory of that brief, terrible visit of the Count on the day of the catastrophe.

Her thoughts were now full of tender memories, sweet sad memories, of the short days of love which her husband had given her; she was always being startled by the unexpected awakening of the past in her mind, and she saw him again as he had been in the days of their engagement and also as she had loved him in the few short hours of sensual passion which she had known in the hot sun of Corsica. All his faults faded away, his hardness softened, even his infidelities diminished in importance when seen across the passage of time over the closed tomb. She felt a sort of gratitude to the man who had held her in his arms and forgave him for her past sufferings, thinking only of the moments of happiness. Also time was passing and months following months shed the powder of oblivion over all her recollections and sorrow like the accumulation of dust; and she devoted herself entirely to her son.

He became the idol, the only preoccupation of the three people round him; he was their tyrant. A sort of jealousy developed in the hearts of his three slaves; Jeanne watched nervously the long kisses which he gave the Baron after the rides enjoyed on his knees; and Aunt Lison, to whom he paid as little attention as everyone else and who was treated as a nurse-maid by the little tyrant who could hardly talk yet, used to go to her room to cry, when she compared the niggardly caresses, which she had to beg for and had difficulty in obtaining, with the hugs which he kept for his mother and grandfather.

Two uneventful years passed peacefully, while they devoted themselves entirely to looking after the child. At the beginning of winter they decided to move to the house in Rouen till the spring and there was a family migration. But when they reached the house, which had been empty and was damp, Paul had an attack of bronchitis so severe that it was feared that it might develop into pleurisy, and his three guardians declared in desperation that he could not do without the fresh air of the Poplars. As soon as he recovered, they took him back there.

Then several years elapsed without incident but very pleasantly. Always together round the boy, sometimes in his nursery, sometimes in the main drawing-room, sometimes in the garden, they went into raptures over his attempts to talk, his odd expressions and gestures. His mother called him 'Paulet' as a pet-name, but he could not pronounce it and called it 'Pullet', which always raised a laugh. The name Pullet stuck to him and he was never called anything else. As he was growing fast, one of the absorbing occupations of his three guardians, whom the Baron called his three mothers, was to measure his height. On the wainscoting near the drawing-room door they had drawn a series of small lines with a penknife showing his growth from month to month. This scale, called Pullet's ladder, played an important part in everyone's life.

There was also a new-comer, who occupied a considerable place in the family, the dog Murder; he had been neglected by Jeanne, who only thought of her son. Fed by Ludivine and housed in an old barrel near the stables, he lived a solitary life, always chained up. One morning Pullet noticed him and wanted to go and kiss him; very nervously they led him up to the dog, who proved friendly, and the child howled when they tried to take him away.

After that the animal was released and brought into the house. He and Pullet were soon inseparable; they rolled about together on the floor and slept side by side on the carpet. Murder was soon sleeping on his new friend's bed and the child would not be parted from him. Jeanne was sometimes worried about fleas, and Aunt Lison was jealous, because the dog monopolized the child's affection, feeling that an animal had stolen much of what she would have liked to enjoy.

Occasional calls were exchanged with the Brisevilles and the Couteliers, but the mayor and the doctor were the only regular intruders into the solitude of the old house. Since the killing of the bitch and the suspicions which Jeanne had conceived of the priest after the horrible death of Julien and the Countess, she had never entered the church again, angry with God for having such a servant. From time to time the Abbé Tolbiac hurled anathemas with direct allusions to the mansion, as haunted by the Evil One, the Spirit of Rebellion, the Spirit of Error and Falsehood, the Spirit of Iniquity, the Spirit of Corruption and Lust. That was how he referred to the Baron.

Moreover he had emptied his church, and when he walked about the fields where ploughing was going on, the peasants did not stop to speak to him or turn round to greet him. He had the reputation too of being a sorcerer, because he had driven out a devil which had possessed a woman. He knew, it was alleged, mysterious words to break spells, which he held were the Devil's little jokes; he laid hands on cows which gave blue milk or grew crooked tails, and by some unintelligible formula he enabled things which had been lost to be found. His narrow fanatical mind led him to a passionate study of religious literature dealing with apparitions of the Devil on earth, the different manifestations of his power, his various occult influences, all the means, the tricks and the wiles at his disposal. As he considered it his special vocation to combat this mysterious fatal power, he had learnt all the formulae of exorcism given in ecclesiastical textbooks. He was always imagining that he sensed the Evil One wandering about in the shadows, and he was always quoting the Latin tag 'Sicut leo rugiens circuit quaerens quem devoret'. (He goeth about like a roaring lion seeking whom he may devour.)

The neighbourhood began to be afraid of him, terrified of his occult powers. Even his fellow clergy, ignorant country priests with whom Beelzebub is an article of faith and who, worried by the intricate ritual laid down to deal with manifestations of the

Evil One, come to confuse religion with magic, regarded the Abbé Tolbiac as something of a sorcerer. They respected him as much for the occult powers which they believed him to possess as for the unassailable austerity of his life.

When he met Jeanne, he did not bow. The position worried and distressed Aunt Lison, who in her timid old maid's soul could not understand not going to church. No doubt she was pious and went to confession and communicated, but no one was aware of it or sought to find out. When she found herself alone with Paul, quite alone, she would talk to him in a low voice of God; he listened, not very interested, when she told him miraculous stories of the creation of the world; but when she told him that he must love God very, very much, he would ask: 'But where is He, Auntie?' She pointed to the sky with her finger: 'Up there in Heaven, Pullet, but you mustn't talk about it.' She was frightened of the Baron. But one day Pullet announced: 'God is everywhere, but He isn't in church.' He had been talking to his grandfather about his aunt's mysterious revelations.

The boy was now nearly ten and his mother looked like forty. He was a strong rough child, fearless in climbing trees, but he did not know much. Lessons bored him and he was always looking for an excuse to interrupt them. Whenever the Baron kept him longer than usual at his books, Jeanne used to come in and say: 'Do let him go and play; you mustn't tire him, he's so young.' She always thought of him as six months or a year old; she hardly realized that he could walk, run and talk like a little man. She was in a constant panic that he would fall down or catch cold or get overheated running about, or that he would eat too much for his digestion or too little for his growth.

When he was twelve, a great difficulty presented itself, the question of his first communion. Lison came to Jeanne one morning and pointed out that the child could not be left any longer without religious instruction and without carrying out his first duties. She argued the question from every side, giving many reasons and, most important of all, asking what their circle of friends would think. The mother, worried and unable to make up her mind, hesitated, saying that there was no hurry to decide.

But a month later, as she was paying a visit to the Vicomtesse de Briseville, the lady happened to say: 'I suppose your Paul will be making his first communion this year, won't he?' Jeanne, caught off her guard, replied: 'Yes, Madame.' That brief word settled the matter and without saying anything to her father she asked Lison to take the boy to the Catechism class. For a month all went well, but one evening Pullet came home with a sore throat and next day he had a cough. His mother asked him anxiously how he had got it and discovered that the priest had sent him to wait at the door of the church in the draughty porch till the end of the lesson, because he had misbehaved. So she kept him at home and taught him herself the ABC of religion. But the Abbé refused to admit him among the first communicants in spite of Lison's urgent request, on the ground that his instruction had been inadequate.

The same thing happened the following year. After this the Baron swore in exasperation that the child had no need to believe all this nonsense, the puerile mystery of transubstantiation, in order to be a decent man. It was decided that he should be brought up as a Christian but not as a practising Catholic and that he should be free to follow his own convictions, when he came of age.

Some time later Jeanne called on the Brisevilles, but the call was not returned. She was surprised, knowing the punctilious politeness of her neighbours, but the Marquise de Coutelier arrogantly explained the reason for this behaviour. Owing to her husband's position, her own well-established title and her considerable fortune, she regarded herself as a sort of queen of the Normandy nobility and ruled them like a queen, expressed her opinions freely, showed herself gracious or cutting as occasion dictated, gave advice, administered rebukes and offered congratulations without inhibitions.

So Jeanne called upon her, and after a few frigid remarks the Marquise said in a hard dry tone of voice: 'Society is divided into two classes, those who believe in God and those who do not. The former, even the humblest of them, are our friends and equals; for us the others do not exist.'

Jeanne, sensitive to this attack, replied: 'But surely one can believe in God without going to Church?'

The Marquise retorted: 'No, Madame; the faithful go to

church to pray to God, as one goes to a man's house to find him.'

Jeanne, hurt, replied: 'God is everywhere; as for me, who believe in His love from the bottom of my heart, I do not feel Him nearer to me when certain priests stand between Him and me.'

The Marquise got up, saying: 'The priest is the standard-bearer of the Church, Madame; whoever does not follow the standard is against God and against us.'

Jeanne got up too, furious: 'You believe, Madame, in the God of one party; I believe in the God of all decent folk,' and she bowed and left the house.

The villagers also criticized her in private for having prevented Pullet making his first communion. They were not regular church-goers themselves or regular communicants, only receiving the sacrament at Easter in obedience to the strict rule of the Church. But it was quite different with children; they would never have dared to bring up a child outside the pale of this universal law, just because religion was religion. Jeanne soon became aware of this criticism and reacted in her soul against all these compromises with conscience, this universal fear, the cowardice deep down in every heart, which wears the mask of respectability when it does reveal itself.

The Baron supervised Paul's schooling and started him on Latin. His mother offered only one piece of advice: 'Above all don't tire him.' She was always prowling anxiously round the schoolroom, Papa having forbidden her to come in, because she was continually interrupting the lesson to ask: 'Are you sure your feet aren't cold, Pullet?' or 'You haven't got a headache, have you?' or in order to stop his master: 'Don't make him talk so much; you'll strain his throat.'

As soon as the boy was free, he went out gardening with his mother and aunt; they had developed a passion for growing things, and they all three planted small shrubs in the spring and sowed seeds, whose shoots and sprouts thrilled them, pruned the branches and cut flowers to make bouquets. The boy's chief interest was lettuces; he kept three large beds in the kitchen-garden, where he very carefully raised lettuces, cos, succory, wild chicory, royals, in fact every known variety of edible salad. He hoed, weeded, pricked out, helped by his two mothers, whom he kept at work like farm-hands. One saw them for hours at a time on their knees in the beds, plastered with mud, their hands busy planting the roots of young plants in holes dug by sticking a finger straight into the earth.

Pullet was now growing fast; he was nearly fifteen, and the ladder in the drawing-room showed five feet, two and a quarter inches. But he was still a child in mind, ignorant and simple, stifled between the two skirts and the kindly old man who belonged to a past age. One evening the Baron talked of sending him to the High School; Jeanne immediately began to sob and Aunt Lison kept out of the way in a dark corner of the room. His mother protested: 'Why does he need to know such a lot? We'll make him an agriculturist, a gentleman-farmer. He will cultivate his property, as many noblemen do; he will live and grow old in this house, where we shall have preceded him and where we shall die. What more can he want?'

But the Baron shook his head: 'What will you say, when he comes to you at twenty-five and says; "I'm a nonentity, I know nothing, and it's all your fault, the fault of a mother's selfishness. I don't know how to work, I shall never be anyone; and yet I wasn't meant for a humble obscure existence, a life of deadly boredom, to which I am condemned by your blind affection"?'

She was always in tears, appealing to her son: 'Tell me, Pullet, you won't ever blame me for loving you too much, will you?'

'No, Mama,' replied the boy in surprise.

'You swear it?'

'Yes, Mama.'

'You want to stay at home here, don't you?'

'Yes, Mama.'

But the Baron took a firm stand and said emphatically: 'Jeanne, you have no right to dictate his life. What you are doing is cowardly, almost criminal; you are sacrificing your son to your own selfish happiness.'

She hid her face in her hands in a paroxysm of weeping and stammered through her tears: 'I've been so unhappy ... so terribly unhappy! Now that I am happy with him, he is to be taken away from me ... what will become of me ... all alone ... as I am now?'

Her father got up, came and sat by her side and took her in his arms : 'And what about me, Jeanne?'

She flung her arms round his neck, kissing him passionately and, still choking, she murmured in a strangled voice : 'Yes, you are right . . . perhaps . . . Papa dear. I was crazy, but I have suffered so much. I agree; let him go to High School.'

Without any clear idea of what was to happen to him, Pullet in his turn began to sob. Then his three mothers all kissed him, smothering him with caresses to cheer him up. When they went up to bed, they were all broken-hearted and cried in bed, even the Baron, who up till then had controlled himself. It was decided to send the boy to the High School at Le Havre at the start of the next school year; and all through the summer he was more spoilt than ever.

His mother was often unhappy at the prospect of the separation. She got his clothes ready as if he was going to be away for ten years. At last, one morning in October, after a sleepless night, the two women and the Baron got into the barouche with him and they set off at a trot behind the two horses. On a previous visit his place in dormitory and class-room had been chosen. Jeanne with Aunt Lison spent the day arranging his things neatly in the small chest of drawers. As there was not room in it for a quarter of what they had brought, she went to the Head Master to ask for a second one; the Bursar was sent for; he pointed out that so much linen and effects would only be in the way and serve no useful purpose, and he refused her request for a second chest of drawers, quoting the School rules. So in despair the mother decided to hire a room in a small hotel near by, instructing the proprietor to take round personally to Pullet at his first request anything that he might need. Then they strolled out to the pier to watch the boats going out and coming in.

The depressing gloom of evening was descending on the town, and lights were beginning to appear; they dined at a restaurant, but none of them had any appetite. They looked at each other with moist eyes, while the dishes were put before them and taken away almost untasted. After dinner they walked slowly back to the School. Boys of all ages were arriving from every direction, escorted by their families or by servants; many were in tears and the sound of sobs was audible all over the dimly lighted quadrangle.

Jeanne and Pullet had a long embrace, while Aunt Lison stood unheeded behind them, her face buried in her handkerchief. But the Baron, who was also beginning to show signs of emotion, cut short the farewells and dragged his daughter away. The barouche was waiting at the gate and they all three got in and drove back to the Poplars in the dark. The next day Jeanne spent in tears, and the following day she ordered the phaeton and set off for Le Havre. Pullet seemed quite reconciled to the separation. For the first time in his life he was with other boys of his own age and he was so eager to be out playing with them that he fidgeted on his chair in the Visitors' Room.

Jeanne went to the School every other day and every Sunday for their day out. Not having anything to do during school hours between the breaks, she stayed in the Visitors' Room, having neither the energy nor the courage to leave the school. The Head Master sent for her and asked her to come less often, but she paid no heed to his suggestion. He then warned her that, if she continued to prevent her son playing games in the recreation periods and getting on with his work by taking up his time with her frequent visits, the boy would have to be sent home. The Baron was also warned in an official letter. So she was kept under observation at the Poplars like a prisoner.

She looked forward to each holiday with greater eagerness than her son. She was becoming increasingly worried and began wandering about the countryside, going for long solitary walks with Murder, day-dreaming. Sometimes she would spend the whole afternoon sitting looking at the sea; sometimes she went down to Yport through the wood, repeating the walks of old days which she could not forget. What a long time it was since she had wandered through the countryside as a young girl intoxicated with dreams ! Every time she saw her son again, it seemed like ten years since the last time. He was growing up all the time and all the time she was aging. Her father was more like a brother now and Aunt Lison, who showed little sign of age, having lost the bloom of youth at twenty-five, was more like an elder sister.

Pullet was doing little work; he took two years to get through the Third Form; in the Fourth he did not do too badly, but he failed to get his remove from the Fifth and did not reach the Sixth till he was just on twenty. He had grown into a tall fair boy with sprouting whiskers and the beginnings of a moustache. It was now his turn to come over to the Poplars every Sunday. As he had been taking riding lessons for some time, he simply hired a horse and rode over in two hours. Jeanne went out quite early to meet him with Aunt Lison and the Baron, who was gradually becoming bent and walked like a little old man with hands clasped behind his back, as if to avoid falling forward on his nose. They walked slowly along the road, sometimes resting on the dyke, scanning the distance for a sight of the rider. As soon as the little black speck came into view on the white road, the three relatives waved their handkerchiefs; and he put his horse to the gallop and came up like a hurricane, terrifying Jeanne and Lison and pleasing Grandpapa who cried: 'Bravo!' with the enthusiasm of one whose riding days were past.

Although Paul was taller than his mother by a head, she still treated him as a small child, asking: 'You're not cold in the feet, are you, Pullet?', and when he was walking about in front of the terrace smoking a cigarette after lunch, she would open the window and call: 'Don't go out without a hat, *please*; you'll catch a cold in the head.' She was tortured with anxiety when he started to ride back in the dark: 'Don't go too fast, Pullet, darling; do be careful, think of your poor mother, who would be desperate if you had an accident.'

One Saturday morning she had a letter from Paul, saying that he would not be coming over next day, because some friends of his had arranged a picnic to which he had been invited. All Sunday she was in a fever of anxiety, as if some misfortune was threatening; on the Thursday, unable to endure it any longer, she set out for Le Havre. He seemed changed, though she could not say exactly how; he seemed in high spirits and his voice sounded more grown up. Suddenly he said as if it was something quite natural: 'Look, Mother, as you have come today I shan't come over to the Poplars next Sunday, because we are having some more fun.'

She was flabbergasted, struck dumb as if he were announcing

his departure for the New World. When she was able to find words, she said: 'Oh! Pullet, what's the matter with you? What's happening to you? You must tell me.'

He burst out laughing and kissed her: 'Nothing at all, Mama, absolutely nothing! I'm just going to have some fun with my friends, like all boys of my age.'

She remained tongue-tied and when she was alone in the carriage disturbing thoughts came into her head. She no longer recognized Pullet, the little Pullet of the past. For the first time she realized that he was grown up, that he no longer belonged to her, that he was going to live his own life without bothering about the old folk. In one day he had changed; could he still be her son, the child who had made her prick lettuces, this young man with a beard and a will of his own?

For the next three months Pullet only came home occasionally and was always obviously anxious to get back as early as possible; every evening he tried to leave an hour earlier. Jeanne was getting alarmed, but the Baron did his best to console her, repeating: 'Leave him alone; he's twenty now, remember.'

Shortly afterwards, one morning, an elderly man, shabbily dressed, came and asked for the Viscountess in French with a German accent. After lengthy formal greetings he took a dirty wallet from his pocket, saying: 'I've got a little piece of paper for you,' and he unfolded and handed to her a sheet of greasy paper. She read it over twice, looked at the Jew, read it a third time and asked: 'What does this mean?' The man in an obsequious tone of voice explained: 'I will tell you the whole story. Your son was in need of ready money and, as I knew you were a good mother, I lent him a little for his needs.' She was trembling: 'But why didn't he ask me?' The Jew explained that it was a matter of a gambling debt, which had to be paid the next day before noon, and that, as Paul was not yet of age, no one would have lent him the cash and 'his honour would have been compromised' without 'the little service' which he had rendered to the boy. Jeanne wanted to call the Baron, but was unable to get up, her emotion paralysing her legs. Finally she said to the money-lender: 'Will you kindly ring the bell?'

He hesitated, fearing some trick: 'If it is inconvenient to you, I will come back later.'

She shook her head. He rang and they both waited, facing each other. When the Baron came, he understood the position at once. The I.O.U. was for 1,500 francs. He gave the man 1,000 and said, looking him straight in the eye: 'And now don't come here again.' The Jew thanked him, bowed, and left.

Grandfather and Jeanne immediately went to Le Havre, but on reaching the school they learnt that Paul had not been there for a month. The Head Master had received four letters signed by Jeanne, saying that the boy was ill and giving full details; each letter was accompanied by a doctor's certificate – of course they were all forgeries. The two guardians were crushed and stood there looking at each other. The Head Master, much upset, took them to the Police Station. They spent the night at a hotel.

Next day the boy was found living with a prostitute in the town. His grandfather and mother took him back to the Poplars, not a word being exchanged between them on the drive home. Jeanne was weeping, with her face buried in her handkerchief; Paul was looking out of the window with no sign of emotion. During the week it was discovered that in the last three months he had run up debts to the extent of 15,000 francs; his creditors had kept out of sight, knowing that he would soon be of age.

No explanations were asked for; they were anxious to win him over by kindness. He was given the daintiest of food and generally coddled and spoilt. It was spring and they hired a yacht for him at Yport, so that he could go sailing when he liked, but he was not allowed a horse for fear he might go off to Le Havre. Having nothing to do he grew irritable and sometimes rude. The Baron was worried at the interruption of his school work; Jeanne, though distressed at the idea of being separated from him, wondered nevertheless what his future would be.

One evening he did not come back. They found out that he had gone out in a boat with two sailors. His mother, dreadfully upset, rushed down to Yport bare-headed in the dark. A few men were waiting about on the beach for the boat's return. A light appeared some way out and came in rocking on the swell. Paul was not on board; he had had himself taken to Le Havre. The police searched for him in vain. The girl who had sheltered him before had also vanished without a trace; her furniture had been sold and her rent paid up. In Paul's room at the Poplars two letters were found from her; she seemed to be madly in love with him and wrote of going to England; she had raised the money, she said. The three inmates of the mansion lived in dreary silence in a grim hell of mental torment. Jeanne's hair, already grey, had turned white; she wondered guilelessly why it was her fate to suffer in this way.

She received a letter from the Abbé Tolbiac: 'Madame, the hand of God has fallen heavily upon you. You refused to give your son to Him, and now He has taken him from you to throw him to a whore. Will you not open your eyes to this lesson from heaven? The pity of the Lord is infinite. Perhaps He will forgive you, if you return and kneel before Him. I am His humble servant and I will open the door of His house when you come and knock.'

She sat for a long time with the letter on her lap. Perhaps what the priest said was true; and all her religious doubts began to stir her conscience. Could God be vindictive and jealous like mankind? If He did not show himself a jealous God, no one would fear Him or worship Him any more. It was in order that we might understand Him better that He revealed Himself with human feelings to men. Cowardly doubt, which drives the hesitant and worried to church, entered into her heart, and one evening she ran secretly to the presbytery and kneeling at the feet of the thin priest begged for absolution. He promised her a partial pardon; God could not shower all His grace upon a house which sheltered a man like the Baron. 'You will soon,' he declared, 'feel the effect of the loving-kindness of the Lord.'

In fact two days later she got a letter from her son, and in the depth of her trouble she took it for the beginning of the consolation promised by the Abbé. 'Dear Mama,' it ran. 'Don't worry. I am in London, quite well, but I'm in desperate need of money. We haven't got a brass farthing left; we can't even afford to eat every day. The girl who is with me and whom I love with all my heart has spent all she had, 5,000 francs, in order to stay with me. You will realize that I am in honour bound to repay her this first of all. It would be very kind of you to advance me 15,000 francs out of Father's money, as I shall soon be of age. This would get me out of a very awkward mess.

Good-bye, my dear Mama; I send my love and kisses to you and Grandpapa and Aunt Lison – Looking forward to seeing you again soon, your son, the Vicomte Paul de Lamare.'

He had written to her; so he had not forgotten her. She never gave a thought to his request for money. As he needed it, the money would be sent. What did money matter anyhow? He had written to her. She hastened in tears to the Baron; Aunt Lison was called, and word by word they read over again the letter giving news of him, lingering over every phrase. Jeanne, rising from the depths of despair to the intoxication of hope, defended Paul : 'He'll come back; he'll certainly come back, as he has written.' The Baron more logically declared : 'I wonder. He left us for this slut; so he must love her more than us, as he had no hesitation.'

A sudden piercing pain smote Jeanne's heart, and in a moment the flame of hatred was kindled in her against the mistress, who was stealing her son away from her, a fierce implacable hatred, the hatred of a jealous mother. Hitherto she had only thought of Paul, she had hardly given a thought to the girl, who had been the cause of his peccadillo. But suddenly the Baron's re-mark had called up the picture of her rival and revealed her fatal power. She felt that between this woman and herself a desperate struggle was beginning, and she felt too that she would rather lose her son than share him with another. All her happi-ness collapsed. They sent the 15,000 francs and heard nothing for five months.

Then one day the solicitor called to arrange the details of the probate on Julien's will. Jeanne and the Baron produced the figures without discussion, even giving up the mother's life interest. On his return to Paris Paul received 120,000 francs. After that he wrote four letters in six months, giving his news briefly and ending with a chilly expression of affection.

'I am working,' he wrote, 'I've got a job on the Stock Ex-change. I hope to come and kiss you at the Poplars one day, my dear parents.'

He did not mention his mistress, and this silence was more eloquent than a four-page letter. In these frigid letters Jeanne felt this woman entrenched, implacable, the prostitute, the eternal enemy of every mother. The three solitary old people had long discussions as to what could be done to save Paul, but they could think of nothing. Should they go to Paris? What good would that do? The Baron used to say: 'We must leave him alone till his infatuation cools; then he'll come back of his own accord.'

Their dreary life continued and a considerable time elapsed without news. At last one morning a desperate letter threw them all into a panic. It ran: 'My poor Mama, I am lost, I can only blow my brains out, unless you come to my rescue. A speculation, which seemed to have every chance of success, has failed, and I owe 85,000 francs. If I don't pay, it means disgrace, ruin; I can never get another job. I am lost. I tell you again, I'll blow my brains out rather than live in disgrace. I should probably have done so already without the encouragement of a woman, of whom I never speak but who is my Good Angel. I send you all my love, dearest Mama – perhaps for the last time. Good-bye, Paul.'

Some bundles of business papers enclosed with the letter gave details of the disaster. The Baron replied by return of post that he would see what could be done, and went off to Le Havre to arrange things. He mortgaged his landed property and the money was sent. The young man replied with three letters of lyrical gratitude and passionate affection; he would come, he said, quite soon to thank his beloved parents; but he never came.

A whole year passed. Jeanne and the Baron were on the point of going to Paris to try and find him and make a last effort to save him, when they heard that he was in London again, floating a steamship company registered as 'Paul Delamare and Company'. He wrote: 'Success, perhaps wealth, is assured. I am risking nothing; that will show you how good the prospects are. When I see you again, I shall have a fine position in the business world. Business is the only way to keep out of difficulties nowadays.'

Three months later the steamship company went bankrupt, and the managing director was prosecuted for irregularities in the book-keeping. Jeanne had a nervous breakdown and took to her bed. The Baron went off again to Le Havre to investigate the matter. He saw barristers, business men, solicitors and bailiffs, and discovered that the debts of the Delamare Company amounted to 235,000 francs. He mortgaged more of his property, including the Poplars, for a large sum.

One evening, as he was completing the last formalities in his solicitor's office, he collapsed in an apoplectic fit. A man on horseback was sent to inform Jeanne. When she got there, he was dead. She brought the body back to the Poplars, so prostrated that her condition was one of unconsciousness rather than despair. The Abbé Tolbiac refused to allow the body into the church in spite of the frenzied appeals of the two women, and the Baron was buried at nightfall without any religious ceremony. Paul learnt of what had happened from one of the officials in charge of the liquidation proceedings of the Company. He was still in hiding in England. He wrote making excuses for his absence; he had not heard of the misfortune in time. 'Besides, now that you have got me out of the mess, my dear Mama, I am returning to France, and I shall soon be with you. I send my love.' Jeanne was in such a state of nervous exhaustion that she did not seem able to take anything in.

Towards the end of the winter Aunt Lison caught bronchitis, which developed into pneumonia, and she died peacefully, murmuring : 'My poor little Jeanne, I will implore God in His mercy to take pity on you.'

Jeanne followed her body to the cemetery and saw the earth fall upon the coffin. As she was on the point of collapsing from a heartfelt desire to die herself, to suffer no more, to think no more, a sturdy peasant woman caught her in her arms and carried her away, as if she had been a small child. Back at the house, Jeanne, who had just spent five nights at the old lady's bed-side, made no resistance when the unknown countrywoman, handling her gently but masterfully, put her to bed, where she fell into the sleep of exhaustion, overcome by weariness and grief.

She woke up about midnight. There was a night-light burning on the chimney-piece and a woman was asleep in an armchair. Who was she? Jeanne did not recognize her and leaning out of bed she tried to get a better view of her features in the flickering light of the wick floating in oil in a kitchen glass. However, she had a feeling that she had seen that face before. But where and when? The woman was sleeping peacefully, her head resting on one shoulder and her cap fallen on the floor; her large hands were hanging down on both sides of the chair and her hair was going grey. Jeanne gazed long at her in that confusion of mind which follows a great shock. She had certainly seen that face before. Was it long ago or lately? She did not know; and she wanted to know, her uncertainty worried her. She got out of bed to take a closer look at the sleeping woman and moved towards her on tiptoe. It was the woman who had picked her up in the cemetery and put her to bed; she remembered that vaguely. But hadn't she seen her elsewhere at some other time in her life? Or was it only the confused recollection of the previous day that made her think that she recognized her? But how did she come to be in her bedroom? What was she doing there?

The woman opened an eye, saw Jeanne and sat up quickly. They were facing each other so close that their breasts were almost touching. The stranger growled: 'Hullo! Why are you out of bed? You'll catch cold at this time of night. Get back to bed!'

'Who are you?' asked Jeanne.

The woman, throwing her arms round her, picked her up again and carried her back to bed with the strength of a man. As she laid her down gently on the bed, leaning over her, almost lying on top of her, she burst into tears and began to kiss her passionately on cheeks, hair and eyes, wetting her face with her tears and stammering: 'My poor Mistress, Madame Jeanne, my poor Mistress, don't you even know me?'

Jeanne suddenly cried: 'Rosalie, my dear girl!' and putting her arms round her neck, she embraced and kissed her; and they both sobbed, embracing and mingling their tears, unable to let each other go.

Rosalie recovered herself first: 'Come now! We must be sensible and not catch cold!'

She picked up the blankets, remade the bed and replaced the pillow under her mistress's head. Jeanne, still choking, stirred by memories that awakened in her mind, at last asked: 'How do you come to be here again, my poor girl?'

'Do you think I could leave you like that, all alone now?' replied Rosalie.

Jeanne went on: 'Light a candle, so that I can see you.'

When the light had been put on the night-table, they looked at each other for a long time without a word; then, holding out her hand to her old maid, Jeanne murmured: 'I should never have known you, my dear girl; you have changed a lot, you know, but not as much as I have.'

Rosalie, looking at this white-haired woman, emaciated and faded, whom she had left in the bloom of her youth and beauty, replied: 'It's true, you are changed, Madame Jeanne, but remember it is twenty-four years since we last saw each other.'

They said no more, thinking of the past. Finally Jeanne stammered: 'Have you at least been happy?'

Rosalie, hesitating for fear of raising too painful memories, faltered: 'Oh, yes ... yes, Madame! I've not got much to complain of; I'm sure I've been happier than you. There's only one thing I've always regretted, that I didn't stay here,' and she stopped abruptly, sorry for this unthinking remark. But Jeanne replied gently: 'What would you, my dear? One can't always do what one wants. You have lost your husband too, haven't you?' And she went on, her voice trembling with anxiety: 'Have you had other ... other children?'

'No, Madame.'

'And he, your ... your son, what has happened to him? Are you pleased with him?'

'Yes, Madame, he's a good lad and is a real hard worker; he was married six months ago and he's taking on a farm of his own, now that I am back here with you.'

Jeanne trembling with emotion murmured: 'Then you're staying with me, my dear?'

Rosalie replied emphatically: 'Certainly, Madame; I've made all my arrangements to stay.'

For some time nothing further was said. In spite of herself Jeanne could not help comparing their lives, but with no bitterness in her heart; she was resigned to the cruelty of her fate. She went on: 'And your husband? Did he make you happy?'

'Oh, he was quite a good sort, a hard worker, who did well for himself. He died of pneumonia.'

Jeanne, sitting up in bed, wanted to know the whole story and said: 'Come now, tell me everything, my dear girl, all about your life. It will do me good after all I have suffered.'

Rosalie, bringing up a chair, sat down and began to talk of herself; she described her house with all the little details that peasants love, sometimes laughing at incidents long past, which recalled happy moments, gradually raising her voice like a farmer's wife accustomed to command. She ended by saying: 'Oh, I'm quite well off nowadays; I've nothing to fear.' Then, worried, she added in a lower voice: 'All the same I owe everything to you. You know I'm not taking any wages. Certainly not! I couldn't. If you don't agree, I'll go away.'

Jeanne replied: 'But you don't mean that you'll be my servant without wages.'

'Yes, I do, Madame. Money! The idea of you giving me money! I expect I've got quite as much as you. Do you know how much you've got now, with your mass of mortgages and borrowings and unpaid interest piling up every quarter? Do you know? No, you don't. Well, I assure you, you've only got 10,000 francs a year coming in, less than 10,000, I tell you. I'm going to take charge of your finances straightaway.'

She had begun to raise her voice again, getting quite worked up about the unpaid interest and the bankruptcy threatening Jeanne. As a faint good-natured smile flickered across her mistress's face, she cried quite crossly: 'It's nothing to laugh about, Madame; without money we're good for nothing.'

Jeanne took her hands and held them, and said slowly, obsessed by her one thought: 'Oh, I've had no luck. Everything has gone wrong in my life. Fate has got a grudge against me.'

Rosalie shook her head: 'You mustn't say that, Madame, you mustn't say that. You made a mistake over your marriage, that's all. One oughtn't to marry as you did, without knowing the sort of man one is marrying.'

They went on talking about themselves like old friends and were still talking when the sun rose.

CHAPTER TWELVE

In a week Rosalie had assumed complete control of everything and everybody at the mansion. Jeanne, quite resigned, was her obedient servant. Weak and dragging her feet, as Mama had done in days gone by, she went out on her maid's arm for gentle walks, while Rosalie lectured and encouraged her in kindly but brusque terms, treating her like a sick child. They always talked of the past, Jeanne with a sob in her throat, Rosalie in a peasant's matter-of-fact tone. The old servant often came back to the question of the interest in abeyance, and later she insisted on having the custody of all the documents, which Jeanne, who knew nothing of business affairs, kept out of sight, being ashamed for her son. Then every day for a whole week she went to Fécamp to have everything explained to her by a lawyer of her acquaintance.

After this, one evening, having put her mistress to bed, she sat down by the bedside, saying curtly: 'Now that you're in bed, Madame, we must have a talk,' and she explained the financial position. When everything was settled, there would be an income of between 7,000 and 8,000 francs left, no more.

'Well, what does it matter, my girl,' replied Jeanne, 'I'm sure I shan't make old bones. There will always be enough for me.'

Rosalie got annoyed: 'Perhaps enough for you, but what about Monsieur Paul? Won't you want to leave him anything?'

Jeanne shivered: 'Don't ever speak to me of him, please; the thought is too painful.'

'On the contrary, it is precisely about him that I want to speak to you. You see, you are a coward, Madame Jeanne; he is playing the fool now, but he won't go on doing that always. Later on he'll marry and have children; and there will have to be money to bring them up. Listen to me now; you've got to sell the Poplars.'

Jeanne sat up in bed with a start: 'Sell the Poplars! What are you thinking about? Oh no! I'll never do that, never!'

But Rosalie was not impressed: 'I tell you, you will sell the house, Madame, because you must.'

She explained her plans, giving the figures and her reasons. Having once sold the Poplars and the two farms attached to it to a purchaser whom she had found, they would keep four farms in Saint-Léonard, which, freed from mortgages, would bring in an income of 8,300 francs. 1,300 francs a year would be set aside for upkeep and repairs; that would leave 7,000 francs, of which they would take 5,000 for current expenses, and 2,000 would be left over to form a reserve fund. She added: 'All the rest has been frittered away and thrown down the drain. I shall keep the key, you understand. As for Monsieur Paul, from now on there will be nothing more for him, absolutely nothing. He would clear you out to your last farthing.'

Jeanne, who was crying quietly, murmured: 'But suppose he is starving?'

'If he's hungry, he'll come to us for food. There'll always be a bed for him and a dish of stew. Do you imagine that he would have played the fool as he has done, if you hadn't given him the wherewithal at the start?'

'But he had debts; he would have been disgraced.'

'When you have nothing left, will that prevent him getting into debt? You have paid his debts; well and good, but you won't do so any more. I mean what I say. Now good night, Madame.'

With that she left the room. Jeanne did not sleep that night, she was so upset at the thought of selling the Poplars and going away, leaving the house with which her whole life had been bound up. When she saw Rosalie come into her room next morning, she said to her: 'My poor girl, I shall never be able to make up my mind to leave here.'

But the maid lost her temper: 'But, Madame, there is no other way. The solicitor will be here presently with the prospective purchaser. Without this money, in four years you won't have a bean.'

Still overwhelmed, Jeanne could only repeat: 'I just can't do it; I shall never be able to sell this house!'

An hour later the postman brought her a letter from Paul asking for another 10,000 francs. What was she to do? Distraught, she consulted Rosalie, who threw up her arms, crying: 'What did I tell you, Madame? You would both of you have been properly in the soup, if I hadn't come back.'

So Jeanne, bowing to the maid's iron will, answered her son: 'My dear son, I can't do any more for you; you have ruined me. I find myself compelled to sell the Poplars. But never forget that I shall always have a shelter to offer you, when you are willing to seek refuge with your old mother, to whom you have caused so much suffering. Jeanne.

When the lawyer arrived with Monsieur Jeoffrin, a retired sugar-refiner, she received them herself and invited them to inspect the mansion in detail. A month later she signed the contract for the sale and at the same time bought a small middle-class house near Goderville on the main road to Montivilliers in the hamlet of Batteville. Then till the evening she walked up and down 'Mama's drive' by herself, her heart bleeding and in deep distress; she addressed desperate, tearful farewells to the distant view, to the trees, to the worm-eaten bench under the plane, to all the things she knew so well that they seemed to have entered into her eyes and her very soul, to the shrubbery, to the bank overlooking the common, where she had so often sat and from which she had seen the Comte de Fourville hurrying towards the sea on the terrible day of Julien's death, to an old topped elm against which she had often leant, and to the whole well-loved garden. Rosalie had to come and take her by the arm to force her to come in.

A sturdy peasant boy of twenty-five was waiting for her at the door. He greeted her in friendly fashion, as if he had known her for years: 'Good day, Madame Jeanne! I hope you are quite well! Mother told me to come and see about the move. I want to know what you're taking with you, so that I can do the job at intervals without interrupting my work on the farm.'

It was Rosalie's son, Julien's son and Paul's brother. Her heart seemed to stop beating, and yet she would have liked to kiss him. She looked at him to see if he was like her husband or her son. He was red-faced and strongly built, with fair hair and his mother's blue eyes. Yet he had a look of Julien. How was it? What gave him that look? She could not define it, but there was something of Julien in the general cast of his countenance.

The young man went on : 'It would help if you could show me now what you are taking.'

But she did not know yet what she would decide to take, as her new house was quite small, and she asked him to come back in a week. After that her days were fully occupied with the move, which offered her a depressing distraction in her dreary life with so little to look forward to.

She went from room to room, looking for pieces of furniture which reminded her of events, those friendly pieces which are part of our life, almost of ourselves, which we have known since our young days and which have gathered round them sad or happy memories of dates in our life, which have been the dumb companions of our hours of joy or sadness, which have grown old along with us and been worn out, whose material is split in places and their lining torn, whose joints creak and whose colour is faded.

She chose them one by one, often hesitating and worried as one is before taking important decisions, and continually changing her mind, weighing the points of two arm-chairs or some old writing-desk against a work-table. She opened drawers, trying to remember the history of their contents. At last when she had definitely made up her mind, she would say : 'Yes, I'll take this,' and it was taken down to the dining-room. She wanted to take everything from her own room, her bed, her tapestries, her clock, everything.

She took some of the drawing-room chairs, those whose patterns she had loved since her earliest childhood, the fox and the stork, the fox and the crow, the grasshopper and the ant, and the melancholy heron.

Then as she was wandering round the odd corners of the house which she was leaving, she went up one day to the attic. There she paused in astonishment; it was a jumble of all manner of things, some broken, some only soiled, others that had been taken up there for no known reason, just because people had got tired of them or because they had been replaced. She saw a thousand knick-knacks, which she had known in former days and which had suddenly vanished unremarked, things which she had handled, trivial little things that had been lying about round her for fifteen years, which she had seen every day without noticing them, and which, when suddenly found again in the attic among others yet older, whose places she remembered in her first days in the house, now assumed the importance of forgotten witnesses of the past and old friends found again. They impressed her like people whom one has known slightly for a long time and who suddenly one evening for no particular reason begin to talk and reveal all the secrets of their life.

She went from one thing to another, experiencing frequent shocks, saying to herself : 'Look ! There's the little cup I cracked one evening a few days before my wedding. Ah ! there's Mama's lantern and the stick which Papa broke trying to force open the garden gate, when the wood had swollen in the rain.' There were also many things in the room which she did not recognize and which recalled no memories; they went back to the days of her grandparents or great-grandparents; they were some of those dust-covered relics which look like exiles in an age quite strange to them. Sad in their loneliness, no one knows their life-story, for no one knows those who chose them, bought them, owned them, loved them and handled them every day and liked to see them about.

Jeanne touched them and turned them round, dirtying her fingers in the accumulated dust; and she spent a long time there, surrounded by these old things in the dim light which came in through small panes of glass let into the roof. She examined minutely some three-legged stools, trying to think whether they recalled any memories, a copper warming-pan, a battered foot-warmer which she thought she remembered, and a mass of worn-out household utensils. Finally she made a pile of the things which she wanted to take, and coming downstairs she sent Rosalie to fetch them. The maid indignantly refused to bring down 'all this trash !' But Jeanne, though she no longer had any will of her own, insisted this time and got her own way.

One morning the young farmer, Julien's son, Denis Lecoq, came with his cart to take the first load. Rosalie went with him to superintend the unpacking and see that the things were put in the rooms which they were to occupy. Left alone, Jeanne wandered through the rooms of the mansion, plunged in despair; in a rush of passionate affection she kissed all the things which she could not take with her, the great white birds on the drawing-room tapestry, the old candelabra, everything that she found there. She went from room to room, distraught, with tears running down her cheeks; then she went out 'to say good-bye to the sea'.

It was late September, and a lowering grey sky lay heavy on the world, and dreary yellowish waves stretched away to the horizon. She stood for a long time on the cliff, her head full of poignant thoughts. At nightfall she returned, having suffered as much that day as in her worst moments. Rosalie had come back and was waiting for her, delighted with the new house; it was a much more cheerful place, she declared, than the grim old mansion, whose only advantage was that it was not on a main road. Jeanne spent the evening in tears.

Since they had known of the sale of the house, the farmers around had only treated her with a minimum of respect, calling her among themselves 'the Mad Woman', not knowing exactly why, probably because they guessed with their animal instinct her increasingly morbid sentimentality, her quixotic dreams, and all the confusion of her sad mind induced by her misfortunes.

The evening before she was to leave she went by chance into the stable. A growl made her start; it was Murder, whom she had entirely forgotten for months. Blind and paralysed, having reached an age which dogs of his breed seldom attain, he lived on a bed of straw, looked after by Ludivine, who never forgot him. Jeanne picked him up, fondled him and carried him into the house. Fat as a barrel, he could hardly drag himself about. His legs were straddling and stiff, and he barked like the toy wooden dogs which children play with.

The last day dawned. Jeanne had slept in Julien's room, her own having been dismantled. She got up exhausted and breathing hard as if she had been running. The cart with her trunks and the rest of the furniture was already loaded in the court-yard. A two-wheeled trap had also been harnessed behind to take the mistress and her maid. Old Simon and Ludivine were to stay there by themselves till the new owner arrived; then they were to go and live with relations, as Jeanne had given them a small pension and they had savings of their own too.

They were old now and past work and very talkative. Marius had married and left some time before.

About eight o'clock it began to rain, a fine chilly rain, driven by a light sea-breeze; the cart had to be covered with rugs. The leaves were already beginning to fall. Cups of white coffee were steaming on the kitchen table. Jeanne sat down before her cup and drank it in little sips; then, getting up, she said: 'Come! Let's be off!'

She put on her hat and shawl and, while Rosalie was putting her into her gum-boots, she said with a tightening in the throat: 'My dear girl, do you remember how it rained the day we left Rouen to come here?'

As she spoke, she had a sort of spasm, pressed both hands to her breast and fell back unconscious. For an hour she lay in a faint and, when she opened her eyes, she was seized with convulsions, accompanied by floods of tears. When she recovered a little, she was so weak that she could not stand. But Rosalie, afraid of another attack if they postponed their departure, went and fetched her son. They took hold of her, picked her up and carried her to the cart, putting her down on a wooden seat covered with waxed leather; and the old maid, getting in by her side, wrapped up her legs and covered her shoulders with a heavy cloak and, holding an umbrella over her head, cried: 'Quick, Denis! Let's be off!' The young man climbed up beside his mother and, balancing on one thigh, as there was no more room, started the horses off at a trot, jolting the two women up and down.

As they turned a corner in the village, they saw a figure wandering along the road; it was the Abbé Tolbiac, who seemed to be looking out for their departure. He stopped to let the cart pass. He was holding up his cassock with one hand to keep it out of the puddles on the road and his spindly legs in black stockings disappeared into huge muddy clogs. Jeanne lowered her head to avoid meeting his eye, and Rosalie, who knew the whole story, lost her temper, murmuring: 'Good-for-nothing wretch!' Seizing her son's hand she cried: 'Give him a good slash with your whip!' But the young man, just as he was passing the priest, made the wheel of the ramshackle old cart suddenly lurch at full speed into a rut, and a spray of muddy water squirted up and drenched the priest from head to foot. Rosalie was delighted and turned round to shake her fist at him, while the Abbé mopped himself with his large handkerchief.

They had been going for five minutes when Jeanne suddenly cried: 'We've forgotten Murder!' They had to stop, and Denis got down and ran back to get the dog, while Rosalie held the reins. At last the young man returned carrying the enormous, hairless, ugly animal, which he put down between the skirts of the two women.

CHAPTER THIRTEEN

Two hours later the cart stopped in front of a small brick house in the middle of an orchard planted with trellis-trained pear-trees on the edge of the main road. Four lattice-work arbours covered with honeysuckle and clematis formed the four corners of the garden, which was divided into small vegetable plots separated by narrow paths bordered with fruit-trees.

A very high quickset hedge surrounded the whole property, which was separated from the next farm by a meadow. There was a forge a hundred yards up the road. The other nearest houses were about half a mile away. The view from the house extended in all directions over the plain of Caux, which was dotted with farms ringed with four double lines of tall trees round the apple-orchards.

As soon as she arrived, Jeanne wanted to rest, but Rosalie would not let her, being afraid that she would start day-dreaming. The carpenter from Goderville was there to help with the move, and they began straightaway with the arrangement of the furniture already there, pending the arrival of the last cart. It was a long job, demanding much thought and long arguments. An hour later the cart appeared at the garden gate and had to be unpacked in the rain. By evening the house was in complete disorder, full of things piled up anyhow, and Jeanne was so harassed that she fell asleep as soon as she got into bed.

She was kept so busy the following days that she had no time for sentimental regrets. She even took a certain pleasure in making her new house pretty, the thought that her son would come back to it being always in her mind. The tapestries from her room were put up in the dining-room, which also served as a drawing-room; and she arranged one of the two first-floor rooms with particular care, thinking of it as 'Pullet's suite'. The second room she kept for herself, while Rosalie settled in on the floor above, next to the attic. The little house, carefully arranged, was attractive, and Jeanne took to it from the start, though there was something missing which she could not define.

One morning the solicitor's clerk from Fécamp brought her 3,600 francs, the price of the furniture left at the Poplars according to an upholsterer's estimate. The receipt of this money sent a thrill of pleasure through her and, as soon as the man had left, she lost no time in putting on her hat, meaning to go to Goderville as quickly as possible, in order to send this unexpected windfall off to Paul. But as she was hurrying along the main road, she met Rosalie coming back from market. The maid had her suspicions, though she had not guessed the whole truth, but when she discovered it, for Jeanne could keep nothing from her, she put her basket down on the ground in order to lose her temper in comfort. With fists clenched on her hips she raised her voice, and seizing her mistress with her right hand and picking up her basket with her left, she continued on her way home.

When they reached the house, the maid demanded the money. Jeanne handed it over, keeping the 600 francs, but her trick was soon detected by the maid, who was now very suspicious, and she had to give up the whole sum. However, Rosalie consented to the odd 600 francs being sent to the boy. A few days later he wrote to thank her : 'My dear Mother, you have rendered me a great service; we were stony broke.'

But Jeanne could not get quite used to Batteville; she always felt that she could not breathe as freely as before, that she was even more lonely, more deserted, more lost. She would go out for a walk, reach the hamlet of Verneuil and return by the Three Ponds, and no sooner was she home than she would get up, seized by a desire to go out again, as if she had forgotten to go just where she had intended and really wanted to go. It was the same thing every day, and she could not understand the reason for this strange longing. But one evening a phrase came into her mind quite unconsciously, which explained the cause of her restlessness. As she sat down to dinner she said : 'Oh ! how I miss the sea !' What was so painfully lacking was the sea, her mighty neighbour for twenty-five years, the sea with its salty air, its storms, the thunder of its waves, the sea which she had looked at every morning from her window at the Poplars, whose air she had breathed day and night, which she had felt close to her and which unconsciously she had come to love like a human being.

Murder too was equally unable to settle down. On his first evening in the house he had taken up his abode in the lower part of the kitchen dresser and refused to budge. He lay there hardly moving, only turning over at intervals with a low growl. But as soon as it got dark, he staggered up and dragged himself to the garden door, bumping against the walls. When he had been out for the few minutes needed for his business, he came in again and sat down on his tail in front of the still warm range, and as soon as his two mistresses had gone up to bed, he began to howl. He went on giving tongue all night with a plaintive, piteous howling, sometimes pausing for an hour, only to begin again with even more heartrending moans. They chained him up in a barrel in front of the house, but as he was ill and had not long to live, they soon put him back in the kitchen.

Sleep became impossible for Jeanne, who heard the old dog moaning and scratching all the time, unable to get his bearings in this new house, realizing that it was not the house he knew. Nothing would keep him quiet. After dozing all day, as if his failing sight and increased feebleness made movement impossible when all other living creatures were alive and active, he began to wander round ceaselessly as soon as night began to fall, as if he dared to live and move only in the hours of darkness, when all creatures are equally blind. One morning he was found dead, to everyone's great relief.

Winter was passing and Jeanne was overwhelmed with increasing hopeless despair. It was not an acute pain torturing the mind, but a weary mournful sadness. There was nothing to distract her and draw her out of herself; no one took any notice of her. The high road in front of the house stretched to right and left, almost always deserted. From time to time a gig trotted past driven by a red-faced man, whose blue smock, puffed out by the wind raised by his speed, ballooned out behind him; sometimes it was a slow-moving cart; or again one might see two peasants, a man and a woman, approaching in the distance. At first they were just two dots on the horizon, presently they grew larger, then after passing the house they grew smaller again, till they were no bigger than two flies far away on the long white road, which went on and on as far as one could see, up and down according to the undulations of the ground. When the grass began to grow again, a young girl with a skirt above her knees used to pass the garden every morning driving two skinny cows, which grazed along the road-side ditches; she returned every evening with the same dawdling gait, taking a step forward every ten minutes behind her animals.

Every night Jeanne dreamt that she was still at the Poplars. She was there as in the old days with Papa and Mama and sometimes even with Aunt Lison; and she did over again all the little things now forgotten and done with. She saw herself supporting Madame Adélaïde as she walked up and down her drive, and on waking up she always burst into tears.

She was continually thinking of Paul, wondering: 'What is he doing? How is he today? Does he think of me sometimes?' She walked slowly along the sunken roads between the farms, pondering in her mind all the ideas that gave her so much pain. But she suffered most of all from an insatiable jealousy of that unknown woman who had robbed her of her son. It was only this hatred that held her back and prevented her from acting, from going to look for him and finding her way to his house. She pictured this mistress standing at the door and asking: 'And what do you want here, Madame?' Her mother's pride revolted against the possibility of such an encounter, and the arrogant pride of a woman who has always been chaste, who has never made a slip, who has always been free from any taint, exasperated her more and more against the dastardly behaviour of man, who is the slave of all the bestial practices of the fleshly lusts, which corrupt the heart as well as the body. Human nature itself seemed to her obscene, when she thought of all the filthy secrets of sensuality, the degrading caresses, all the mysterious connexions that cannot be broken off, at which she guessed.

Spring and summer came and passed. But when autumn came with its weeks of rain, grey skies and heavy clouds, she became so tired of the life she was living that she determined to make a supreme effort to recover her Pullet; the young man's infatuation must surely be spent.

She wrote a tearful letter: 'My dear Boy, I am writing to implore you to come back to me. Remember I am old now and ill, entirely alone all the year round with one maid. I'm now living in a small house on a main road. It is very depressing, but if you were here, everything would be quite different for me. I have no one but you in the world, and I haven't seen you for seven years. You will never know how unhappy I have been and how entirely wrapped up in you I am. You were my life, my dream, my only hope, my only love, and you have failed me and deserted me. Do come back, my darling Pullet, come back and kiss me, come back to your old mother, who stretches out her arms to you in despair. Jeanne.'

A few days later he wrote back: 'My dear Mother, I should like nothing better than to come and see you, but I'm stony broke. Send me the money and I'll come. I've been meaning to come and find you to discuss a plan which would allow me to do exactly what you ask. The disinterested love of the woman who has been my helpmate in the bad times I am going through remains boundless towards me. I cannot remain longer without making public acknowledgement of her faithful love and devotion. Moreover her manners are such as you would appreciate; she is well educated and is a great reader. In fact you have no idea what she has always been to me. I should be a callous brute, if I did not show my gratitude. I therefore formally ask your permission to marry her. You would forgive my peccadilloes and we would all live together in your new house. If you knew her, you would give your consent immediately. I assure you, she is faultless, a perfect lady. You would love her, I am certain. As for me, I could not live without her. I await your answer anxiously, my darling Mother, and we both send our love and kisses. Your son, the Vicomte Paul de Lamare.'

Jeanne was completely crushed. She sat without moving with the letter on her lap, guessing the wiles of this woman, who had kept such a close hold on her son and never once let him come and see her – waiting for her chance, when the old mother, in desperation, no longer able to resist her longing to embrace her son, would weaken and consent to everything. Poignant grief at Paul's obstinate infatuation for this slut pierced her to the heart; she kept saying to herself: 'He doesn't love me! He doesn't love me!'

Rosalie came in and Jeanne stammered: 'Now he wants to

marry her!' The maid started in surprise: 'Oh, Madame, you'll never allow that! Monsieur Paul can't go and pick up that girl out of the gutter!'

Jeanne, overwhelmed but revolted at the idea, replied: 'No, I'll never allow it, my girl; and since he won't come to me, I'll go and find him, and we shall see which of us two will win the battle.'

She wrote immediately to Paul, saying that she was coming to Paris and wanted to see him, but not in the lodgings where that slut lived.

While waiting for Paul's answer she made her preparations. Rosalie was packing her mistress's underwear and dresses in an old trunk, but as she was folding one of the dresses, an old country frock, she cried: 'The trouble is, you've got nothing to wear. I can't let you go like this. Everyone would be ashamed of you. The ladies in Paris would take you for a servant.'

Jeanne let her have her way and the two women went to Goderville, where they chose a green check material, which was left with the dressmaker to be made up. From there they went to the solicitor, Maître Roussel, who went to Paris for a fortnight every year, to get information from him, as Jeanne had not been in Paris for twenty-eight years. He gave them all sorts of advice, how to avoid the traffic and how to escape pickpockets, telling her to sew her money up in the lining of her dress and only keep in her pocket what was immediately necessary. He gave full details of moderately priced restaurants, mentioning two or three where women went; and he suggested the Hôtel de Normandie near the railway terminus, where he used to stay himself; she could mention his name there.

The railway that everyone was talking about had been running for six years between Paris and Le Havre, but Jeanne in the depths of her grief had never even seen one of these steam trains, which were revolutionizing the country. Meanwhile there was no answer from Paul. She waited a week, then a fortnight, going to meet the postman every morning and asking him, quivering with excitement: 'Haven't you got anything for me today, Malandain?' But he invariably replied in a voice hoarse from exposure to bad weather: 'No, still nothing, my dear lady!' It was certainly that woman who was preventing Paul from answering! So Jeanne made up her mind to go at once. She wanted to take Rosalie with her, but the maid refused to go, in order to cut down the expenses of the trip. Moreover she only allowed her mistress to take 300 francs with her : 'If you need more, just write and I'll get the solicitor to send it to you. If I give you more, it will only find its way into Monsieur Paul's pocket.'

So one morning in December they got into Denis Lecoq's light cart; he had come to drive them to the station, Rosalie escorting her mistress so far. First they inquired about the price of the ticket and, when everything was fixed up and the trunk registered, they waited on the platform, trying to make out how everything worked, so interested in this mysterious invention that they forgot the tragic reason for the journey. At last a whistle in the distance made them turn their heads and they saw the black engine growing larger and larger. It came in with a deafening roar and moved past them, drawing behind it a long string of small wheeled vehicles. A porter opened a door and Jeanne, after kissing Rosalie, climbed into one of the carriages.

Rosalie, deeply moved, shouted : 'Au revoir, Madame! Good luck! See you again soon!'

'Au revoir, my girl!'

Another blast on the whistle, and the string of carriages began to move, slowly at first, then faster, then at a terrifying speed. In Jeanne's compartment there were two gentlemen asleep leaning back in two of the corners. She looked out of the window as they passed fields, woods, farms, villages, dazed by the speed, feeling herself caught up in a new life, swept into a strange world that was new to her, so different from that of her quiet youth and the monotony of her early life.

When the train reached Paris, it was getting dark. A porter took Jeanne's trunk and she followed him, scared and hustled, unused to threading her way through the bustling crowd, almost running behind the man for fear of losing sight of him.

When she reached the reception desk in the hotel, she announced: 'I have been recommended to you by Maître Roussel.'

The manageress, a large solemn woman, asked : 'Who is Maître Roussel?'

Jeanne, disconcerted, replied: 'Why, he's the Goderville solicitor, who stays here every year.'

The portly woman replied: 'Quite likely. I don't know him. Do you want a room?'

'Yes, Madame.'

A page picked up her luggage and led the way upstairs. With a heavy heart she sat down at a small table and ordered soup and the wing of a chicken to be sent up; she had had nothing to eat since dawn. She ate sadly by the light of a candle, with memories crowding through her mind. She recalled her journey through this same town on the way back from her honeymoon, and the first indications of Julien's character that had appeared during their stay in Paris. But in those days she had been young and confident and brave. Now she felt old and worried, even frightened, weak and easily upset. When she had finished her meal, she went to the window and looked out on the busy street. She would have liked to go out but she did not dare; she would inevitably get lost, she was sure. So she went to bed and put out the light.

But the noise, the feeling of being in this strange town, and the worries of the journey kept her awake. The hours passed; gradually the din outside grew less, but still she could not sleep; her nerves were strained by the absence of complete quiet inevitable in every big town. She was used to the peaceful, sound sleep of the countryside dominating everything, man, animals and plants; now she felt all round her a restless stirring. Voices, barely audible, reached her, as if they had penetrated the walls of the hotel; sometimes a board creaked, a door banged, a bell rang. Suddenly, about two o'clock in the morning, just as she was beginning to drop off, a woman screamed in a room not far from hers; Jeanne sat up in bed with a start and thought she heard a man's laugh. As dawn was breaking, she thought of Paul and dressed as soon as it began to get light.

He was living in the Cité, in the Rue du Sauvage. She decided to go there on foot, in order to obey Rosalie's instructions not to waste money. It was a fine morning and the keen air pricked the skin; people in a hurry were scurrying along the pavements. She hastened along the street that had been pointed out to her, at the end of which she was to turn to the right and then to the left. When she reached a square, she would have to inquire again. She failed to find the square and asked at a baker's shop, where she was given quite different directions. She started off again, missed the way, wandered about following other suggestions, and was soon completely lost. Distracted, she was now walking almost blindly and was on the point of calling a cab, when she sighted the Seine. Then she walked along the quays. After about an hour she found the Rue du Sauvage, a little dark alley. She paused at the door, so disturbed that she could not take another step. *He* was there in this house, Pullet was there.

She felt her knees and her hands shaking. At last she entered, saw the porter's lodge and offering him a coin asked: 'Could you go up and tell Monsieur Paul de Lamare that an old lady, a friend of his mother, is waiting down here?'

'He doesn't live here any longer, Madame,' replied the porter.

She shivered and stammered: 'Oh! Where ... where is he living now?'

'I don't know.'

She felt dizzy, as if she was about to fall down, and remained tongue-tied for several minutes. At last by a great effort she pulled herself together and murmured: 'When did he leave here?'

The man gave her full details: 'A fortnight ago. They went out one evening without saying anything and never came back again. They owed money all round; so you will easily understand why they left no address.'

Jeanne saw flashes, great tongues of fire, as if shots had been fired in front of her eyes. But her firm intention supported her and enabled her to stand, apparently calm and able to think. She wanted to know and find Pullet.

'So he said nothing, when he went away?'

'Not a word; they just cleared out, you see, to avoid having to pay.'

'But he must send someone to fetch his letters.'

'Yes, and more often than I have any to give him. They don't get ten a year. But I did take one up for them a couple of days before they went away.'

That no doubt was her letter.

She hastened to reply: 'Listen! I'm his mother and I've come to look for him. Here's ten francs for you, and if you have any news or any information about him, let me know at the Hôtel de Normandie, Rue du Havre, and I'll make it worth your while.'

'You can rely on me, Madame.'

With that she went away and began walking, not caring where she went. She walked fast as if on some important business, hurrying past the shop-fronts and bumping into people with parcels. She crossed streets regardless of the traffic and was sworn at by the cabbies; she tripped over the pavement kerbs, not noticing them, scurrying along with her mind a blank. Suddenly she found herself in a garden and felt so tired that she sat down on a seat. She must have stayed there a very long time apparently, in tears without realizing it, as passers-by kept stopping to look at her. Then she felt very cold and got up to move on, but her legs would hardly support her, she was so weak and exhausted.

She wanted to go and get some soup at a restaurant, but she dared not go into these places, seized by a kind of shame for the grief which she realized was visible on her face. She would stop for a minute in front of a door and look in and see all the people at the tables eating, and pass on, too frightened to enter, saying to herself: 'I'll go into the next one,' but when she came to the next one she did not go in.

Finally she bought a small crescent-shaped roll at a baker's and nibbled it as she walked along. She was very thirsty, but she did not know where to go for a drink and did without it. She went under an archway and found herself in another garden surrounded by arcades and recognized the Palais-Royal. As the sun and her walk had warmed her up, she sat down for another hour or two.

A crowd was thronging into the garden, a well-dressed crowd, talking, smiling, bowing, a crowd of those happy people whose women are pretty and whose men are wealthy, who live only for clothes and pleasure. Jeanne got up to escape, terrified of this brilliant assembly, but suddenly it occurred to her that she might meet Paul here, and she began to wander round scanning the faces, going backwards and forwards from one end of the garden to the other with quick unobtrusive steps. Some people turned round to stare at her, others laughed, pointing her out to each other. She noticed this and slunk away, thinking no doubt that they were laughing at her appearance in her green check chosen by Rosalie and made to her order by the Goderville dressmaker. She did not dare even to ask her way of the passers-by, but at last she screwed up her courage and finally reached her hotel.

She spent the rest of the day sitting without stirring on a chair at the foot of her bed. In the evening she had a meal of soup and a piece of meat, as she had done the day before; after that she went to bed, performing each action mechanically.

Next day she went to the Police Station to ask them to look for her son. They could not promise anything but said they would do their best. After that she wandered about the streets, always hoping to meet him. She was more conscious of her loneliness in this bustling crowd, more lost, more miserable than in the depths of the empty country.

When she returned to the hotel in the evening, they told her that a man giving Monsieur Paul's name had been to ask for her, and that he would come back next day. The blood rushed to her heart and she did not close an eye that night. Suppose it was *he*? Yes, it must be her son, though she would not have recognized him from the description which they gave her.

About nine o'clock next morning there was a knock at her door and she cried : 'Come in !' ready to rush to embrace him. But the man who came in was a total stranger; and while he was making his excuses for disturbing her and explaining his business, which was to claim payment of one of Paul's debts, she felt herself weeping, but not wishing this to be noticed she wiped the tears away with her finger, as they welled up in the corners of her eyes. The man had heard of her arrival from the porter in the Rue du Sauvage and unable to find the young man himself he was approaching the mother. He held out a piece of paper, which she took mechanically. She read the figure of 90 francs, took out her purse and paid. That day she did not go out.

Next day other creditors appeared. She paid out all the money she had left, keeping only 20 francs, and wrote to Rosalie explaining her position. She spent the days wandering about, not knowing what to do to kill time and pass the dismal endless hours, having no one with whom she could have a friendly word, no one who understood her misery. She walked about at random, harassed by the urge to get away and go back to her little house in the country on the edge of the lonely main road. A few days earlier she had been unable to stay there, so overwhelmed had she been by her loneliness, but now she realized that on the contrary she could live nowhere else than in the place where her dreary life was rooted. At last one evening she found a letter with 200 francs. Rosalie wrote: 'Madame Jeanne, come straight home, for I shan't send you any more money. As for Monsieur Paul, I will go and find him, when we get some news. Your faithful servant, Rosalie.'

Jeanne started back for Batteville one morning when it was snowing and very cold.

CHAPTER FOURTEEN

AFTER this she gave up going out and never left the house. She got up every morning at the same time, looked out of the window to see what the weather was like and went down to her chair in front of the fire in the living-room. She spent whole days there not moving, gazing into the fire, making no effort to control her depressing thoughts, recalling all the misfortunes of her life. Darkness spread into the small room and she had not stirred since morning except to put a log on the fire. When Rosalie brought in the lamp: 'Come now, Madame Jeanne,' she cried, 'you must rouse yourself or you won't have any appetite again this evening.'

She was often the victim of delusions which obsessed her and she suffered tortures over trifling worries, silly little things which assumed great importance in her sick brain. In particular she lived over again her past life of long ago, haunted by memories of her girlhood days and her honeymoon in distant Corsica. The scenery of the island, long forgotten, suddenly rose up before her in the flaming logs in the grate, and she recalled every detail, every little incident, every face she had seen there. She could not get the face of the guide, Jean Ravoli, out of her mind and sometimes she could even hear his voice. Then she ranged over the blissful years of Paul's childhood, when he had made her prick lettuces and she had knelt on the moist earth by Aunt Lison's side, rivals for the child's approval, competing as to which of them would make the plants strike root quickest and give the most seedlings.

She kept whispering: 'Pullet, darling little Pullet!' as if she were talking to him. His name sometimes put an end to her dreams, and she would spend hours trying to write the letters of his name in the air with an outstretched finger. She traced the letters slowly in front of the fire, imagining that she could see them; then, thinking that she had made a mistake, she began again with the P, her arm trembling with fatigue, forcing herself to complete the name; when she had finished it, she began all over again. In the end she gave it up, mixing up all the letters and tracing other words, worrying herself nearly into fits.

She was possessed by all the crazes of the recluse, and she became irritable if the position of the smallest object was changed. Rosalie often forced her to take exercise and took her out for walks on the road, but after twenty minutes Jeanne always declared: 'I can't go on, my girl,' and sat down on the edge of the dyke. Soon she began to avoid all movement and stayed as long as possible in bed.

There was one habit she had stuck to since early childhood, that of jumping out of bed as soon as she had drunk her bowl of white coffee; she absolutely insisted on this mixture and she would have felt being deprived of it more than anything else in the world. Every morning she waited for Rosalie to appear with an impatience that was almost sensual; and as soon as the full bowl had been put down on the night-table, she sat up and gulped it down greedily. Then, throwing off the bed-clothes, she began to dress. But now gradually she formed the habit of dreaming for a few minutes after putting the empty bowl back on its plate. Later she started lying down again in bed and stayed there longer and longer each day, idly dreaming, until Rosalie came back furious and dressed her almost by force.

Moreover her ability to make up her mind seemed to have left her; and every time the maid asked her advice or put a question or wanted to know what she thought about anything, she only replied: 'Do just as you like, my dear girl.' She thought of herself as so directly dogged by persistent bad luck that she became as fatalistic as an Oriental, and she was so used to seeing her dreams fade and her hopes come to nothing, that now she dared not make any decision and hesitated for whole days before doing the simplest thing, convinced that she was always on the wrong track and that nothing would go right for her.

She continually repeated: 'I have no luck in life.'

But Rosalie would retort: 'What would you say if you had to earn your living and had to get up at six every morning to go out to work? There are plenty of women who have to do that, and when they are too old to work, they starve to death.'

'But remember,' answered Jeanne, 'I am quite alone and my son has abandoned me.'

At this Rosalie got furiously angry: 'That's a bad business, I know. But what about the sons who are away on military service and those who emigrate to America?'

To the maid America was a vague country, where one went to make one's fortune and never came back. She went on: 'There always comes a time when a family must break up, because the old and the young are not made to live together,' and she added fiercely: 'What would you say if he were dead?'

To that Jeanne had no answer.

When the air got warmer in the first days of spring, she felt a little stronger, but she only took advantage of her renewed energy to plunge deeper into her fits of depression. One morning, when she had gone up to the attic to look for something, she opened by accident a box full of old calendars, which had been kept according to the custom of many country-folk. She felt that she was rediscovering the actual years of her past life, and she stood seized by a strange emotion in front of this pile of squares of cardboard. She picked them up and carried them downstairs to the living-room; they were of all sizes, big and little. She began to arrange them in years on the table. Suddenly she found the first one which she had brought to the Poplars. She looked for a long time at it, with the days which she had crossed out on the morning she had left Rouen, the day after she had left the convent; and she wept slow sad tears, the pitiful tears of an old woman, faced with her unhappy life spread out before her on the table.

Suddenly an idea came into her mind, which soon developed into a terrible, permanent, haunting obsession. She wanted to recall almost day by day everything she had done. She pinned up those soiled sheets of cardboard on the tapestry on the wall, and spent hours in front of one or the other, asking herself: 'What happened to me that month?' She had underlined the important days in her life, and sometimes she managed to recover a whole month, putting together day by day, by grouping and connecting one day with another, all the little incidents that had preceded or followed the important date. By carefully focussing her attention, by efforts of memory and concentration of will-power, she succeeded in reconstructing almost in their entirety her first two years at the Poplars, the distant memories of her life coming back to her with surprising ease and a sense of relief.

But the following years seemed to lose themselves in a fog, become mixed up and encroach on each other. Sometimes she remained for hours bending over a particular calendar, pondering over the past, unable to decide if such and such a memory could be fixed on such and such a date. She went from one calendar to another all round the room, which was ringed with these pictures of past days like the Stations of the Cross. She would suddenly put down her chair in front of one of them and stay till nightfall gazing at it without moving, absorbed in the effort to remember.

Then suddenly, when the sap began to rise in the warmth of the sun and the crops began to sprout in the fields, the leaves to shoot on the trees, when the apple-trees in the courtyards began to blossom like pink balls and scent the countryside, she could not keep still, she had to be on the move. She wandered about, went out and came back twenty times a day, roamed far afield over the farms in a quixotic frenzy of regret. The sight of a daisy peering out of a clump of grass, of a ray of sunlight slanting through the leaves, of a puddle in a rut reflecting the blue sky stirred her, touched her heart, upset her, rousing again the emotions of long ago, an echo of her romantic girlhood, when she had wandered about the country dreaming. She felt the same thrill, enjoyed the same caress and the exciting intoxication of the spring warmth, just as when she had had a future to look forward to. She felt the same exhilaration now, though she had no future; she still had the same joy in her heart, but at the same time there was an element of pain in her joy, as if the eternal happiness of awakening nature, as it penetrated her wasted flesh, her chilled blood and her crushed soul, now only cast a feeble, even a painful spell.

Everything round her too seemed somewhat changed; the sun was a little less warm than in her youth, the sky a little less blue, the grass a little less green, the flowers paler and less scented, less intoxicating than of old. However, the joy of life sometimes took such a hold on her that she began to dream again, to hope, to look forward; for surely, in spite of the grievous harshness of fate, one can always still hope when the weather is fine. She walked on and on for hours, spurred on by the excitement of her heart; and sometimes she would stop and sit down by the roadside to think sad thoughts. Why had she not been loved as many other women are loved? Sometimes she could still forget that she was old and had nothing to look forward to except a few dreary years of loneliness, that her race was run; and she still built castles in the air as she had done at sixteen, making plans for future happiness. But soon the cruel realities of life fell heavy upon her and she got up, as if crushed by a falling weight too heavy to bear, and walked home more slowly, murmuring: 'Oh, what an old fool I am! What an old fool!'

Rosalie was always saying to her now: 'Don't worry, Madame! What have you got to get so worked up about?'

'What can you expect?' replied Jeanne sadly, 'I'm just like Murder in his last days.'

One morning the maid came into her room earlier than usual, and putting down the bowl of white coffee on the night-table, she said: 'Come along, drink it up quick! Denis is waiting for us at the door. We're going over to the Poplars; I've got some business to do there.'

Jeanne almost fainted from excitement; she dressed trembling with emotion, frightened and ready to swoon at the thought of seeing the beloved old house again. It was a brilliantly sunny morning and the pony, feeling frisky, kept breaking into a gallop. When they reached the neighbourhood of Étouvent, Jeanne found considerable difficulty in breathing, her heart was beating so fast, and when she saw the brick pillars of the garden gate, she ejaculated two or three times quite unconsciously: 'Oh! Oh! Oh!' as one does in moments of great excitement. The trap was unharnessed at the Couillards' farm, and while Rosalie and her son went about their business, the peasants suggested that Jeanne should go and have a look over the mansion, the owners being away, and they gave her the keys.

She went off by herself and when she reached the front of the house on the seaward side, she paused to look at it. Nothing outside was changed. The stained walls of the great grey building were bright in the cheerful sunshine. All the shutters were closed. A twig from a dead branch fell on her dress and she looked up; it was the plane tree; she went up to the thick trunk with its smooth pale bark and stroked it as if it were an animal. In the grass her foot struck a piece of rotting wood; it was the last fragment of the bench, on which she had so often sat with the family, the bench which had been put there on the day of Julien's first visit.

When she reached the double door of the porch, she had great difficulty in opening it, as the heavy rusty key would not turn. At last the lock gave with a harsh grinding of springs, and the leaf of the door, itself stiff, opened at her push.

Jeanne immediately went up to her room, almost running. She hardly recognized it with its light wallpaper, but after opening the window she stood deeply stirred before the view she loved, the shrubbery, the elms, the common, and the sea dotted with brown sails, which hardly seemed to move in the distance.

Next she roamed over the great empty house. She looked at the marks on the walls that she knew so well. She paused in front of a small hole in the plaster made by the Baron, who often amused himself, remembering the fencing days of his youth, by making passes with his stick against the wainscoting, as he walked by. In Mama's room, in a dark corner behind a door near the bed, she found a tiny gold-headed pin, which she had stuck in – she distinctly remembered doing it now – and which she had looked for for years; no one had ever found it. She took it as a priceless relic and kissed it.

She went all over the house, searching for and finding almost invisible marks on the hangings of the different rooms, which had not been changed; she saw again the strange figures given by the imagination to the patterns of the material, the marble and the shadows on the ceilings blackened by time. She walked quietly all alone in the huge silent mansion, as if she were in a cemetery, in which her whole life lay buried.

She went down to the drawing-room; it was dark behind the closed shutters and it was some time before she could make anything out, but, as her eyes got used to the gloom, she gradually recognized the tall tapestries with birds walking about.

There were still two arm-chairs in front of the fire, as if their occupants had just left them. Even the smell of the room, the smell that it had always kept, as human beings have their own particular smell, a faint but easily recognizable smell, the pleasant smell of all old rooms, entered into Jeanne, laden with memories, intoxicating her mind.

She stood there gasping, breathing the atmosphere of the past, with her eyes fixed on the two chairs; and suddenly in a quick hallucination induced by the thoughts that were never out of her mind, she imagined that she saw, nay, she did see, her father and mother warming their feet before the fire as she had so often seen them. She started back terrified, struck her back against the door and leant against it to avoid falling, with her eyes still fixed on the arm-chairs. The vision had disappeared.

She stood there dazed for several minutes, but slowly recovering herself she was anxious to get away, afraid of going mad. Her eyes by chance fell on the panelling which she was leaning against and she caught sight of 'Pullet's ladder'; the lines on the paint went up at different intervals and the figures scratched with a penknife gave her son's age in years and months and his height. Sometimes it was in the Baron's large writing, sometimes in her smaller script, sometimes in Aunt Lison's rather shaky hand. She pictured him there in front of her, a fair-haired boy, as he was in those days, pressing his little forehead against the wall for them to measure his height. 'Jeanne!' cried the Baron, 'he's grown half an inch in the last six weeks,' and she began to kiss the panel in a frenzy of affection.

But someone was calling her outside; it was Rosalie's voice: 'Madame Jeanne, Madame Jeanne, they're waiting for you for lunch!' She went out, quite lost to the world. She did not take in what was said to her; she ate what was put before her, heard people talking without understanding their words, no doubt answering questions about her health, let them kiss her and herself kissed the cheeks that were offered her, and then got back into the trap. When the mansion's high roof disappeared from view behind the trees, she felt a sharp pain in her breast; her heart told her that she had said good-bye to the house for ever. They returned to Batteville.

Just as she was entering her new house, she saw something

white under the door; it was a letter that the postman had slipped in, while she had been out. She saw at once that it was from Paul and opened it in a fever of anxiety. It ran: 'My dear Mother, I haven't written before, because I wanted to spare you an unnecessary journey to Paris, as I was just coming to see you myself. At the moment I am suffering from a terrible misfortune and am in great difficulties. My wife is dying after giving birth to a girl three days ago. I haven't got a penny and I don't know what to do with the child; my porter's wife is feeding her on a bottle as best she can, but I'm afraid of losing her. Couldn't you take care of her? I don't know what on earth to do with her and I haven't got the money to put her out to nurse. Do answer by return of post. Your loving son, Paul.'

Jeanne collapsed on a chair, hardly able to call Rosalie. When the maid came, they read the letter together again and sat facing each other in silence for some minutes. 'I'll go and fetch the baby, Madame,' said Rosalie at last, 'we can't leave her like that.'

'Yes, do go, my girl,' replied Jeanne.

After a silence the maid went on : 'Put on your hat, Madame, and we'll go to the solicitor in Goderville. If the woman is going to die, Monsieur Paul must marry her for the sake of the child later on !'

Jeanne put on her hat without a word. Her heart was submerged by a wave of shameful joy, a criminal joy which she was determined to conceal at all costs, one of those discreditable joys which make one blush but give the keenest pleasure in the secret places of the soul : her son's mistress was going to die.

The solicitor gave the maid detailed instructions, which she made him repeat several times; when she was sure that she understood exactly what she was to do, she declared : 'Don't worry; I'll see to everything.'

She left for Paris that evening.

Jeanne spent the next two days so upset that she was incapable of rational thought. On the third morning she got a line from Rosalie, saying that she would be back on the evening train; that was all. About three o'clock she ordered a neighbour's trap and was driven to Beuzeville station to wait for the maid.

She stood on the platform, straining her eyes to follow the lines

200

of the rails, which stretched away till they met on the horizon. From time to time she looked at the clock – ten minutes to wait – five minutes to wait – two minutes to wait – time. Nothing was visible on the track. Suddenly she saw a cloud of white smoke, then under it a black spot, which grew larger as it approached at full speed. At last the huge engine, slowing up, roared past Jeanne; she kept her eyes on the carriage doors. Several of them opened and passengers got out, peasants in their blouses, farmers' wives with baskets, small shopkeepers in soft felt hats. At last she caught sight of Rosalie with what looked like a roll of linen in her arms. She wanted to go to meet her, but her legs were tottering so much that she was afraid of falling. When the maid saw her, she came up to her with her usual placid air, saying: 'Good evening, Madame; here I am back, after rather a difficult time.'

'Well, what news?' stammered Jeanne.

'Well, she's dead,' answered Rosalie, 'she died last night. They got married; here's the baby.'

She held out the infant, which was entirely hidden in its wrappings. Jeanne took the child mechanically and they left the station and got into the trap. Rosalie went on: 'Monsieur Paul will be coming immediately after the funeral; tomorrow at this time, I expect.'

Jeanne murmured 'Paul', and that was all.

The sun was westering, lighting up the grassy plain, dotted here and there with the gold of the rape-flowers and the blood-red of the poppies. Absolute peace reigned over the earth, in which the sap was rising. The trap travelled fast, the peasant clicking with his tongue to urge the pony on. Jeanne was looking straight before her at the sky which was criss-crossed by the curving flight of the swallows, when suddenly a gentle warmth, the warmth of life, reached her legs and penetrated the skin; it was the infant asleep on her lap.

Then an uncontrollable emotion gripped her and she quickly uncovered the child's face, which she had not yet looked at; it was her son's daughter. As the tiny mite, awakened by the bright light, opened its eyes and moved its lips, Jeanne began to kiss it passionately, picking it up in her arms and smothering it with caresses. But Rosalie, pleased but surly, stopped her: 'Come! Come! Madame Jeanne, that's enough! You'll make her scream.'

Then she added, no doubt in answer to her own thoughts: 'You see, life is never as good or as bad as one thinks.'

MORE ABOUT PENGUINS, PELICANS, PEREGRINES AND PUFFINS

For further information about books available from Penguins please write to Dept EP, Penguin Books Ltd, Harmondsworth, Middlesex UB7 0DA.

In the U.S.A.: For a complete list of books available from Penguins in the United States write to Dept DG, Penguin Books, 299 Murray Hill Parkway, East Rutherford, New Jersey 07073.

In Canada: For a complete list of books available from Penguins in Canada write to Penguin Books Canada Ltd, 2801 John Street, Markham, Ontario L3R 1B4.

In Australia: For a complete list of books available from Penguins in Australia write to the Marketing Department, Penguin Books Australia Ltd, P.O. Box 257, Ringwood, Victoria 3134.

In New Zealand: For a complete list of books available from Penguins in New Zealand write to the Marketing Department, Penguin Books (N.Z.) Ltd, Private Bag, Takapuna, Auckland 9.

In India: For a complete list of books available from Penguins in India write to Penguin Overseas Ltd, 706 Eros Apartments, 56 Nehru Place, New Delhi 110019.

GERMINAL
Zola

Germinal was written by Zola (1840–1902) to draw attention once again to the misery prevailing among the poor
in France during the Second Empire. The novel, which
has now become a sociological document, depicts the grim
struggle between capital and labour in a coalfield in
northern France. Yet through the blackness of this picture
humanity is constantly apparent, and the final impression
is one of compassion and hope for the future not only of
organized labour, but also of man.

L. W. Tancock's translation successfully conveys the
earthy clarity of Zola's style.

Also published

L'ASSOMMOIR
THE DEBACLE
NANA
THÉRÈSE RAQUIN

SCARLET AND BLACK
Stendhal

Stendhal's *Scarlet and Black*, which on its publication and for long after received practically no recognition, now has assured rank as a masterpiece. André Gide almost gave it first place among the ten greatest novels of the world: it was only after much hesitation that he put the same author's *La Chartreuse de Parme* above it. Taine said that in it Stendhal revealed himself as a master novelist and the greatest psychologist of the century. According to Bourget, 'this extraordinary book either revolts or fascinates' (it was too strong meat even for Maupassant). The hero, Julien Sorel, is a man of genius handicapped by the circumstances of his birth; determined to get his due place by whatever means, he is always at war 'with the whole of society' as Stendhal himself says.

There is not only subtle dissection of motive in this book; there is seduction, highly passionate love, tortuous intrigue, shootings, and finally the guillotine: those who like excitement will not be disappointed.

Also published

THE CHARTERHOUSE OF PARMA

LOVE

MADAME BOVARY
Flaubert

Flaubert's 'story of provincial life' in nineteenth-century Normandy has been something of a legend ever since it was first published in 1857. Or rather it has been two legends. The first is that of Emma Bovary, the embodiment of desires yearning beyond their inimical environment, failing to escape it, and finally breaking themselves upon it. The second is the legend of Gustave Flaubert, saint and martyr of literature, who shut himself up for over four years in his room at Croisset to make of Emma's story a novel that should be also a model of stylistic perfection.

'Style' to Flaubert was no mere pretty play with words, but a search in words for the very tone and texture of life. 'The form of a thought is its very flesh.' In that search the writer must 'become' whatever he writes of, as Flaubert 'became' not only 'the lovers in the wood' but 'the leaves, the wind, the horses . . .'

Also published

BOUVARD AND PÉCUCHET
SENTIMENTAL EDUCATION